APHRODITE RISING

"Aphrodite Rising"

Edited by Bear Wiseman Internal illustration by Rosie Jaen Cover stock image by Tim Rebkavets/Unsplash
Hardcover ISBN: 979-8-9921023-1-4
Paperback ISBN: 979-8-9921023-0-7

ACKNOWLEDGMENTS

This is for all of those who don't quite know where they fit. There is enough room amongst the stars in the sky for you and everyone else in this world.

Specific thanks to:
- My wife Bee for always listening to my plots and ideas with only minor grumbles.
- Bear Wiseman for the moral support, editing, and motivation to keep on going.
- Rosie Jaen, Gaby Magaña, Hayley Hoffman, Syd Cronin, and Ichneumon Leising for their artwork.
- Thrash Unreal for giving me the feline energy that only a black cat could.
- Everyone who has ever made me feel safe enough to create.
- All the little angels in my life who constantly remind me how loved and appreciated I am.

Contents

1. Chapter 1   1

2. Chapter 2   9

3. Chapter 3   23

4. Chapter 4   33

5. Chapter 5   41

6. Chapter 6   51

7. Chapter 7   65

8. Chapter 8   73

9. Chapter 9   85

10. Chapter 10   97

11. Chapter 11   103

12. Chapter 12   113

13. Chapter 13   119

14. Chapter 14   125

15. Chapter 15   135

16. Chapter 16   145

17. Chapter 17   161

18. Chapter 18   175

19. Chapter 19   187

20. Chapter 20   201

21. Chapter 21   219

22. Chapter 22   233

23. Chapter 23   245

24. Chapter 24   259

25. Chapter 25   271

26. Chapter 26   281

27. Chapter 27   293

28. Chapter 28   309

One

F auna was about to be set on fire.

Though, it really wasn't her fault.

It wasn't her fault that she could read and that the Matron had banned any form of literature. Fauna was surprised the measly village was even allowed to have a school. However, they only wanted to teach her how to darn socks and cook—neither of which interested Fauna in the slightest. Fauna's mother, who passed away when Fauna was only two days old, had rebuked everything the Matron stood for and refused to worship her.

This was why Fauna found herself strapped to a pole while a particularly rotund farmer dipped a torch into the kindling below Fauna's feet. To go against the Matron was practically begging for a one-way ticket to Castle Verity, which meant a lifetime of torture—mental and physical. That was where the criminals went before they disappeared forever. Being set on fire seemed to be the more pleasant of the two.

Corporeal but rarely seen at all, the Matron was someone who ruled from her golden castle, which sat atop an island so high in the sky that no one had ever survived the journey to see it. She flew (though the stories couldn't decide if she had secret wings or a charmed cloak) and would descend from the sky at random. Draped in wealth while her people starved, the Matron commanded crowds to bend to her will with only a single glance. Sharp eyes the color of smoke and skin so fair that it was obvious she never saw the sun, the Matron struck fear and compliance into the people of the village. Men and women fell to their knees and offered their meager belongings in hopes of staying in the Matron's good graces.

Except for Fauna, who now wiggled in her bindings, trying to break free. Down below, she watched as a crowd grabbed the book she'd been caught with and passed it back and forth. There were only a handful of people in the village who could read or write, but they could get enough context from the illustrations.

Fauna was lucky on that front. Her father never spoke about her uncouth habits. Even though he was illiterate and incredibly pious, he still turned a blind eye when the local merchant secretly taught Fauna how to read and write. Books were hidden under her bed and read by candlelight once the village was asleep. Even when she moved into an abandoned silo in her teenage years, she still found herself choosing books over people. No one noticed her and it was wonderful.

Until today.

The silo was a poor excuse for a home—quite chilly for such a small space, and the makeshift door didn't shut properly, but it was the closest thing to solace that she had ever known. She still cared for her father, who stopped speaking to her when she turned thirteen and lost his ability to walk soon after, though she kept to herself.

When her father quietly died, Fauna sold his belongings and pulled completely away from society. The village didn't bother her and no one seemed to acknowledge her outside of a polite nod after shopping. Even she and the merchant hardly spoke, though that was mostly for their safety. He hid books in his kiosk and Fauna left money in their place.

Just an hour prior, Fauna had walked into the village with joy in her heart. She'd freshly braided her hair and tucked the gray streak behind her ear. Her dress was clean and her shoes were polished. It was going to be a good day. There was a new book waiting in the secret compartment, and she was so excited to read it!

The book, the last in its series, was written by an author who wrote long and beautiful poetry about their many loves in life. Sometimes it was a love for men or love for women, but sometimes it was love for the birds in the sky or the petals of flowers. There were lines about the moons and stars that painted such visceral pictures in Fauna's mind that she forgot who she was while she read.

In between the pages of love were adventures! Swords and dragons and fairies with elves. The short stories were perfect, as they united under an enchanting plot! She finally had the last one needed to make sense of it all! It was a perfect mix of fascinating subjects and pretty prose and though she was sad for it to end, rereading her books was one of Fauna's favorite pastimes. She knew how hard the Merchant worked to acquire it for her, so she had vowed to bring a treat the next time she visited. Hence, the little bit of chocolate that now sat in her secret compartment in his stand.

She opened the book as she walked away, too excited to wait and deliberately ignoring the rules. The Matron didn't care about her, she never had. She'd be fine. An illustration made of simple lines curved in places and ragged in others formed two bodies draped across each other in such a passionate embrace that Fauna began to blush at the mere implication of it. The beautiful art alone made her heart beat *very* quickly.

Could such love be real? To want to drape yourself over someone? The idea of sharing space at all seemed uncomfortable. Fauna liked her privacy and liked having her own safe place. However, she'd also never been presented the opportunity to do so.

And as soon as she'd begun to get invested, it was snatched from her hand.

"NO!"

Her voice—unfamiliar to almost everyone—called attention to her immediately. The man's eyes widened when he looked at the pages.

Fauna, too stunned to move, simply sat and watched as a crowd began to form around her. Something told her that she'd finally stepped over the line that she'd been toeing for years. Was it *wrong* to read? Were they surprised that she had come outside? Or were the people surprised that she could think for herself? Perhaps it was her quiet demeanor or the dark shadow that seemed to follow her wherever she went. Regardless, she watched in fear as a crowd of people began to close in on her.

A sharp tug on her braid pulled Fauna painfully into the dirt below. She kicked and screamed as she was suddenly hauled to the pole where thieves and murderers were displayed before being shipped off to die. Farmers who had sold her eggs whispered and jeered all around her.

She flailed and growled when they cut her dress, revealing her slip to the whole village. She'd recently spent days mending it and now it hung in tatters around her waist. A rope fastened her legs to the pole and her arms followed soon after.

Higher and higher, they pulled her until her toes were just above her captor's belt. A chilling sensation began in her feet as the wind began to sway her dress back and forth against her body. The smell of fuel burned her nose and she wondered if anyone could justify the wasted cost of it for her unimportant death. She posed no risk to anyone—she simply enjoyed poetry about love and minded her business. What threat could she pose to a village? Nary a word had been shared with those cretins and they dared to charge her with *what*? Reading?

As the villagers began stacking lumber around her feet, time slowed down for Fauna. For an emotional beat, she realized that she left no legacy, no family. There was nothing in her silo but vegetables and old books.

Men and women cheered as if the world would be better once she died.

She hated them all.

When the next torch was thrown, Fauna felt a gust across her face. It was still early in the day and while the weather was unpredictable, the swipes of wind were nevertheless quite curious. High above the crowd she stuck out her chin bravely and refused to cry. She always knew this day would come—that the village would tire of her inability to dull herself down to their level. She was not *better* than them, she was just smarter—she landed well outside the Matron's grasp. She was not afraid to die. The only thing she was afraid of was a lack of knowledge. There were so many things she would never learn, and that was the true heartbreak of it all.

Oh, if only her mother could see her now. Burning at the stake for reading a book.

As the flames touched her well-worn boots, she finally screamed. Not for her own life, but because she never got to read the book she'd waited months to receive. Such a shame; perhaps a villager would find it and realize that there was a world out there—one where love was a force of good and not exchanged for a dowry. Hopefully, every little maiden who needed to see it would find it and leave the destitute village riddled with the stink of sweaty men and deliberate ignorance.

Fools! They were all fools in the trivial games that were played with them! Just wait until their monstrosity of a leader got bored with them and wiped them all out. Perhaps, in that case, Fauna would be the winner for having escaped much earlier.

She growled as the anger built in her chest. How *dare* they cut her life short!

Her legs began to tremble and she wet herself in fear. Not fear of death—oh she didn't fear death one bit. She was scared of the pain though, of how the flames would slowly char her flesh before actually killing her. It was ridiculous that even the village's livestock would die by a gentler hand than she would. Even her father died in his sleep.

As the torches were thrown and the wood ignited, the frigid winds slowed alongside time itself as a massive raven, nearly as big as a pig, swooped down and began pecking the eyes out of the men who cheered gleefully as the wood ignited. The flames seared her legs, making her eyes roll back into her head. Foam began to tumble from her mouth as her lungs heated like coals under the fire.

The leather that bound her began to wither away and soon she felt a popping sensation as she pitched forward off the pole, falling towards the pyre. The moment before she hit the ground, she felt a painful snag between her shoulder blades. Fauna looked up as best as she could against the glaring sun and noticed what seemed to be the same oversized raven carrying her up toward the afternoon sun and away from her personal bonfire. Fauna, stunned and in shock, struggled to see or understand what was happening. What was this raven? Where did it come from? Where was it taking her?

The raven came into focus as it flew past the sun, and Fauna could see the claws stuck into her shoulders. When she looked back down, the raven let her go and sent Fauna careening towards the ground. She landed in a broken heap on the stoop in front of a grand wooden door, boots still smoking with piss-soaked stockings, freezing in a sudden blizzard that seemed to overtake the area around her. She was in so much pain that she could only shake and moan. Just a second prior, she'd been ready to die. Now she was heaving amongst the silence of nature. Was this death?

She tried to move her legs but only her feet responded. The tip of her boot was desperately close to the castle doors. She didn't dare look down for fear of the grotesque burnt lump that was her body. She took a deep breath that sounded more like paper ripping than much else and used every grain of energy she had to knock her boot against the door two times. The impact banged her foot inside her boot, and the pain that radiated from the rip of her skin inside made her gag and retch.

A woman holding a woven basket opened the door and gasped. Her eyes widened as she shut the door quickly and screamed so loudly that her voice could be heard through the thick wood. Fauna, too dazed to do anything, silently begged for help. As her eyes began to close, she heard some muffled voices and felt herself being lifted and moved. Almost immediately, she was picked up and cradled against something incredibly *soft*. A low voice mumbled things to her but she could not make out any of the words. All she knew was that the ground was gone and she was moving.

Fauna sighed as she was carried gently down what seemed to be a long hallway. Her pain had lessened to a resounding ache, which was still awful but manageable if she focused on anything else. Her eyes closed and opened as her consciousness began to flicker and exhaustion filled her scorched bones.

After a few pitiful attempts at speaking, Fauna gave up and silently cried as her lungs ached and her mouth tasted of soot. Whoever was carrying her wiped away her tears, brushed something off of her face, and said something in a kind tone, but Fauna was already slipping into a deep sleep. As she began to fade away, she heard a door slam behind her and a lot of screaming. It would make sense that her appearance would startle someone. In fact, it would have been an interesting plot, had she not been the one living it.

Two

When Fauna woke, she was wrapped in linen and felt like one large, throbbing scab. Her limbs, heavy and immobile, felt as if she'd been bathed in molasses and laid out to dry in the sun. A jolt of pain lanced through her when she tried to stretch or move even the smallest bit. The ache was manageable, but there was a deep, penetrating sorrow in her bones that weighed her down from within. Her ribs felt like skewers in her sides, while her flesh was the main course. Tiny pockets of air stuck uncomfortably in her chest as she tried to breathe. Breath rattled through her throat and hit every tender patch of flesh as it escaped. At that moment, Fauna felt more like a set of time-worn hearthside bellows than a human being.

The next few minutes were spent coughing and grimacing until little stars twinkled in her peripherals. When they finally cleared, the tears of pain eventually fell down her cheeks as she spotted a glass of water on a table next to her, looking like the most beautiful grail in existence. It was her new goal, her greatest purpose in life, to reach it. Never in her thirty-five years had she wanted something more than *that* glass of water.

With a pitiful moan, Fauna tried to move her upper body, bit by bit, until she heard a sickening crunch and a searing hot pain shot through her shoulders. She raised her newly freed arm and saw that a nasty bit of skin had been stuck to the bed and now revealed vulnerable pink flesh, not yet ready for the world. The sight of her mottled skin against the sheets made her gag and knock her hand against the corner of the table. She watched with defeat as the glass of water slid off the edge, smashing against the hardwood floor below. The echo of the shatter bounced off the walls and mocked her as she tried her best to swallow her frustrated sobs. She sat back against the sheets and gagged again when the stuck-on skin poked her in the back.

Immediately, a woman in an incredibly tidy maid's outfit scurried in with a horrified look on her face. Portly, but with rose-tinted cheeks and a splash of freckles the same earthy color as her hair, the maid immediately knelt beside the bed to avoid the glass and inspected Fauna's open wound with careful fingers and a frown of sympathy. The woman looked around the room and saw what she was looking for. She stood and quickly went towards a simple writing desk and retrieved a tin and rag that were hiding just out of view. Fauna did her best to look past the edge of the bed, but her skin protested and she was not keen to repeat her earlier mistake.

A cold touch to her skin made Fauna startle until she realized that the maid was gently guiding her to sit forward. Deft fingers pressed and prodded at Fauna's open wound but did not cause any more discomfort than before. Quiet in her steps, the maid switched her attention between tending to all of Fauna's injuries and a basin of water that seemingly appeared out of nowhere.

After some humiliating care, a *very* painful change of sheets, and a few extra pillows, a cool rag was placed over Fauna's eyes and a gentle nudge against her lip begged her to drink from a cup. The water relieved the itch in her throat but stung like a million little shards scraping against her windpipe. Drinking while only slightly inclined was incredibly difficult, but she did it nonetheless.

The woman—who never muttered a word but spoke volumes with her looks of sympathy in the moments when the rag on Fauna's eyes was removed to be refreshed—laid Fauna back down against the pillow and seemed to bustle about the room doing this or that. Little bouts of shuffling and the sound of chores being done fluttered around in a calming tune while the rhythmic pendulum swing of a broom kept Fauna company. Soon, she was dozing and let herself sink into the sheets. Swaddled like an infant and as comfortable as was possible, she felt herself drift off into a deep sleep.

When she awoke a second time, Fauna noticed two things. One, that the towel was missing from her eyes, and two, that she had been asleep for quite a while. The moon hung heavy in the sky, graciously illuminating her room with supple beams that gave off an ethereal feel. How long it had been, she didn't know, but the moon's height indicated that it had been quite a while. Bright and bulbous with a particular epochal fanfare into her new life, the moon calmed her breathing and eased off Fauna's fear of this strange new place.

She sat up just a bit, groaning as her skin protested. It was strange—she didn't recall being burned all over her body when she'd been saved, but she felt like she'd been cooked like freshly hunted game. A glance downwards made her grimace—her chest and everything that wasn't encased in bandages and a simple white shift looked at best like tanned leather. It was far too grotesque for her to examine for more than a second. There wasn't a sliver of her normal skin to be seen. Never in her life had she cared about how she appeared but the shock of seeing herself in such a state turned her stomach.

"You were almost killed," a voice rumbled from a rocking chair in the corner. "Such a shame."

"I-," Fauna tried to speak but coughed instead. She grunted in frustration and squinted toward the dark corner. She began to speak again but growled in defeat when all that came out of her throat was a thick sigh of whistling air.

"Don't worry about speaking, you took a lot of damage here," the voice said, standing up and walking toward her with a finger to her throat. "The maid said you might not be able to talk for quite a while."

Unable to respond in any civilized manner, Fauna sighed and laid back against the blankets. She huffed petulantly and looked at the young woman, who seemed quite amused by her pain.

"Beatrice. Call me Bea. I'm the oldest daughter. I'm the one you should thank—my sister wanted to kill you. I convinced her otherwise. You'd be smart to remember that." Bea sauntered forward, revealing eyes the color of freshly polished gold. A midnight blue dress swirled around her pale ankles like ocean spray. Her icy-white hair flitted light and airily around her and Fauna knew that if she could reach and touch it, it would be softer and thinner than anything she had ever felt.

Fauna nodded and raised a bandaged hand in surrender. She was in no shape to even reply.

"What's your name?" Bea asked before her lips turned up in an amused grin. "Oops! I forgot you can't speak. Can you write? I don't want to think about how little the villagers learn anymore. They're kept quite dependent, aren't they?"

Fauna nodded but grimaced when she raised her hand to show Beatrice. It looked better than the rest of her body but even wiggling her fingers felt like it was cracking open her skin. How they managed to take so much damage after being strung up above her head baffled her.

"I suppose I could find something—my sister does enjoy collecting writing utensils. I'll be right back. Don't say anything to anyone. Oh, that's right," Bea chuckled again. "You can't!"

With that, the woman spun around and seemingly turned into a fine mist as she walked toward the shadow-covered door. She must still be exhausted, Fauna told herself. Her body was weak from her injuries and her mind was simply ill-equipped to process what had happened to her, which made her see things that weren't there in a desperate attempt to rationalize it.

To calm herself down and distract her wayward mind, Fauna laid back against the pillow and took in the hazy details of her dark room.

Paintings in frames the color of red wine were hung against the walls with prudent precision. Ornate filigree decorated the doors and windowsills, akin to the castles Fauna frequently read about in her books. A large floor-to-ceiling window took up half of the wall that she faced and let in quite a bit of natural light, even at night. There, the moon looked so plump and ripe that Fauna felt like she needed to pick it from the sky lest it become too sweet. When she squinted, she noticed that there seemed to be a balcony of sorts outside the window.

The ceiling in itself was hard to see in detail. Wide, swooping streaks of creamy paint glittered in the light like damp stones. Was she in a bedroom or a chapel? Perhaps a mausoleum, considering her state of health. There was *something* painted on the ceiling too, but the moonbeams did not quite stretch high enough to identify it. Before she could wallow in self-pity for too long, the same mist appeared in the corner once more as Beatrice stepped through the doorway. Though, the door didn't seem to open as she came in. Again.

Quickly, a handful of mismatched pens of varying sizes appeared in her lap alongside a nondescript but well-made journal.

"Sorry, I had to dig this out of Scarlet's room without waking her. She hoards these supplies, as if she has anyone to write to. Idiot. But, then again, that's my sister for you. She has *stacks* of blank notebooks and journals filled with nothing. But does that stop her from getting more? Never. She won't miss this one."

Fauna pressed the journal against her sheet-covered lap and tried her best to grip the large pen that felt more like a small mallet in her bumbling grasp. Eventually, she scrawled out her name in blocky letters. By the time she was finished, her hands were in so much pain that she'd begun to sweat and shake.

"Fauna?" Bea asked with an impressed look. "Cute. Oh! I have to go—Mother is adamant about keeping you a secret up here. Can you believe that? I'm her eldest daughter and she still won't confide in me. She said you died of 'natural causes' when you were dragged to her. I didn't believe her. Regardless, thanks for the company. We *never* have visitors!"

Fauna tried her best to smile at Beatrice, who grabbed the writing supplies and tucked them into a desk drawer across the room. Footsteps sounded outside her door so Beatrice held a finger to her lips and opened the window before sliding out onto the balcony.

The door clicked open and Fauna creaked her head around to peer at the door. A woman, familiar but just barely so, entered with only a click of her heels to announce her. Her hair was slightly darker than Bea's but wasn't as long. Her dress, too dark to truly discern, seemed to fit her quite well. Sharp features with a single dimple on her cheek gave her a spooky but serene quality.

"Burnt to bits and yet you defy pain to smile at me? How cute. It's good to see you awake. I was sure you would die when I brought you up here." The woman walked to the bed and loomed over

Fauna, blocking out all of the moonlight. Even in the darkness, her intense gaze and fluid movements reminded Fauna of an apex predator. Most of her body was obscured by the darkness, but there seemed to be an air of otherworldly energy about the woman. However, she'd saved Fauna and given her a room to recover in, so she tried her best to stay calm and assume the best.

"Can you speak?" the woman asked. When Fauna shook her head, she sighed. "Well, I must fill the silence then. I am Lady Aphrodite—the Countess of the Castle. Have you heard of Castle Verity?"

Fauna would have blanched if her skin had allowed it. *Castle Verity!* Lady Verity's reputation painted her as a sadist who fed upon screaming men as she hunted her prey in a fatal bacchanalia. Once again, as someone who was also tragically labeled a deviant, Fauna hesitated to believe the woven tales of wayward bards. But, given the Lady's imposing demeanor, she was not going to rule anything out.

"The Matron?" Fauna tried to speak, but only let out a pathetic wheeze. Thankfully Aphrodite seemed to understand what she'd been attempting to say.

"Ah, you've been listening to the pesky rumors running around the village," Aphrodite hummed quietly before sitting gently on the edge of the bed at Fauna's feet. "She is not here, nor does she live here. She lives at *Hurmehovi*, her highly guarded island in the sky. It's so high above us that you walk upon stairs made of clouds to get there."

Realizing that she had been still for too long, Fauna quickly nodded and made a writing motion with her hand. When the Lady understood, Fauna pointed to the same desk drawer from earlier. Aphrodite slid to the edge of the bed and opened the drawer to reveal the supplies.

"Did the maid bring these?"

Fauna, not willing to cause any issues between family members, nodded earnestly and waited.

"Well, that was fortuitous thinking on her part. I should give her a bonus."

While Lady Aphrodite's back was turned, Fauna's mind began to race. Had she imagined this woman rescuing her only hours prior? Was Fauna at the precipice of being consumed entirely by the woman? Were the tales fabricated by village elders to keep its residents in check? Was she in danger? Before she could ponder it further, Aphrodite set the pen and notebook in Fauna's lap.

"I will try to only ask yes or no questions to save your hands from exertion, but I do think some questions will require you to explain as much as you can." Aphrodite searched the room, grabbed the large rocking chair from in front of the window, and dragged it over to the bed. She sat with perfect posture and crossed her ankles before tucking her legs to the side. Fauna was concerned—had that rocking chair been there the whole time?

"What is your name?" she asked gently, a hand reaching to smooth out the twisted sheets on the bed. "Do not look so frightened. If you tell only the truth, you will be more than comfortable here."

With a thankful nod, Fauna opened the notebook and pointed to the name she'd scrawled earlier.

"Ah, such a pretty name," the Lady replied with a sly smile. "Are you a woodland creature? Do you grow in the forest?"

Fauna felt her already burnt skin warm at the compliment and shook her head at the playful question. Such kind words were foreign to her. In all honesty, she felt uncomfortable being noticed at all. Much of her life had been spent clinging to the strangely enticing solitude of darkness and the warm blanket of the moon at its highest spot in the sky. She did not *know* this woman yet, so all banter felt suspicious.

"May I look at your neck? I want to see how badly you were burned from the shoulders up."

Every instinct, every synapse begged her to slide under the blankets and hide from the woman. However, that was childish and she was very obviously *not* a child.

Aphrodite waited calmly for Fauna to agree before reaching out with a soft hand and gently grasping her chin. Her fingers were soothing and unnaturally cold against Fauna's injuries. It frightened her for a moment, but she quickly cast it aside as her body began to relax under the gentle touch. It had been ages since anyone had touched her, except to tie her to a stake. Her first instinct was to shy away, but unfortunately, she was unable to do so.

"You stayed hidden for so long," Aphrodite mumbled, though it seemed to be more to herself than to Fauna. "How, I wonder. Regardless, you'll be safe here. That much is certain."

Fauna squeezed the pen in her hand and scribbled out a wobbly and barely legible "thank you" on the page in front of her. The Lady removed her hand and moved it back to sit in her lap while Fauna struggled to move the book so she could read it better.

"You're quite welcome," Aphrodite snapped her fingers and waited for a beat. "We don't get much company here but I do try and keep tabs on the villagers so the Matron doesn't have to overwork herself. She's a busy woman, you know."

A soft rap against the door interrupted what she was going to say next and almost immediately, a tray with a tea set was pushed into the room. Before Fauna could see who it was, the door was shut and Lady Aphrodite stood to fetch it.

Fauna nodded and accepted the teacup. She took extra care to grip it only by the handle to avoid any extra heat to her healing palms. The thick bandages made it hard to hold so she tried her best to support the bottom of the cup with her other hand. It was clunky and uncomfortable, but she persisted anyway.

"Born and raised in the village?"

Another nod. She blew on the tea and sipped on it and smiled when she realized it was just a simple green tea at a medium-warm temperature. Nothing too heavily spiced for her burnt throat, but still incredibly soothing.

"Why didn't I know of you?"

Fauna set the cup down and spent a bit scrawling an answer. *I hid. From everyone.*

"And why would you need to hide? Did something happen to you? You don't seem hysterical or sickly to me."

I read and write.

Aphrodite, clearly impressed, hummed her surprise. "I see. Is that the *only* reason?"

Short, panicked breaths stuck in Fauna's aching chest, stretching the tender skin and making her eyes well with tears. She did not want to lie, especially now. Why had she admitted that?

"You seem to have your wits about you, Fauna. What did you do?" she asked quietly. Fauna surmised that she already knew but was just provoking her. She licked her rough lips and tapped the pen against the paper, making little black dots all over the page. The teacup still cooled in her other hand, barely even touched. Eventually, she forced out a sigh and shakily wrote down her damning crime.

I got books from outside.

"Oh, is that all?" the Lady seemed quite surprised by that information. Fauna braced herself in case she decided to swing at her. Instead, the Lady's eyes softened and her head tilted to the side. She set her teacup down and looked at her quite affectionately. "No harm will come to you." She put a large hand gently on each of Fauna's burnt shoulders. "You are safe here."

Fauna, extremely relieved but unable to conjure words, nodded in return and finished her tea. When she emptied the cup, it was gently taken from her and set on the nightstand.

"You have many injuries, inside and out." The Lady spoke matter-of-factly. "You're probably rather uncomfortable?"

Fauna nodded.

Aphrodite looked towards one of the walls in the dark.

"Lay back, I'll grab something to help a little bit."

Disappearing out of sight but reappearing just as quickly, Aphrodite stepped back into a moonbeam which gave Fauna the briefest hint of a well-fitting outfit.

"May I touch you?" Aphrodite asked gently. When Fauna very obviously froze at the idea, she held up her hands in surrender. "I won't hurt you. What if I promise to only touch your hands? This will take the sting out. It looks like the bandages on your fingers could come off too—you have to air out these types of burns." The Lady held the tin out for Fauna to sniff as it that would placate her. How could she explain that being around other people in a foreign place was already teetering on the edge of far too much for her?

It smelled of aloe and the twine they used to secure things in the village, but mashed into a puce sort of colored cream.

"Dip a finger into it, so you can know how it feels," the Lady offered. "I know what it's like to loathe being handled. I spend much of my life playing nice and polite amongst those who are not."

That made Fauna look up at the woman and her proffered tin. She nibbled on her lip and took a deep breath. Summoning every ounce of self-preservation she could muster, Fauna lifted both of her hands to Aphrodite, who set the tin in Fauna's lap and gently undid the bandages on her palms.

"Now, your hands will still hurt after this, but the nagging pain when you move them will be gone. Also, it's a bit slippery so writing immediately after will be difficult. May I take your hands?"

Fauna agreed, trying her best not to be anxious despite her nervousness about being touched.

"That's good." The Lady smiled and applied a small dollop of the salve to the upper palm of Fauna's left hand. A tingling chill moved through her hands and did indeed take away a lot of the discomfort.

"I'm so proud of you, especially for telling me so much about yourself," the Lady murmured while gently pressing the cream in between Fauna's fingers. "We will get you all healed up. You've already overcome so much."

Fauna, who had no means of communication when her hands were busy, bowed her head to the woman and shrugged her shoulders before looking away. So much praise was foreign to her. How was she supposed to react to it? There weren't books that dealt with what she was experiencing.

"Sleep now and keep your hands outside the blankets so they can dry. I'll try to get you something to wear over your bandages and see about getting you a personal attendant. Everything will seem much more manageable in the morning."

Fauna nodded as she laid back against the pillows. Once again, she found comfort in seeing the moon so clearly.

"Welcome to Castle Verity, little Fauna of the Forest. No harm looms ahead, so please sleep if you can."

As the door was shut, Fauna finally let loose the deep breath of anxiety she'd been holding in her chest. Her hands did feel much better and she almost couldn't feel anything when the Lady touched her fingers. The woman was a stranger and a dangerous one at that.

So, why was she so kind? And why did she so kindly ask Fauna if she was okay with being touched?

What was happening?

Why would anyone want to take care of her? She was the feral child raised by books in the hidden alcoves of the village. She was the haggard homely woman who wore only black and didn't speak a word to anyone. She was the oldest person in the village not to wed, choosing instead to read of mystical beings and grand romances atop magical mountains. And though she was no damsel, she was surely distressed. As she pondered her life, the moon began to sink once more, and Fauna fell fast asleep.

Three

The next few days passed in a medicated blur. Lady Aphrodite had assured Fauna that being asleep while she healed would make her days pass more quickly and to trust her with everything. Mornings and nights blended into one another until Fauna had no idea how much time had gone by. She only woke to drink her medicine mixed with cooled oats and have tepid broths tipped down her throat. She did all with an uncharacteristic optimism—at least she wasn't dead.

Gifted with a mind that dreamt in extremely detailed quality, Fauna genuinely enjoyed dreaming for hours on end. There were, of course, nightmares about being burnt, but she found that she had very little in the way of memories about her trauma. Most of her dreams were of her mother, which wasn't a *new* occurrence per se, but it did seem a little odd. The strange thing was… no matter how hard she tried, the details of her near-fatal escape from the village eluded her. It was as if it never happened. Once, she thought too hard about it and gave herself an awful headache. Perhaps it was her mind's way of self-soothing, or perhaps everything had happened too quickly for her to process any of it.

One drizzly and damp morning, Fauna woke to a tray of solid breakfast on a stand next to the bed. Behind the food, there was a small pack of much nicer pens. They had sleek black barrels with silver engravings and a very thick grip. They did not have removable nibs, for which she was very grateful. The finesse needed to write with a utensil like that was beyond her physical capability at the moment. She looked around the room and noted that nothing obvious had changed while she had rested for so many days. A glance down at herself revealed that her skin looked much healthier than it had. She still had discoloration and a painful tugging when she moved too quickly, but many of the scabs had come off and she no longer resembled something cooked upon a spit.

A couple of pillows had been tucked around her hips and a few more sat on the opposite corner of the expansive bed. Her dark hair hung in singed chunks around her head. Where it used to be near the middle of her back, it now barely skimmed her shoulders. Had the fire burnt her braids completely off? Hair was not something Fauna generally cared about, but a change so severe that she did not make made her extremely uncomfortable... and a little self-conscious. When she looked at the very edge of her peripherals, Fauna noticed that her gray streak had been stained with soot. She would need to wash that soon.

Fauna slid the tray onto her lap and grimaced as its warmth and pressure irritated her tender thighs. At least now it was more of a nuisance than outright pain.

Little by little, she cleared the plate and sighed in delight as she ate solid food for the first time in ages. She still had no idea how long she'd been out, but the memories of her resting period were blurry and disjointed. However, she had woken in much better shape than before, so she grabbed her notebook and began to scrawl a thank you note to Aphrodite and the staff for taking such good care of her.

It was strange, to speak with someone regarded as the most dangerous of villains. Even if Aphrodite was not overly kind or animated, Fauna still found herself comfortable. It could be because she had no other choice, but regardless, it wasn't the worst thing Fauna had experienced. She did miss having books to fill her time though. While her surroundings were new, there were only so many times she could memorize the ceiling. Granted, there was quite an interesting painting on it—one that featured two women reaching for each other. When she had first awoken, it was too dark to see, but in the daylight, it was an extremely beautiful piece of artwork. There was a certain somberness about it, but that also could have been Fauna's overactive imagination that was desperate to romanticize anything it could. Still, there was *something* that made her stare at it and wonder for hours on end.

The rumors of the Castle were aplenty in the village but Fauna had paid them little mind. Too eager to be in her silo, secluded from society, and too eager to dive into a book and leave the villagers behind, she missed almost all of the whispers about much of anything. To be honest, she didn't quite believe that Lady Aphrodite existed until she had been saved by her. It was strange that the villagers even spoke of her, considering they were so adamant that everything they believed in was right under their noses. Perhaps it was the Matron's ties to the Verity castle that made the story reputable to them.

All she had previously known about Aphrodite Verity was that she (or a witch, depending on the tale) loved stringing men up by their tendons and leaving their bones to dry by the fire. It was a silly rumor, one that Fauna frequently heard while she shopped in the village. Though, her favorite of the wives' tales was that the Castle was inhabited by soul-stealing ghosts that took on their victim's forms and walked around as them until their bodies died. Now, *that* was a story with potential.

She wanted to get up from the bed—wanted to stretch her legs. But, her knees could barely bend and her toes were still numb from the damage to her nerves. So, she settled for laying her tray on the bedside table and lying on her back.

A noise, familiar but not exactly so, vibrated outside her door, and a small knock rapped against it. Suddenly a giggle rang out and the door opened to reveal the young woman from before, only slightly less intimidating this time.

"Sorry, forgot you couldn't talk. I was waiting for you to invite me in," Bea chuckled as she walked into the room and looked over Fauna with an amused expression. "You should hear some of the rumors going around the castle about your little stunt. They're pretty entertaining. You're an enigma already. It's become a game to talk about you without Mother hearing—even the maids are in on it. How fun!"

Fauna cocked her head to the side, quite confused at what that could mean. All she wanted was to get better. There was little else in her future, considering she had nowhere left to go. What stunt had she pulled? Other than being nearly cooked, of course.

"Everyone keeps saying that you're *so* dramatic and you love attention. Do you like poetry?"

The sudden change in topic threw Fauna for a loop. She couldn't even correct Bea on reading her personality completely wrong. In her frustration, Fauna gave up and played along with the conversation, as confusing as it was.

"Poetry?" Fauna mouthed. It was easier than scrambling to write things down.

"Yes, it's where you use letters to make words," Bea teased obnoxiously while walking around Fauna's room. She purposefully turned a painting a *little* off-center and made a little mess here and there. "Well, do you? Scarlet writes poems in her spare time, which she has an abundance of considering she doesn't actually do anything. She's never paying attention to anything but her silly poems. I wonder if she's written about you yet. She gets very defensive over Mother's attention, as all little sisters do. Anyway, I don't think Mother likes you much. She won't tell us about you and she tells us *everything*."

Fauna reached into the bedside drawer for her journal and pulled it out quickly. Her hand began slowly amble across the page. She raised the journal to show it to Bea, but when she didn't look, Fauna slapped the book with her bandaged hand until Bea finally looked at her.

"God, you're annoying. *What?*"

What are you talking about?

"We don't keep secrets in this castle, we never have," Bea explained evenly. She sat down on the bed and pushed Fauna's leg brusquely out of the way. "And suddenly Mother pretends that we didn't see you at all.

Fauna was quite certain she did not remember that.

"Oh did you forget?" Bea clapped. "Well, one of the little maid things—I don't remember their names anymore—found you and screamed. But, never once did anyone tell us a single thing. Scarlet knows you're here, but she's shy, and I don't like trouble."

The implication that Fauna meant trouble irritated her to no end, but there was little she could do to prove Bea wrong.

"This is boring. You're boring. Well, maybe not really, but you can't tell me otherwise can you?" When Fauna didn't laugh, she tried something else and ripped the sheets off Fauna's body. "Are you really burnt everywhere?"

Fauna cried out pathetically and hissed when her throat began to spasm. She tried to grab for her last shred of privacy and began to cry out of frustration. Yes, she was still covered in bandages, but that didn't matter!

"Ha!" the girl laughed. "Humans have so many stupid feelings. You're just human, it's not like I haven't seen skin before. I just wanted to see how you were healing."

Fauna ripped the sheet out of the girl's hand. She brought it up to her bandaged chest and tried to shrink away from her. Why was this daughter being so rude? Was this some sort of game? She did not seem so wretched the last time.

"Oh, I hear footsteps. See you later!"

With that, Bea walked backward with a sly smile and snuck out the large window at the end of the bed, careful to avoid the rocking chair in front of it.

As soon as the window clicked shut, the bedroom door opened to reveal Lady Aphrodite, looking regal and refined. Another well-tailored dress—this time in a deep royal blue—made for a wonderful contrast against her fair skin. She looked around the mussed room and began fixing each thing one by one without even acknowledging Fauna. Why was everyone being so cold today?

Aphrodite continued to correct everything that Bea had disturbed until she looked around the room and nodded in acceptance. She swept the hair off of her neck and let the flaxen waves fall against her dress as she grabbed the rocking chair and turned to Fauna.

"Good morning," Aphrodite greeted her as she sat in the chair and crossed her legs professionally. "My schedule is tight today, but your wounds need to be tended to. I have assigned a personal maid to help you now."

Fauna sighed. She couldn't very much tell Aphrodite about Bea's mistreatment without causing an issue, so she just laid back against the pillows. She wasn't fond of people anyway, so it really shouldn't have bothered her so much.

"How are you feeling?" Aphrodite asked, then pointed to the sheet. "May I? I need to unwrap your burns."

Fauna nodded and reached for her notebook. At least the Lady had asked permission and gently removed the sheet, instead of ripping it off of her like her daughter had. Gentle fingers traced the bandages and lifted the edges just a bit, to judge the skin underneath. The vulnerable feeling alone had Fauna's heart beating wildly and her breaths sputtering in short gasps. With shaking fingers, she reached for her notebook and tried to be concise. There wasn't time or energy to explain why skin-to-skin contact with others made her uncomfortable.

Skin is sensitive. No sting, just ache.

"I'm glad to hear it," Aphrodite replied as she gently unwound the wraps around Fauna's chest. Fauna looked away, still viscerally swathed in discomfort at being looked at like a specimen. Being the center of attention was high on the list of things she did not enjoy.

"I see the rest has been good for you," Aphrodite said quietly. "You're healing nicely and there's more color in your skin. You were dreadfully pale when I found you."

Fauna, preoccupied by the urge to turn away in shame and the discomfort of being studied, tried her best to smile but couldn't muster one. Every muscle in her body wanted her to move away, but her injuries kept her still.

Taking the hint, Aphrodite stood and walked over to open the large window to reveal the sounds and scents of midday. Birds chirped off in the distance and the brush strokes of someone sweeping below immediately helped Fauna relax.

"Some fresh air will be good for your skin. You cannot walk, but if you'd like I could scoot the chair over to the window and carry you there. It would only be for a few minutes if I stay with you, or then for several hours if I were to send someone up later to help you back to bed. I don't want you to be helpless, but I don't have time to stay here much longer."

Fauna mulled it over. She did miss seeing outside, even if she'd chosen not to spend much time there. It was almost as if her love for the outdoors was rekindled the moment she was forced inside. After a minute, Fauna looked at the woman and smiled as she nodded. In return, the woman fondly smiled back. Never once had anyone paid such gentle attention to her. While it wasn't unwelcome, it still was very strange.

Aphrodite stood and moved the chair back to the corner, but swiveled it towards the window. Afterward, she grabbed Fauna and jokingly tickled her cheeks with the sheet until a breathy chuckle emitted from her. She was picked up, sheet and all, and carried to the chair like a bride over the threshold. Fauna looked down and saw the vulnerable pink skin that was peeking out between the slowly healing cracks that were fading on her legs.

She was gently placed in the chair and the blanket from the bed was deposited in her lap.

"Lay back. Relax. I know you've been through quite an ordeal, but you are safe in this castle—no harm will come to you. This chair holds a lot of memories and has been used by many people. Enjoy the sun and rest a little," Aphrodite said as she turned toward the door. "I'll be back later."

Fauna nodded and wrapped her arms around herself. The sunlight warmed her skin but did not burn, as the sun journeyed from the east to the west. She must have fallen asleep at some point because she woke to herself being lifted and deposited back in the bed.

Fauna furrowed her eyebrows and turned her head to look up at who was moving her.

"It's just me," Aphrodite hummed in delight as she stepped back. "Seems like a nap in the sun was just what you needed. Perhaps you are a little flower from the forest, withered without any sunlight."

Fauna wanted to ask about simple things like meals and bathing but found that when she tried to form the questions in her mind and reach for her notebook, she was simply too tired.

"Rest while you can," Aphrodite told her. "You have a lot of recovering to do. Sleep. Sleep."

Four

When she woke up tucked gently into the bed, Fauna found a small plate of sandwiches and a leather-bound book on her nightstand. Completely disregarding the food, she grabbed the book and turned to the first page. As soon as she opened it, the blissfully familiar scent of fresh parchment wafted around her. Fauna closed her eyes and took a few breaths, reveling in the momentary happiness. She was comfortable, healing, and had a fresh book to read.

The sandwiches, which were unfortunately tasteless and not remarkable, went down quickly. She wasn't one to spend too much time thinking about sustenance anyway—cooking for one was a waste of time. What was she trying to prove and who was she trying to impress?

When the plate was cleared, she set it back down and laid back once more. Her limbs already felt better, so she tried to stretch them and grimaced when her muscles tightened in protest. Still, she pressed on, using her hands to knead the muscles in her thighs and taking deep breaths until she felt as if the crumbs in her bones had disintegrated.

Soon, her focus traveled up to her arms and she began to simply *move*. It felt divine to release all the tension she'd been holding onto. She looked ridiculous, slowly moving her limbs like a sloth, but she was incredibly proud of herself for even trying. The pain was minimal, but still uncomfortable enough for her to be tired soon enough. Freshly motivated, Fauna grabbed the book and slid it into her lap. As soon as she began to open it, a knock on her door interrupted her.

"Good afternoon, Fauna," Aphrodite greeted her as she walked into the room. Her outfit was similar to the day prior, though colored in a deep burgundy instead. Perhaps she owned the same clothes in multiple colors. That did seem to be a smart idea. There was no shame in knowing what worked.

Fauna tried to greet her but was only met with an infuriating *wheeze* instead.

The attempt brought a polite chuckle out of Aphrodite. "You'll speak soon, I am sure. Do you like the book? I saw that you were writing, so I assumed you enjoyed reading as well. Was I correct?"

Unable to contain her smile, Fauna bashfully nodded at Aphrodite and silently whispered her thanks.

"Will you write something for me soon?" the Lady asked and pointed towards Fauna's journal. "When you are better? I would love to see what you could come up with. I like reading too."

Fauna paused. She had never truly penned anything but bits of embarrassingly lovelorn poetry with a variety of subjects. What kinds of things could she even write about? She had little in the way of life experience and almost everything she had written before were journal entries. Aphrodite looked quite pleased with her reaction, so she nodded slowly and tried to hide her blush.

"Did you have a good nap?"

Fauna nodded with an innocent smile and pointed to the chair in the corner.

"Ah, you liked the rocking chair. It has claimed many victims. Not a single soul can sit in it without falling asleep," Aphrodite chuckled softly. "I miss the days when the girls were so small, they both fit into my lap. We would count the stars and they would be snoring on each other before we even reached one hundred."

Fauna grabbed the notebook and began to write in better handwriting than her days prior. Her fingers seemed to understand their purpose better and the aches in her hands were more manageable. It still was barely legible, but the letters at least looked like something other than wobbly shapes.

I still don't like being touched.

If Aphrodite was confused about the topic change, she did not show it. "May I ask why?"

Fauna took a moment to decide how best to explain her aversion to other people. She scooted upright, thankful that she had just stretched.

Never done it. Feels strange.

Aphrodite's look of pity was almost too much for Fauna to handle. "You haven't even hugged someone or shaken their hand? Never had someone scratch your back as they pass you or lay their head against your shoulder?"

Fauna paused for a moment. Was she *supposed* to do those things? She had spent the vast majority of her life in her mind, avoiding anything that could interact with her. She knew that being alone had deprived her of some experiences, but she could gain those experiences from books.

Aphrodite took a deep breath in. "Well... what *do* you like? You're going to spend quite a bit of time up here, so you might as well have something to do."

Books are fine.

Aphrodite looked at the journal Fauna held up. "Anything else? Puzzles? Games?"

Fauna shrugged and shook her head.

"Then, someday you will see the libraries here. We have four—three of them are in private wings and one is accessible to anyone in the castle. However, I would be willing to show you around mine. There are books of all shapes, sizes, and topics. I think you would have quite a bit of fun there."

The idea of *four* libraries bombarded Fauna with a curious wonder that made her heart leap! The enthusiasm with which reading was spoken about filled her with a resounding joy. Oh, she was *excited* to get better and go exploring!

Quickly, with only a slight shake in her hands, Fauna began to write once more. Aphrodite's intense gaze made Fauna so nervous that she fumbled the pen several times. Eventually, she was able to write out what she had been trying to say.

Thank you. I miss reading. Books were not allowed. I hid them.

The lines took longer than they should have, but between her shaking hands and the pen sliding around the page, Fauna was just glad she was able to write it at all.

"Books are not allowed?" Aphrodite asked gently. "Who made that rule?"

The Matron.

"The villagers must have lied! Oh, those simple-minded pious fools!" Aphrodite shook her head in disapproval. "They almost killed you over a book? And they dare to lie about the Matron's rules?"

Fauna shrugged and nervously fingered the pages of her new book. The corner of the page creased a bit and she cursed herself for already bending it. There was a doubt in the back of her mind that the villagers had lied. They were annoying and simple, but they did not lie. It was exactly what she had always thought to be true—an educated population was dangerous and a dependent one was loyal. That was how all the rulers came to power in her books.

"Well, if you're comfortable, write down some things you like to read about," Aphrodite offered kindly. "I will look through our libraries and see if there are any books that might catch your eye."

Fauna nodded softly before focusing on making sure she was able to write something that Aphrodite would be able to read. Once she was finished, she gently ripped the page away from the binding and handed it over.

Aphrodite read through the list and tapped her finger against each line as if committing it to memory. She folded the piece of paper in half and regarded Fauna.

"Consider it done, though please be patient. I will be leaving for a few days—the castle's business never ends. I am called away quite a bit, you'll come to know that. You just happened to be here at a very opportune time. Once I'm home, I'll come to see how you're doing."

Fauna nodded again. It had only been a few days but she was so tired of nodding and shaking her head to get her point across. Her throat needed to heal as soon as possible.

Aphrodite reached out but hovered over her shoulder. "May I?"

Curiosity got the best of Fauna, so she agreed. Aphrodite placed a warm hand on Fauna's shoulder and squeezed. A curious warmth spread through Fauna's body and made her cheeks turn pink. It was the most innocent of gestures, but she was so new to even being *seen* that all attention embarrassed her.

"Do you hurt? You're very tense."

Fauna picked up her pen again. Perhaps tomorrow she would try out the nice new ones.

Stiff. My skin feels tight.

Aphrodite set the paper on Fauna's nightstand and reached out once more. "I suppose I could spare a few more minutes. Could I help?"

When Fauna tentatively permitted her, Aphrodite pressed her thumb gently into the meat of Fauna's shoulder. There was no pain—more of an insistent pressure. Slowly, Aphrodite's focus moved across Fauna's upper back, releasing a lot of the tension. The relief immediately improved Fauna's mood. Never once had she ever tried to do something like that for aching muscles. Her father had always taught her that a good night's sleep would do the trick but that clearly wasn't working, considering all she had done lately *was* sleep.

Gently, Aphrodite peeled away some of the bandages on Fauna's skin. "You're looking good here. Perhaps soon we could remove these wraps and get you into an actual piece of clothing. How does that sound?"

Instead of nodding or writing her answer, Fauna chose instead to give Aphrodite her brightest smile—even if it was a little awkward. There had not been many chances in Fauna's life to do such a thing, but it seemed as good a time as any.

"Could I peek a bit more? I would like to see your neck and upper arms."

Fauna took a deep breath and allowed Aphrodite better access to her wounds. She gently lifted some of the bandages and peeked at Fauna's skin underneath. Bit by bit, she inspected the burns and when she was finished, she tapped Fauna's shoulder gently.

"Your newly healed skin is irritated, likely from being in the same position for too long. We're lucky that it's not broken open. I'll send your new helper up with some salves to treat that and I'll make sure she helps you sleep in a different position to air out your skin." With that, Aphrodite grabbed Fauna's book list from the bedside table and stepped backward. "I do need to be going. Will you still write something down for me while I'm gone? It would make my

dreadfully boring trip much sweeter if I knew a nice letter was
waiting for me at home."

Fauna stretched to read her journal again.

Okay. Can I take a bath?

"The maid will help you with that too. She's quite friendly and
also loves to read. I will tell her to bring a few personal recommendations so you can get to know each other. You can write down
how you feel about the books in your journal if you'd like. You're
under no obligation to show those entries to me, but I would love
to know your thoughts, should you be willing to share them."

Beside herself at the generosity this woman had bestowed upon
her, Fauna simply gazed up at the beautiful woman and mouthed,
"Thank you."

"You're quite welcome. You are safe here, please remember that."

When she left the room, a warmth bloomed in Fauna's chest.
Why would Aphrodite Verity be so kind to a stranger? That was
not the woman that the village had made her out to be. Sure, she
was a little cold at first, but so was Fauna. They were strangers
brought together by a traumatic incident that had nearly killed her.
Now, she just had to win over the daughters. Well, so far only Bea
had introduced herself. She was interesting, to say the least. But,
Aphrodite promised she was safe and Fauna had no other option
than to believe her. She had nothing to offer the castle, so there
really wasn't any reason to lie to her.

Her thoughts were scattered—what would she write down for
the Lady to read? How would she even address it? Was "Aphrodite
Verity" improper? Would the maid be someone willing to respect
Fauna's aversion to contact? Would she finally get a bath? How
could she have a bath without contact if she couldn't walk? So many
questions were spiraling around her mind that she had to close her

eyes and take even breaths to try and concentrate. So much was happening for someone so accustomed to a slow life.

Being incapacitated made Fauna realize that perhaps having someone to talk to wasn't the worst thing that could happen. Perhaps, the terrifying women of Castle Verity weren't as bad as the stories made them seem. Maybe there was more to the story, maybe not. Either way, she had a new book, some things to write with, and a maid coming to potentially help with a bath... so life wasn't all terrible.

Five

*L*ady Verity,

    You asked me to write you a letter but I don't know what to say. My writing is very messy and I doubt you'll be able to decipher most of this. Maybe I'll never deliver this to you and just address my journal entries as such. Is that strange? I don't recall ever wanting to write things down about my life. I am purposely nothing, I barely exist. I live through the stories others have written and I am fine with that. I am just someone meant to read and imagine. I take comfort in the mundane.

    So, hello to you, I suppose. I am Fauna. My father was silent most of my life, and my mother died before I knew her. I am older than I look but that is not on purpose. I tell time by the sun in the sky and I smell when it's going to rain. I once went one hundred and sixty-five days without leaving my home and I still yearn for the tranquility brought to me by that solitude. I watch people with wonder and ponder what fuels their desire to do the strangest of things. What makes them fall in love? What makes them violent? Why do they not question what the Matron tells them? Why don't they think for themselves?

    People are frightening and ridiculous and I think that I will never understand them.

    My hands hurt when I sleep. I have tingles everywhere and anywhere on my body. The arch of my foot became terribly itchy last night, but it was too uncomfortable for me to try and scratch it, so I suffered. I feel as if my bones are made of bricks.

The painting on the ceiling is pretty, as is the rest of the room. What is outside that window? I cannot see properly as the trees are too tall. I haven't spotted any birds, but I can surely hear them.

I hope the Merchant is well and likes the chocolate I left him, even if he thinks I am dead. I hope he doesn't blame himself. I blame the Matron for just about everything.

I hate the Matron. I apologize if you do not. She stole my mother from me, of this I am certain. My mother was the bravest woman that I have never met. She dared speak out against a tyrant ruler and she died for it.

I am Fauna and I am not a sheep.

I am Fauna and I still smell my burning flesh as I fall asleep.

I am Fauna, but I have no idea what that means anymore.

With the last sentence done in her journal, Fauna gasped at the cramp in her hand when she set down the pen. Her fingers contorted without reason and a sharp pain shot into her elbow. She clutched her arm to her chest in hopes of relieving the pain, which it *did*, but only a bit. It frustrated her to no end that her only means of communication was so agonizing. Not only was her voice reduced to a hoarse cough, but now her hands were betraying her. She shut the heavy cover and slid it down the bed by her calves. The letter had taken her seven hours to write and every other minute, she debated whether it was too much information to give Aphrodite when she returned.

Just as her hand began to relax and the sun began to set, the sound of footsteps came from outside her door. Fauna tried to cover herself up with the bedsheet, to preserve some of her dignity. But even with the rest of the bandages that covered most of her body, she still felt rather exposed. Before she could tuck herself into the sheet, she heard a solid knock, and her door was opened.

"H–hello?"

When Fauna didn't answer, she heard footsteps enter her room.

"You sure don't look okay," the voice said as it drew nearer to the bed. "The staff said you didn't look very good. I said you weren't screaming, so it couldn't be too bad. Bea called me an idiot."

Screaming? What kind of atmosphere did the Castle normally have? Fauna, intrigued by the gentle tone that was paired so casually with talk of screaming death, angled her body in the other direction to see who had entered the room. The only light was from the fleeting sunset, so she squinted to try and figure out who was speaking to her.

A stocky girl, with curly hair the color of autumn leaves and eyes the color of fog, smiled and slid into the oversized rocking chair. The girl touched the wooden arms as if remembering something, pulling her slippered feet up cross-legged beneath her.

"Hi, I'm Scarlet," the girl whispered, though no one else was in the room. "You're Fauna, yes?"

Fauna nodded.

"Does Mother know you've been talking to us?" Scarlet undid her legs to rock using a foot on the ground.

The gentle creaking to the back and forth made Fauna a little sleepy. A yawn built in her chest but got stuck halfway up, which made her chest spasm in the most distressing of ways. When she was able to breathe, Fauna shook her head and held a finger up to her lips.

"Oh, it's a secret?" Scarlet's eyes widened. "I love secrets. I can keep them *forever.*"

Fauna smiled nervously and grabbed her journal. She tucked the bedsheet under her armpits and began to write in the book. She raised the page to show Scarlet, who stood and moved a bit closer to read it.

I was hurt and saved. No one can know that I'm up here.

Scarlet read it and nodded in understanding. She looked at Fauna's bandages with a strange amount of scrutiny and eventually spoke.

"I see. What happened?"

Burned.

"Oh, what a foul way to nearly die." Scarlet flopped on her back, making herself at home on Fauna's bed. "Not the least bit romantic. Makes for a good story though."

Fauna's eyebrows shot up.

Not romantic at all. How old are you?

Scarlet snickered. "Older than you, that's for sure. But, isn't it rude to ask that? Anyway, what's in an age anyway?"

The rhetorical question made Fauna pause. What was Scarlet even talking about?

"You're all right in the head, I take it?" Scarlet asked. "Well, as right as any of us could be. That's good to know. You really can't talk?"

Fauna shook her head. Scarlet began to eye her incredulously before her head shot up.

"Oh, someone's coming! I can hear them on the stairs! Bea and I have to take turns, so you'll see her later tonight or tomorrow." Scarlet winked as she slid out of the window, which was still cracked, and disappeared into the fresh night. "Goodbye, new friend!" her voice whispered in her wake.

A gentle knock stole Fauna's attention as a bright mop of curly red hair made its way into the room, attached to a softly rounded woman with a large satchel at her hip and a thick towel in her hand.

"Hello, I'm Rhiannon. Lady Verity asked that I bring you dinner and a book. Dinner isn't for a few hours, but I was bored of waiting around so I just grabbed a book instead. I was *very* curious to meet you. Not many people, especially those from the village, read much. Sorry, I talk a lot when I meet someone new and I heard you can't talk so I thought that I would make up for that." Rhiannon suddenly looked a little embarrassed. "I think I'm done babbling now."

The way Rhiannon acted, as if Fauna was the first friendly person she had ever met, made Fauna breathe a sigh of relief. She smiled, which she had been doing more and more whilst in the Castle, and made a gentle grabby motion to the book. The woman's pink cheeks were scattered with freckles just like hers, and her eyes were the deepest shade of green that she had ever seen. It hadn't taken much but a book and a friendly smile and Fauna found herself uncharacteristically charmed.

"Lady Verity asked if I would bring my favorite, but I don't read as much as I used to," Rhiannon lamented. "I could bring more once you're finished. I don't have a dedicated station here, but I was raised in the castle so I'm very familiar with how things work. I'm more of someone who fills in when needed. I've been assigned to you!"

A small bit of light started to shine into the darkness of her heart. Fauna nodded so earnestly that her hair fell from behind her ears and covered her face. She shook it away, which made Rhiannon laugh and point towards the empty half of the bed.

"Care if I have a seat? My feet hurt and I brought my book too. I thought maybe you could use some company tucked away in here. If not, I can use the rocking chair, but I always seem to fall out of those. I get too aggressive in rocking and I tumble. I know, not very mature of me."

Fauna reached for her notebook and scribbled furiously. She wanted to tell the maid to go away, but that seemed a little rude for someone tasked with helping her.

I'm not used to having visitors.

"Oh! You can write? Amazing. I thought that I would have to stick to basic yes or no questions. Okay. Which book do you want first?"

Fauna pointed to Rhiannon and mouthed *you pick* to her. The maid smiled devilishly as she grabbed a thin one and handed it over.

"This is a short story, but I found it in the library and Scarlet let me keep it. Oh, she's one of the daughters here. I don't think you'll meet them, given that you're tucked up here. They're both very nice, except if you cross them too often. Then they can be fickle and you'll find yourself staying in the cellar for a bit."

Fauna's curiosity was piqued. What was in the cellar?

Rhiannon's face contorted. Clearly, she had said too much. "Oh, pay me no mind. You're as far away from the cellar as you can be. Besides, with you stuck in a bed and locked in a room, I hardly think you'll be any trouble for anyone."

Fauna made sure there was quite a bit of room between them on the bed. She still was leery of having someone so close to her, but it seemed to be something she would need to tolerate now that she was dependent on others to do most basic things.

But, Rhiannon seemed docile and kind-hearted, so Fauna felt safe enough to try. The maid slid onto the bed and gently rearranged the pile of stuff that had begun to accumulate. The large journal still sat open between them. She had no idea what else to write in it. Especially since she could only write a paragraph at a time before her hand began to cramp. Instead, she shut the journal and slid it aside to make room.

"I have to mark pages in advance to prevent me from getting too lost in my books, I wouldn't want to forget to feed you!" Rhiannon laughed and got comfortable. "I'm sure you understand what it's like to lose yourself in reading. Are you okay like this?"

Fauna nodded to her and cracked open the first page of her short story. She began to read and immediately felt a strange kinship with the protagonist. The author painted a strong picture of just how much the main character loved her father. Though it was a bit up in the air as to what happened to him, the character was lost when he died.

As the story went on, Fauna found herself relating a little bit *too* much to the character and memorized the page she was on before shutting the book a bit louder than she had intended. It startled her and made her tuck the sheets around herself defensively. Perhaps that wasn't the best book to read after such a traumatic event. Vulnerability was *not* something Fauna was used to and feeling so raw and exposed was extremely unsettling.

"It's a morose one, isn't it?" Rhiannon asked as she checked the time. "Makes you think though. Parents are important to us, and they form how we grow up. But, how much is too much? I'm lucky in that department—my mother was great."

Fauna opened the journal and turned to a fresh page while contemplating how much she wanted to tell this random woman. She tapped the pen against the pages for a while, working out what exact words to use.

My father died years ago.

"I'm sorry about that," Rhiannon said softly. "Were you close?"

Fauna shook her head.

Not in the end. We were familiar strangers.

"A conundrum. Familiar strangers. I like that. Then please, take your time with the book. Savor the words, don't swallow them whole," Rhiannon advised. "I'll bring another book when you are finished. You just let me know. I believe Lady Verity left one for you too?"

Fauna pointed to the two books that had been shuffled down to the foot of the bed. Remembering something, she got Rhiannon's attention and scribbled in her book.

I might need help bathing.

"I have a bath planned for later tonight, if that's okay? I need to get the creams that Lady Verity was using before I take the rest of your bandages off. I think she said that you'd be okay to air the wounds out overnight though! So, you can either sleep naked or I can grab you a shirt. I know I'm a bit larger than you, but it's the most I can offer you until we get you some clothes made. It would at least be extra comfortable!"

With that, Rhiannon slid off of the bed and pointed to her bookmark nestled in her book. "See, it works! I'll go fetch your dinner and give you some time to yourself. Thanks for letting me hang out here."

Fauna watched the maid leave and once the door closed, she opened the book again. This time, she was more prepared, but still felt a sinking feeling in her gut as she read onward.

When she turned to the last page, Fauna let a few tears fall. Never had she grieved her father, but for some reason, reading about the poor woman who was so attached to her father that she would actively keep her house intact down to the last bit of dust just didn't sit well with her. But then she wondered… was that what she was *supposed* to do? Was it normal to mourn someone so viscerally that any changes were not acceptable? Fauna had sold her father's things for practicality's sake—she didn't need them and the money was nice. Even her father's small collection of her mother's belongings had dwindled over the years until it was all gone.

She didn't miss her father the way the woman in the book had, though occasionally things reminded her of him. The whiff of alcohol or burning tobacco always brought back a feeling of comfort, which was strange because once she was able to talk about her lack of faith in Matron, he no longer comforted her. Her father never beat her or forced her into anything, he simply just let Fauna raise herself in her mystical imaginative world. While he never hurt her physically, his silence nevertheless took a very distinct toll.

She tried to remember the last time he'd hugged her... and she couldn't. Fauna couldn't remember which came first—her aversion to touch or her father's death. She was so used to taking care of him in silence that she barely remembered what he even sounded like. It didn't seem like he hated her, but it also seemed that his love for her tapered off as well. During the last few years of his life, he felt like more of a stranger than much else. Fauna always assumed he was simply too disappointed in her to try and make an effort.

It was baffling that the castle felt safer to her than her village. The castle, rumored to have such awful people within it, had so far been the best thing to happen to her. The people were kind enough, that was for sure.

Rhiannon also made her feel safe, which was bewildering to Fauna. Even after only a few hours, the plump little maid had been quite fun to be around. Fauna would go out on a limb and call Rhiannon an acquaintance. Granted, she was also a caregiver and hired help, but she was still cheery and talkative. Also, Fauna was pleasantly amused that she'd finally found someone more awkward than herself—a challenging feat.

Lady Aphrodite had told her that she was recovering quickly and Fauna believed her—what could she gain from lying, after all? She wouldn't tell her about the libraries and the people in the castle if she didn't have plans to introduce them. Beyond healing, Fauna had no idea what she would do. Perhaps Lady Aphrodite would let her cook or clean. Oh! Maybe she could be a *librarian!*

Going from a hardened recluse in the isolated darkness to a woman wrapped in bandages and forced to depend on strangers had thrown her for a loop. However, despite it all, Fauna was content and healing.

Six

While Rhiannon was gone, Fauna found herself lying sideways across her bed and staring out into the night. The moon sat high in the clouds and she wanted nothing more than to crack open the large window and take a breath of the brisk nighttime air. Even if it brought a bite of chill, she did not care. She missed being outside—missed being able to take a walk or simply stand.

It hadn't been very long, but she was starting to realize all of the things she took for granted. Not wanting to go outside was a choice, but now it was a decision that was not hers to make. Choosing to read books all day instead of being social was her decision, but now that was her only option. Loneliness wasn't something she ever truly felt, but she did feel a pang of something in her chest when she wanted to ask a question but had no one to ask. Lady Aphrodite was busy, her daughters were a secret, and Rhiannon spent time with her, but not every waking moment.

So, instead of picking up the book, she grabbed her pen and wrote down what she was feeling.

Lady Verity,

I have not decided if I will give you these letters, or if my journal will simply be named after you. You are the first person to insist that I keep in contact, even via writing. It feels weird to name my journal, but I suppose no one can think it's weird if I never show them.

I am angry today. Not at anyone who still walks among us, mind you. And even then, I think my anger is misplaced.

I am angry at my mother for leaving me in the care of a man who could barely get himself out of bed, let alone raise a child. What kind of father stops speaking to their child at fourteen? A wretched one!

I am angry that the only things I know about my mother were things I was told as a child and little snippets my father muttered when he drank too much. I wish I remembered her. I wish I could have known her. I wish she could see me and all I have amounted to. I wish she could know that I never caved—never fell on my knees for everyone else's idol. I hope she is proud of me.

I only know she was beautiful, and that she loathed the Matron so aggressively that she was shunned because of it. I always thought my father was so devoted to the Matron to cancel out my mother's ire, but that seems even more pathetic! I cannot recreate my mother's beauty, but I can channel her lust for independence and freedom—both of which I had until this wretched attack.

Why did my mother hate the Matron so much, I wonder? I know why I hate her, but those reasons are obvious. She's a tyrant, a dictator, addicted to power. She lures the simple-minded to their graves and robs them blind. She steals their children and kills their husbands. No one ever lives to tell the tales of their interactions with her, and it drives me crazy! She's no larger than myself but her presence alone can make people do the strangest things.

Or do I hate her because my father loved her more than he loved me? He polished his sacred texts and hung her photograph above the mantle but never had anything to do with me. He never even tried to reach out to mend our relationship.

He gave his life to the Matron and I, in return, was in charge of everything he neglected.

I am angry at him for dying.

I am angry at myself for not caring more. Why am I so twisted in the head? Why am I suddenly—after thirty-five years—wondering if everything I have ever based my moral compass on was wrong? Why do I suddenly find myself wanting to talk to people when I cannot? Why do I want to sit in the rocking chair and put my head on Aphrodite's shoulder while she tells me about the stars? When did I suddenly become so vain that I care what I'm wearing?

Perhaps I'll never know.

When she finished her last word, Fauna set her pen down and slammed the journal shut. She did *not* like the things she was feeling. To her, wanting help was shameful. She'd practiced for years and years to be self-reliant. Now, she couldn't even move off the bed or change her clothes. What would happen if she fell? Would she lay on the floor crying until Rhiannon came to her rescue?

As soon as she started to spiral, she heard someone knock. Rhiannon rolled a tray of food into the room and wiped her hands on her apron. Eager to hide her impending tantrum, Fauna brushed the tears away from her eyes and scooted into her normal position on the bed. It was surprisingly easy to fake a smile. Part of her felt disingenuous for lying to her new helper, but she didn't want to talk about it—writing it all down would take far too long and she was *not* showing anyone her letters.

"Okay, here's your dinner. I've got mine too. I'll be honest, walking up and down those stairs is taxing so forgive me if I spend a lot of time here. There is a lift for those with carts and trays, but it's quite busy at this time of day and you're not technically part of the castle yet."

Fauna, with more than a little effort, heaved her legs over the side of the bed. Rhiannon slid the cart to her and pushed it flush against her knees like a makeshift table. Rhiannon grabbed the rocking chair from the window and took her spot on the other side of the cart. She smiled from across the expanse, her green eyes twinkling with some unknown delight. Fauna felt compelled to smile back, something she was dreadfully unused to. Rhiannon blushed at the friendly gesture.

"Thanks for letting me eat up here," Rhiannon admitted in between bites of food. "The other maids are nice enough, but they are much older than me and we don't have much in common."

Fauna did not like the idea of someone purposefully upsetting Rhiannon.

"I know you can't talk much, but I can read lips if that helps," Rhiannon sounded as if she'd just remembered that. "I have problems hearing in one of my ears, so when it's loud I have trouble separating noises around me. I learned how to read lips so Lady Verity didn't have to tell me things twice. She doesn't like repeating herself and I don't like upsetting her, so it just seemed beneficial to us both."

"What happened?" Fauna mouthed, exaggerating the words in a way that seemed *very* silly but seemed to work.

"It's not as dramatic as it sounds," Rhiannon laughed. "I pulled on a cow's tail when I was young and it kicked me in the head! My grandmother always said that it bruised my brain too, that's why I'm so funny even when I'm not trying to be."

Fauna laughed for perhaps the first time in as long as she could remember. It didn't hurt her throat or turn into a cough, even though it sounded like a painful wheeze. That alone made her laugh even more. She continued to laugh until she clutched her sides with little amused breaths. When was the last time she'd found something so funny? And for that to happen after all that she'd endured? Simply wonderful.

"See? You agree," Rhiannon teased. "I'm hilarious."

Fauna replied with a very fake serious nod before bursting into silent but contagious giggles.

"Did you have many friends before?" Rhiannon asked as she patted the corners of her mouth with a napkin. "On the outside? You're easy to get along with."

Fauna grimaced and made a circle with her fingers to show that she had zero friends at all.

"None?" Rhiannon sounded surprised. "But you're so nice!"

Fauna shook her head again as she looked down at her plate awkwardly. She had never *tried* to be nice because no one had ever been nice to *her*. Perhaps an opportunity for growth was unfurling.

"You're not nice?" Rhiannon asked gently. "I think you are."

Fauna shook her head and continued to look down. Soon, the creak of a chair broke the silence and the bed dipped next to her.

"Do you like hugs?" Rhiannon asked. "Lady Aphrodite warned me that you were a bit skittish to touch."

Fauna grimaced but took a second to think it over. She'd had such a good time so far and Rhiannon seemed so kind. So, she nodded once and gasped when two strong arms wrapped around her frame. The embrace, while quite surprising, was kind of… nice. What made it even better was how little it hurt. The scabs had fallen free and while her skin was still very raw, she was able to move without constant pain. Rhiannon clung to her and eventually let go with a very sentimental look.

"Whoever told you that you aren't kind is an idiot," she said with a bit of sass. "I'm not sure why I'm crying but I do it often so you should probably get used to that."

Fauna fell back a little bit and reached around the maid for her journal. Soon, she held it up with three simple words.

I told myself.

"You told yourself that you aren't kind?" Rhiannon asked sadly. "Why would you do that?"

Fauna shrugged. Even *if* she could speak, she wouldn't have been able to answer that question. There were too many parts to explain and not enough words and eventually Rhiannon wouldn't want to listen and then she would leave.

Rhiannon patted her on the shoulder affectionately and let her hand linger for a moment. She chewed on her lower lip and looked as if she was having an internal debate on what to say.

"Could I ask a personal question? I don't want to upset you. I'm just curious."

Fauna indicated that it was okay and prepared herself for whatever could spill from the maid's mouth.

"You're so beautiful… why are you here?" Rhiannon seemed to genuinely wonder. "Not that I'm sad to meet you. But, you could have your pick of anyone in the village to marry, so why are you alone?"

Of all the things Fauna expected Rhiannon to ask, that was absolutely not one of them. She had never cared about looks—vanity was something reserved for those who wanted to gain something. She did not. There was no prim about her and not a single moment of her life would be wasted on something so shallow. Unwilling to explain it all, Fauna reached for her journal again.

I don't care about being beautiful. I don't want to win affections. I want to read.

"Are you not interested in anyone?" Rhiannon seemed to pick her words carefully. "At all?"

No. I never have been.

"Oh." Rhiannon said glumly.. "Well, you're quite pretty—even if you don't care. I like your hair. The gray streak is very unique. And your cheeks are so cute! I want to pinch them."

Fauna stared at her.

"But I won't!" Rhiannon assured her. "That would be mean! I get nervous around pretty people."

"Pretty," Fauna mouthed and pointed at the bashful maid. *"You."*

"Stop!" Rhiannon covered her face and laughed a hearty belly laugh. "Be careful, I'll never go away if you keep being so sweet to me!"

Before Fauna could say anything back, Rhiannon was up with a chuckle and clearing the dinner mess. She stacked all the plates together and set them on the bottom shelf of the rolling tray. When she turned around, she clapped her hands and motioned to another door on the opposite side of the room.

"Are you okay if I carry you?" she asked as she moved the cart away from the bed. "I need to get you to the restroom and into the bath before I go back downstairs. Or, I could help you walk. I'm not sure how well that would work out, though."

Fauna looked down at her legs and willed one to move. When it did not move, she sighed and began to lift the sheet off of herself. It was frustrating that her legs seemed keen on healing some days, but as soon as she had hope, they were unresponsive once again. Her skin looked like it was healing rapidly, so why wasn't the rest of her?

Rhiannon placed a hand under Fauna's knee and scooped her up into her arms. "And before you complain, I had to carry double sacks of potatoes to and from the garden for most of my life, so you are hardly an effort for me. Don't be shy, we all have the same bits and bobs when it comes down to it."

As she was transported from her bed to the bathroom, Fauna glanced back and saw the dried rusty splotches where she had been sleeping. It disgusted her to think that she had been lying in her own blood. Had one of her wounds opened up? Did she need more cream for her skin? When had *that* happened? She didn't feel like she was bleeding.

"Can I set you on the toilet and go change your bedding? Will you be okay?" Rhiannon asked and carefully set Fauna on the cold seat when she agreed.

While she did her business, Fauna took a moment to look around the small bathroom. Briefly, she pondered why she was only seeing the room *now*, but chalked it up to days of sleeping and dehydration. The walls were a bright white instead of the warm royal colors of her room. The bath, the towels, the shower, and what looked like a steam room in the corner of the mid-sized room. Little vials of powders and bulbous glass bottles of liquids lined a large shelf that ran around the entire wall.

"Extravagant, isn't it?" Rhiannon mused as she took in the room. "I haven't been up here but maybe once? I think the room is protected by something that makes it impossible to find unless you're a member of the family. I'm joking, but the Lady told me exactly where to go and I still almost got lost. This castle is a maze that only the most seasoned of workers can navigate. I still have to go to the center of the castle sometimes to reorient myself."

"Wow," Fauna mouthed, her eyes still transfixed on the mirrors around the room.

"Are you finished? I can find something else to do for a bit?" Rhiannon asked. "I find it more comfortable to put someone in the bath and then run the water, just so you don't get shocked by the temperature. Also, it keeps you safe from sliding out of my arms."

Fauna indicated that she was done by raising her arms and waiting to be picked up. When Rhiannon lifted her and set her on the edge of the tub, the cool porcelain of the rim of the bath made her body break out in goosebumps.

"I need to unravel the bandages around you, is that okay?" Rhiannon asked.

Fauna waved a hand to signify she was fine and hissed as Rhiannon's nimble fingers skimmed her skin. The contact was minimal but even so, being touched in such vulnerable places like her ribs or knees, had her body desperate to get away. She wasn't offended by it, not in the slightest. Being cared for was a new experience but so far it wasn't unbearable. It was just... new and necessary if she wanted to feel clean. The fresh skin was extra sensitive in the crisp air of the bathroom, making Fauna shiver more than once.

As the bandages were undone to reveal her chest, Fauna grimaced at the red scars that were very bright against her skin. When her torso was unraveled, Fauna looked down once and quickly looked away. Mottled red wounds and the remains of huge, gross scabs inhumanly covered her skin. She looked like a monster. Granted, her scabs had already healed quite quickly thanks to Lady Aphrodite's medicines and the stellar care given to her. But, it was still uncomfortable to see herself in such a state.

Rhiannon tossed the pile of bandages into the nearby garbage. "I promise, no matter what happens, I have seen so much worse. Being in this castle has yielded some strange experiences, that's for sure.

"No one has seen me naked," Fauna mouthed twice when Rhiannon missed the first attempt at communication.

"Well, that's okay, I'm not here to peek," Rhiannon assured her. "The maids share a bath so I promise you this isn't hard for me."

Fauna was curious. "Share?"

"We have a communal bathing room," Rhiannon explained. "We mind our business all take part in keeping it clean. We're provided with the necessities and whatever else anyone brings is their decision. I usually help make scented soaps, but the ingredients sometimes make my head hurt if I spend too long there."

A heavy and incomplete silence followed for a minute or two.

"Also, no one wants to look at me," Rhiannon admitted and waved at Fauna's body. "I'm not much to look at."

Fauna, unaccustomed to being perceived as a whole, took a moment to decipher if Rhiannon's words were a compliment to her or an insult directed at her own body.

"I'm sorry, that was rude of me," Rhiannon sighed as she took off the top dress of her maid's outfit along with her shoes and socks. She stood in her shift and bare feet, ready to start the bath. "I didn't mean for it to come out that way. I just… sometimes get envious of others. It's a bad habit that I would be smart to get rid of."

"Pretty," Fauna reassured her with a poke to Rhiannon's shoulder.

Rhiannon flushed, her cheeks taking on a rosy tint.

"Thank you," she whispered bashfully before changing the subject. "How about we pick a scent? Who knows, maybe Lady Verity will visit later? Wouldn't want her to think you smell bad!"

Fauna laughed silently and pressed her toes into the cool bottom of the empty tub. When she felt Rhiannon behind her, she turned around and looked at all the scents laid out.

"Pick one!" She offered the vials to Fauna, who uncorked them all and gave them a sniff. When she got to the last one, she debated and selected one filled with soft pink powder.

"Fresh Blossoms? Good choice," Rhiannon nodded and handed her the vial. "Just a pinch works wonders and you'll smell like a garden."

Fauna sprinkled a bit into the empty bath and giggled when the pink powder settled on her pale feet. As Rhiannon went to put the powders back, Fauna realized something.

She didn't have any scarring on her feet, even though that's where she'd originally been burned the worst. Her toes were all intact and her feet were unscathed compared to the rest of her body. Maybe her boots had saved her skin. But... she'd felt her skin tear inside her boots when she'd been dropped at the castle and now they looked normal. Perhaps sleeping for such long bouts had truly jumpstarted her healing process.

"Do you like hot baths?" Rhiannon asked. "We can't go too hot because of your freshly healed skin but I can try."

Fauna shook her head. *"Cold."*

"How cold?" she asked as she turned on the faucet. "Is this okay?"

The lukewarm water quickly dissolved the powder on Fauna's feet. When the water touched her skin, she lamented that it was still warmer than she was used to, but she didn't feel like complaining so she smiled at Rhiannon and nodded that it was fine.

"Okay, I'm going to slide you in the bath so be careful not to let yourself smack the bottom. I know your muscles must ache from everything. I'll tell you what, if the Lady doesn't come up to say goodnight, I'll bring up some salves and work it into your muscles. Otherwise, if she's on her way up here, I'll send it up with her."

Fauna groaned as the water lifted her and caressed her skin. She was glad that she'd not had Rhiannon re-run the bath because even the smallest amount of warmth was just enough to soothe her aches.

"Can you wash yourself?" Rhiannon asked. "I know your hands were damaged the most. So, if you can't grip the cloth, it's okay, I can help out. I promise to make it quick and painless."

Fauna reached out for the cloth and came very close to being able to grip it but eventually gave up when her hand began to cramp. She'd already written so much and exhausted her muscles, so it made sense that she was taxed for the night.

"Here," Rhiannon took the cloth and dipped it into the water. She then grabbed a bar of soap that smelled of pine and lathered it up before gently touching the cloth to Fauna's healing shoulders.

"Does that feel okay?" Rhiannon asked. When Fauna nodded, she began to gently scrub at her body.

"You aren't very dirty, but I do need to get the sticky residue off of you from being wrapped in those bandages. Are you alright if I reach around you?" Rhiannon spoke gently. "I'll get the gunk from the old salves off of your skin at least. You've got a bit of a build-up of grime."

Able to gather at least a shred of strength, Fauna uncrossed her arms and lifted them gently. She turned away, embarrassed, as the maid wiped at her skin.

"I know it's mortifying," Rhiannon looked guilty. "But you'll get sticky and smell if I don't do it. So, I would rather it be like this than get any worse. I promise I'm not judging or anything."

The conversation stopped there as Rhiannon washed her stomach and ribs while expertly avoiding any other intimate areas. When she dunked the cloth and moved around to the other side, Rhiannon began to tell a story.

"If it makes you feel any better, my whole family has worked here since the castle has existed—or at least that's what my grandmother told me. My mother worked in the castle as well, but she spent all of her free time trying to raise me while working. I was a very rascally child—a magnet for mischief! It wasn't my fault that I wanted to learn about everything and if I didn't get my answers right away, I went looking for them myself!"

Fauna silently chuckled and relaxed a bit as Rhiannon continued her story.

"I wasn't supposed to work in the castle, but Lady Aphrodite insisted. She has a soft spot for little girls. I wasn't old enough to properly do maid tasks, so I was assigned little things. I learned to sew to help the seamstress. I learned to read and write to help in the libraries. I was also in the process of learning how to tend to the gardens, but it turned out that I was rather afraid of spiders. Now, I've since grown out of that fear, but it was pretty bad back then. That's why I'm so helpful around the castle—I've done practically everything. Well, everything except being a caregiver. So this is very interesting for me!"

Hearing it phrased like that eased some of the guilt from Fauna's shoulders. This was a job Rhiannon was excited about, so who was she to doubt her? Besides, if she'd been at the castle since she was born, she probably knew just about everything about the family, should Fauna need to know.

"I think your hair looks fine for now, the uneven parts will soften as it grows out. Next time you bathe, we can scrub it but for now, we'll give it a good rinse. How's that sound?" Rhiannon bent over to look at Fauna's face. "I can't trim to save my life, but I might convince one of the workers to loan me the good shears unless you want to try it yourself once your hands get better. We can figure it out then."

When Fauna nodded for what seemed like the thousandth time, Rhiannon gently eased her back until her head skimmed the water. She was pulled up again, like a baptism by bathwater, and Rhiannon soon pulled the plug. As the water ran down the drain, Fauna scrunched her nose up at the dirt and grime that muddied the water.

Freshly scented and relaxed, Fauna lifted her arms and pressed her legs against the edge of the bath so she could help Rhiannon lift her to the rim of the bathtub. Rhiannon dressed her in a robe and picked her up with ease. This time, instead of being put on the bed, Rhiannon set her gently in a chair at the writing desk.

"I need to find you a nightgown, so I'm going to keep you in the robe while I leave with the tray. Here's your journal and the pens to tide you over until I get back."

Rhiannon handed over the stack of things and gathered her mess on the bottom tray of the cart. She then wrapped her arm around Fauna's chest and hugged her close for a moment. The back of

"I'll be right back," she sang as she trotted out of the room.

Fauna, filled with many emotions and a strong motivation to heal, grabbed the familiar pen and wrapped her hands around the thick base, even if it made her muscles ache. She began to write again, though she did not address it to anyone as she had done prior.

I've been in the castle for a while and so many things have happened. Today, I accepted an embrace from a stranger.

Rhiannon is so kind to me. At first, she unnerved me by being so friendly, so quickly. I'm so used to being alone that my first thought was, what she could want from me in return? I can see us becoming close. Or not. Who knows?

I still can't feel my legs. It's like, if I tell them to move, they listen for a fraction of a second. I can feel them but they're… almost like dead weight. My arm strength is coming back slowly. I think my wounds are healing, but I believe that might be the least of my worries right now.

Why am I locked away? Am I actually in danger? Why did I feel so weird when Rhiannon touched my skin? I don't find her touch alluring in the way the books describe it. Perhaps I am just that unused to being touched that simple contact makes me skittish. Two people have touched me so far and neither of them scared me. But to enjoy it? Not quite.

Perhaps I am healing in more ways than one.

Hopefully, I will find out soon enough.

Seven

When the door opened once more, Fauna quickly shut her journal and whipped around with a smile. She jumped when she saw Lady Aphrodite instead of Rhiannon. A blush skittered across her cheeks at being caught off guard.

"I found Rhiannon trying to pick a night shirt for you so I sent her off to the tailor to have some made instead. Until then, here are some things from the maid's storage closet. I'm sorry to have been gone most of today. There is a lot to do when you run a castle." The lady set a bundle of garments down on the bed and smiled widely at her. Her normal dress had been traded for a rather luxurious robe and gown set. Her feet were encased in lush but plain slippers. How someone could make pajamas look regal was a feat in itself.

"Look at you, writing away at the desk. So precious." The Lady held out her arms to her. "Are you ready to be back in bed? Could I help?"

Fauna nodded and gasped when the woman hoisted her up as if she weighed nothing. Something about the women in Castle Verity must make them extra strong because Fauna was neither delicate nor petite.

The fresh sheets were cool against her freshly bathed legs. Fauna eased herself out of her robe and let it fall down her back as she slid under the blankets. Aphrodite handed over a night dress from the stack and let Fauna dress herself. Soon the duvet was laid over her as Aphrodite tucked in Fauna's legs and feet.

"Now, I heard that you and Rhiannon get on well?" she asked as she grabbed the rocking chair and lifted it before setting it in front of the bed.

Fauna nodded once and pointed to the desk where her journal still was. Aphrodite returned it to her and waited patiently in the rocking chair for Fauna to write down her feelings.

She's very nice and quite funny.

It seemed like a dreadful understatement but her hands could only handle so much writing before they began to ache. The short sentence would surely get her point across anyway.

"She is quite funny," Aphrodite agreed. "Her mother was the same way. She was on the staff here as well. When you are able, I will introduce you to the rest of the castle. Then you'll have so many people to meet and remember, it will be overwhelming. I'm sure you'll love them so very much. Tell me, Little Fauna of the Forest, are you comfortable here?"

One nod.

"Are you fed and clothed appropriately?"

A second nod.

"And you have things to keep you busy? Books? People?"

A final nod. Guilt began to spread throughout Fauna, as to why had she been so arrogant about her saviors. Even if they were just thoughts, it still didn't feel right. It was clear that the castle was her best option to get better, she would have the best care available to her therein.

Aphrodite seemed to mull something over before extending her hand to Fauna.

"I know I've just tucked you in, but how about we look at the stars?" she used her other hand to point to the large window. "Afterwards, I'll leave the salves for you to apply if you'd like."

Instead of writing an answer or nodding *yet again*, Fauna offered up both arms. Aphrodite helped slide her out from under the blankets and raised Fauna to her full height. It was nice to finally be upright, but Fauna knew that the moment she tried to move, she would collapse. Aphrodite helped her swivel a few times and slowly lowered Fauna to the base of the rocking chair

"Have you written any letters to me?'

A blush skittered across Fauna's cheeks as she decided how to answer. She had not quite made up her mind about anyone seeing her journal. She'd been quite vulnerable with them and while these people were taking good care of her, she still didn't trust anyone fully. It was hard to transition from a life of solitude to relying on others; the trust aspect would come in due time.

Aphrodite stood behind the large rocking chair and gently squeezed Fauna's shoulder.

"Well, if you do decide to write me a letter, just have Rhiannon bring it to me," Aphrodite kindly requested. She maneuvered around the chair and leaned forward to undo the clasp of the large window. "Let's get a nice breeze in here."

As soon as the cold night air hit Fauna, she took a breath so deep that it seemed to never end. On the exhale, she felt every bit of pain and dread disappear, and a sense of serenity washed over her.

"You smell nice, Little Fauna," Aphrodite remarked. "There isn't much that a bath cannot fix. I hope that you are feeling better now."

Fauna smiled back. And while smiling was not something she had done much of most of her life, she recently felt the need to do it quite often. Blushing, too. When had she become so bashful? Either way, Fauna was used to being able to hide her emotions behind a stony face but now she seemed incapable of doing such a thing.

Before Fauna could stop and delve into why she felt that way, Aphrodite moved away from the window and stepped behind the chair once more to watch the night descend alongside her.

For the second time, Aphrodite's hand touched her shoulder and Fauna did not flinch. It was… comforting. There was no violent twitch of her body, no clench of her muscles. Only a calmness and stillness she was not used to experiencing. It was nice and not at all unwelcome.

"I heard Rhiannon brought you a book. I would love to read about it sometime if you're willing to tell me about it?" The Lady spoke from behind the chair. Fauna nodded but continued to look out the window to marvel at the moon hanging lazily in the night sky.

"I think you two will be great friends," Aphrodite said. "Two hearts, so filled with love for everything. Only one is too shy to admit it, and one is too lost in her anger to even know that she is capable of love."

What did *that* mean?

Was she lost in her anger? She surely wasn't the one who was too shy. But to be lost in anger? Sure, she had resentment from her past… but *anger?*

Without missing a beat in the conversation, Aphrodite changed the subject. "You do look a lot better than you did yesterday. Perhaps within the week, you could try walking from the bed to the desk. You could regain your ability to walk much sooner than I anticipated."

Fauna heard Aprhodite offer her a sliver of independence but was still thinking about her feelings.

Lost in thought, Fauna nodded once and kept thinking about the offhand comment about anger in her heart. Was it that obvious? Should she feel guilty? When she was alone, dealing with things was much easier. Now she had to consider her actions and how they affected other people—especially ones that she wanted to remain close to.

Together, in silence, they gazed outside until the sun finally slept and the room was illuminated by only a single beam of moonlight. Out in the garden, owls perched astutely on high branches, ready to start their work as all the cicadas began their twilight lullaby. As time went on, Fauna's internal debate settled temporarily as she felt a sense of peace she had not known in a very long time, if ever.

Occasionally, Aphrodite's hand would slide up and down her shoulder, not daring too far in each direction. After quite a while, she began to hum a low tune, one that Fauna had never heard. It was mournful and swayed like the movements of the sea. And although Fauna had never seen the sea, she'd read about it enough to envision it quite well.

When the song ended, Aphrodite stilled the gentle comfort on Fauna's shoulder and tapped her once before moving away.

"Let's get you to bed," the Lady whispered, as if she were on an emotional precipice.

Wordlessly, she scooped up Fauna and laid her gently on the bed before grabbing the rumpled duvet and bringing it upward.

"Goodnight, Little Fauna of the Forest."

With that, she hurried out but made sure to close the door gently in her rush. Fauna simply peered out over her blanket-covered feet and continued to stare into the pearlescent night sky. When sleep did not come quickly, she began to count the swirls in the paint on her bedroom walls. Each time she tried to get lost in the pattern, her eyes went to the painting on the ceiling. The longing depicted was incredible, even down to the details in the faces.

As she finally fell asleep, she reveled in the feeling of her soft gown around her. How something like that could be considered just some 'silly old thing' confused her. Used to scratchy fabrics and whatever sewing she was capable of, Fauna truly appreciated anything made by hand. She had been repairing her long gown since she could remember and there was a lingering sadness that it had been burnt away.

Her dreams that night were quite pleasant. Instead of writing stories in her mind or dreaming of her books, Fauna dreamed she was twirling on an outdoor dance floor illuminated by fireflies in the navy blue twilight sky. The words to the music were unintelligible, but it sounded very familiar. The way she swayed and twirled without hesitation felt so *good*. The dress was silky against her legs and she took deep breaths of such pure air that she could *taste* the freshness of it all.

And as Fauna danced, the lights blurred into a string and the stars did so too. A hand grabbed hers and gently tugged her out of a spin. Fauna stopped and turned to look at a strange woman, about the same age as her, dressed in a simple gown the color of foamy sea froth. The mysterious woman said nothing but smiled so warmly that Fauna found herself immediately at ease. Fauna waited respectfully for an introduction, but one did not come.

With a giggle, the woman tugged at Fauna's hand, still in hers, and led her toward the middle of the dance floor. As they jogged jubilantly, the woman's hair swung like a pendulum of fire, swaying back and forth with each hit of her bare foot against the ground. Her dress moved in the same way, creating such a beautiful scene that Fauna did not want to wake from it!

When they reached the right spot, the woman smiled impishly, like she'd done something mischievous, and looked back and forth. Before Fauna could even speak, she raised a finger to Fauna's lips and shushed her.

"Can you hear that?" her voice sounded like the twinkle of stars. "Can you?"

Fauna closed her eyes but heard nothing; not even the wind in the grass or their breaths. With her eyes still closed, she shook her head.

"Exactly. There's nothing there, nothing at all," she said knowingly, although Fauna had no idea what she seemed to *know*. "So much nothing, that it wraps us up and keeps us safe."

Once again, before she could speak, the woman shushed her by placing a slender finger against Fauna's lips. She leaned in so close that Fauna could see the prettiest blue eyes peering right back at her.

"Just pretend," the woman urged Fauna. "Pretend. It helps."

The music picked up in the background and the woman's eyes lit up with youthful glee. She grabbed Fauna's other hand and pulled her into a dance. It wasn't coordinated or even *good*, but it was fun to spin and smile amongst the stars. The woman began to sing softly with the music and it was then that Fauna realized it was the song that Aphrodite had been humming as she put Fauna to sleep.

"Who are you?" Fauna eventually spoke, though she could not hear her own voice.

"Pretend." the woman ignored her question and looked at Fauna with a very serious expression. "Promise me."

It took a moment for Fauna to make a decision, but when she agreed silently, the woman looked extremely relieved. She reached out and grabbed Fauna's hands in her own before squeezing them gently.

"Thank you."

Immediately, the lights around them turned off and the stars flickered to nothing. The moon flickered and faded away, and the fresh air turned dank and stale.

As Fauna began to choke on the harsh air, she felt a gentle touch on her shoulder. Unable to see, she simply turned in that direction and jumped when a gentle kiss was placed on her cheek before turning into a whisper.

"Just pretend."

Eight

Fauna sat up in bed before she knew what was happening. Clutching her hand to her rapidly beating heart and glancing around the room, she did her best to inspect her space. Coral rays of the sunrise were beginning to spill over the trees in the distance. Frustrated by her lack of mobility, Fauna scanned the room as best as she could. Shapes and angles were starting to come into focus as the light poured in, but most of the room was still heavy with sleepy darkness.

"Boo!" One of the daughters jumped up and scared her senseless. She tried to scream but her throat surged with pain when she tried. Desperately, she reached around her nightstand until she bumped into the glass of water and began to drink it quickly. When she was done, she burped slightly and set it back down. Her hand trembled as she let go of the glass.

"Wow, I got you," Bea whooped. "I never get to scare people anymore. Mother says it's not good for business or something."

"Business?" Fauna mouthed.

"We have very important trade agreements," Bea offered as she jumped up. "Just…we can't afford to not have the patrons that we do, is all I meant."

Fauna shook her head and shrugged. Her only experience with business was slowly selling off her father's livestock and heirlooms. Money had no value to her, truly. She moved her hands around the bed, looking for her journal, but found nothing. When she opened the drawer, she noticed it was empty as well.

"Okay, I'm sorry. I hid your book and I'll grab your pens," Bea sighed dramatically. "Scarlet said you were faking your injuries to get close to our mother, but I don't think you are. Well, I did for a little bit, but now I don't. She thinks everyone is always out to get us. Don't you think that's exhausting? You don't seem to be good at faking much anyway."

Faking? Why *would* she fake something like that? How *could* she fake something like that? Instead of giving the girl a response, Fauna sighed and rolled onto her side before laying back down and closing her eyes. She refused to play the games Bea wanted to play. To think that she'd gone through hell just to do what—get a free room? She shut her eyes and hoped the girl would leave.

"Mother still hasn't told us about you," Bea spoke from around the room."She tells us everything. But not about you. I don't know why."

Bea kept pacing around the room. The sound of the drawer at the writing desk opening filled the silence and immediately Fauna felt her journal hit her in the behind as each pen was tossed her way. They bounced off her body and landed all around the large bed. She reached out and grabbed the ones that she could before stretching to grab the journal behind her.

I don't know why she hasn't said anything. I don't even know why she saved me.

Fauna raised the book and set it down on the bed for Bea to grab.

"You mean you weren't lying about any of it?"

Fauna rolled over dramatically and grabbed the book back.

Why would I lie?

"People have lied about stranger things to try and get into Mother's good graces. In case you didn't see, she's very pretty. And rich.

I think some people want to court her. She's off the market though, *permanently*."

The intensity of the last word started Fauna. When she looked up at the daughter, Bea looked away, clearly embarrassed at her outburst.

"Never mind that. You didn't want her money? Or her? Do you think she's ugly?"

Fauna gasped. Well, it was an attempt at a gasp, considering she was still a little raw from her accident. Instead of the dramatic effect, it gave a feeble airy whine. How could someone think Aphrodite Verity was ugly?

Bea laughed gently. "So you *do* think she's pretty. How old are you? A crone by the village standards."

I'm 35. I think.

"How are you *around* 35?" Bea asked incredulously. "One fiery day in the air and your brains got scrambled for the rest of time? Or did the village only teach you numbers you could count on fingers and toes?"

I forgot and stopped counting.

"You stopped counting your birthdays?" Bea asked, seemingly appalled. "I've had *so many* and I refuse to let anyone forget them. Doesn't your mother keep track?"

She died when I was born. How many birthdays have you had?

"Oh," Bea's tone completely changed and her face softened. "I'm sorry. I didn't know. Losing a parent is tough."

"How many?" She tapped the line again for emphasis. There was no way Bea could be older than eighteen.

"An exaggeration, sheesh!" Bea slipped out of the chair and onto the bed. This time her eyes were much less wild and her demeanor a lot less playful. "No one lives to be very old here. Don't be an idiot."

You're strange.

"Well, you're not exactly normal either. What's with all the books?"

"I don't have friends or family. Only books."

"No one?" Bea looked surprised. "None?"

Fauna shook her head.

"Doesn't it get lonely?" Bea asked gently, all traces of her earlier bravado long gone. "With just you and your thoughts?"

I often pretend I'm someone else. It makes life more fun.

"All books are always pretend. All of them," Bea smiled sadly before rising gently from the bed. "Do you know what I would give to just walk in the village without anyone noticing? I wish I could be someone else, even for a day."

Bea looked at her, confused. Could she not? The people in the village knew very little about Lady Verity's personal life.

"I would give anything to be nobody. But I cannot. And you can. Well, you could before. Not so sure about now. I'm forced to stay here in the castle. Sure, people come and go, but I sometimes wish they wouldn't."

You're kept here because of your mother?

"No, because of *hers*."

Fauna shook her head in confusion—was there a grandmother in the mix somehow? Bea rolled her eyes and held out her hands to explain.

"Our family tree is bizarre." She made a triangular shape in the air. "The Matron is technically my grandmother, but I don't like to think about that. Not at all."

"Why?" Fauna mouthed due to her lack of a notebook.

"She doesn't like when Mother shares her attention," Bea recalled sarcastically. "The Matron gets jealous easily. I don't understand it,

I just leave them alone. Sometimes I think she hates Scarlet and I just because Mother loves us."

"Father?" Fauna mouthed, pointing to a faint line that Bea had gently drawn next to her mother's.

"No," Bea looked out towards the garden. "No father. Not any-more. I only have one parent."

The ache in Bea's tone was palpable. There was something sad there, but Fauna was careful not to pry—she barely knew this girl and didn't want to upset her. It was kind of nice to have a visitor or two during her stay. Even if she was perplexing, to say the least.

Fauna grabbed her journal back and shut it. She reached for the book she was reading and held it out.

Bea inhaled sharply. "Do you want me to read aloud?"

Fauna nodded happily.

"Well, why not?" Bea shrugged. "I don't have anything to do until breakfast. And even then I'm sure Rhiannon is bringing yours up after ours. I'm sure the Castle would collapse if we told Mother that we knew you were up here."

When Bea began reading from the chapter where Fauna had left off, she heard the cheer return in the dips and sway of her voice. The conversation about parents had clearly touched a nerve. What made it more curious, however, was Aphrodite's longing looks into the garden as well. The mystery and ache of it all scratched at the plot-driven part of Fauna's brain as she began to devise little ideas of what could have happened. The garden was only barely visible from the bed—she would need to be in the chair again to get a proper look.

"Of course Mother had this brought to you. She's so silly," Bea laughed as she stopped reading. "She's such a romantic. Men and women throw themselves at her feet all of the time and she rejects them all. She still believes in true love, even after everything that's happened to her. Besides, she's not the easiest person to live with. I would know."

Fauna found her journal again.

Is she not married?

Bea ignored the question.

"Have you ever been in love, Fauna?"

She shook her head and flipped to the next page in her journal.

I don't think I'm capable of love.

"Haven't you ever just seen someone that caught your attention so suddenly that you just had to know them?" Bea breathed in and out as if she was smelling the most delicious flower. "Wanted to know the little things and experiences that have come together like little puzzle pieces, that make them who they are at that very moment? Have you ever had your cheeks flush when someone smiles? Even if they don't know you exist, everything they do brings you such joy that you can't imagine a world where they don't exist?" When Fauna shook her head, Bea looked surprised. "Sheesh, you really were tucked away and hidden from the world. I can't imagine."

I never let myself think about it.

"You haven't even practiced kissing?" Bea asked, mystified. "When I was younger, I thought my first kiss would be something magical. Like, french horns blaring and larks singing. That type of thing. I was mistaken, but it was a nice delusion while it happened. I've been lucky enough to see real, passionate, and honest love in my lifetime, just not for me. Still, it was wonderful to watch."

Fauna continued to listen as Bea went on about romance and how love was hard. When the girl looked up and realized how much she'd divulged, she changed the subject.

"I'm sorry, I didn't mean to go off like that," Bea admitted while taking a deep breath. On the exhale she seemed to calm down. "I think I heard the breakfast bell. I need to go. Take care."

Fauna offered a small smile as Bea wandered out of the door. When the latch clicked, she tore a scrap of paper from her journal, inserted it into the pages that Bea had stopped at and laid it down beside her in bed. As she laid down for a small nap, Fauna thought of Aphrodite and how Bea had described her as such a romantic, yet refused to engage in any romance at all. The contradictions of it had Fauna's head spinning. How could someone be so invested in love and companionship, but sequester themself off from the world in a castle? Or, at least that's how it seemed from their brief meetings.

The sound of the door banging open startled Fauna so badly that her whole body contorted in surprise.

"Oh! You're already up, good!" Rhiannon, oblivious to Fauna's fright, appeared pushing a rolling cart. "I heard the Lady's out for a bit so it's just us. Do you want me to stay here for a few nights? I know she's tucked you in the last few days and I don't want you to get too lonely. I think she has some big business going on and won't be able to make it up here at all."

Unaccustomed to people wanting to spend time with her, Fauna took a moment to answer. Why would someone want to spend any extra time with her? But, if Rhiannon was offering, she could accept the company. Maybe just for a little bit. A very little bit.

"Sure," Fauna mouthed. *"Hungry."*

"Of course, the food here is *so* good," Rhiannon laughed as she separated their plates. "It helps that I know all of the cooks. So, if you find something you like, let me know so I can have it added to your rotation."

Fauna smiled in between bites and signaled that she'd been listening. Most of their meal passed with Rhiannon telling Fauna all about the stories of the kitchen staff. At this point, she would know everything about them before ever meeting them. Now, *that* would be a strange situation.

"I know your throat is scratched up, but I wonder if this would put a little pep in your step… er… metaphorical step. Water is so boring. I wish we had honey mead but the Lady would not let something so *vile* into her castle," Rhiannon sang the last part as if she'd heard it many times before. "She hates anything but wine and lots of it. Sometimes I wonder how she stays upright all of the time."

Fauna accepted the small glass and was quite surprised when it went down just fine. She tried to speak but once again found that no sound came out. Granted, the pain was less obvious but it was still irritating. Rhiannon looked quite pleased when Fauna smiled afterward.

"Well, we have a few hours before you get lunch. What do you want to do?

Fauna pointed to the rocking chair and her book. Rhiannon seemed to understand.

"I could open the window if you'd like?" Rhiannon asked. When Fauna nodded she agreed. "Or is it too cold?"

Fauna shook her head and pointed to the rocking chair. She smiled bashfully as she remembered the kindness she experienced while sitting in it—and the naps. The wonderful chair naps in the sun were almost blissful.

"Do you want to finish your short story?" Rhiannon pointed to the book she'd discarded the previous night. "Or should I give you a new one?"

Fauna pointed to the book that Bea had been reading and smiled in thanks when Rhiannon handed it over.

"Here, try to stand," Rhiannon held her hands out. "I have one of the fresh gowns from the pile over there."

Fauna put her hands on Rhiannon's shoulder—careful to avoid the springy curls that seemed to bounce out of whatever she tied her hair back with every day—and let herself be hoisted upwards.

It wasn't *painful* to stand, not in the normal sense. Her legs didn't hurt, which was fine. The odd part was that she couldn't feel them at all. Not a dull ache, not even an itch on her nearly-healed skin. It was as if they didn't exist. But, glancing downward, she knew that without a doubt she did indeed have legs.

"Can you balance?" Rhiannon asked gently, dipping her head down to make eye contact with Fauna. It was a little uncomfortable to have someone so close to her, but it wasn't a bad discomfort. Just... new.

When she took a step, she had no idea how to move her legs, so it turned into a sort of slump against Rhiannon, who took it in stride.

"Progress is progress, don't be too harsh on yourself," Rhiannon assured. "You stood up, which must have been frightening in itself. Now, let's get you back on this bed to get changed and then we can bask in the midday... rain."

Fauna smiled shyly as she took off her nightgown and sat nude on the edge of the bed. The pink burns on her skin were fading nicely, turning into faint white blotches. It was nice to know that she would be seemingly healed soon. There were libraries to see and people to meet!

"You're quite pretty, you know," Rhiannon said softly, unprompted. "There's something so beautiful about people who just experience the world without a single care of how they seem to others. I'm a little envious if I'm being honest. I think too much about how others see me. But, you already know that—we've talked about it before.

Fauna struggled to respond. Bea had called her lucky for going unnoticed and Rhiannon had called her pretty for not caring about her appearance. Neither of those statements seemed true, but she didn't want to argue.

"I care too much. It's what I do, don't think too hard about it," Rhiannon admitted as she handed over some nondescript garments. "That's why I'm a good caregiver. Looking after other people's needs comes naturally to me."

"Thank you," she mouthed to Rhiannon, unable to make eye contact. Instead, she tugged the clothes on and held her arms out for help.

"Here, wrap your arms around my neck," Rhiannon guided her. "Just like when we went to the bath."

From there, she deposited Fauna in the oversized chair, opened the balcony windows, cast a longing look into the garden, and ambled back toward the bed. With a *flop,* Rhiannon fell against the bed and giggled when she bounced back up. Fauna watched it happen with a persistent smile and joy in her heart.

They sat like that for hours, just reading and enjoying each other's company. Sometimes Rhiannon would laugh quietly under her breath at something in her book. Fauna finished hers and found herself just gazing out into the damask cloudy sky, inhaling the crisp fresh air. The top of the garden was mostly obscured by tall trees, but it was pretty nonetheless.

"Ready for lunch?" Rhiannon asked quietly from across the room. Unable to voice her affirmation, Fauna nodded and gave an affirmative gesture from her chair.

"You know," Rhiannon began as she lifted Fauna out of the seat. "You're very interesting for someone who is practically silent."

Fauna wanted to laugh. She was not interesting in the slightest. There was solace in obscurity.

"I can't wait until your voice heals," Rhiannon admitted as she set Fauna down and grabbed for the cart. "I can't wait until we get to be better friends."

"Me too," Fauna mouthed, and for once it didn't feel like a lie.

Nine

When Rhiannon brought up lunch, the pair spent the rest of the day perched on their tummies on the bed, writing notes back and forth. Rhiannon found it quite fun to show Fauna little games like tic-tac-toe and a game involving dots and boxes. Eventually, her journal was pushed to the side while they scribbled little notes back and forth on the margins of the game pages they had drawn and ripped out.

They began a word guessing game, which resulted in a wonderful written conversation where they both drew things and had the other guess. Neither of them was very good at drawing, which made the game so much more fun. They were so amused at the crude drawings that they began to snort in laughter. This led to Rhiannon rushing Fauna to the toilet, still laughing the whole way. That alone sent them into such a fit of giggles that they both ended up on the tile floor of the bathroom with their backs pressed to the bathtub as their giggles eventually died down.

They stared at each other with thin-pressed lips and shaking shoulders until Rhiannon cracked and began to giggle again.

Fauna fell victim to Rhiannon's laugh soon after and found herself in silent stitches. Rhiannon's snorts faded while she let her head fall onto Fauna's shoulder. The woman's curls felt strange against her face, but the sensation was not entirely unwelcome.

Usually, her body would jerk violently away from anyone touching her, but this time it was… tolerable.

Exhausted after almost an hour of erratic laughter, Fauna's limbs were heavy and her stomach ached from the exertion. A smile stayed stamped to her face and she laid against the cool porcelain until it had warmed to match her skin.

After a short while, Rhiannon stood up and reached to pick Fauna up. Once she was deposited back in her spot, Fauna fell against her pillows with a soft smile still plastered on her face. She nudged Rhiannon's shoulder and nodded to the ceiling.

"I don't know when that appeared," Rhiannon admitted. "No one has been in this room for quite a while before you got here. I think maybe Lady Aphrodite painted it. Did you know she's quite a talented artist?"

Fauna shook her head. It seemed that Lady Aphrodite was good at almost everything. Was there anything she couldn't do?

While she stared at the ceiling painting, Rhiannon tied her hair up and sifted through the stack of books on the other edge of Fauna's bed, tucked against the wall. Some time later, she announced that it was time for her to fetch dinner and she would be right back. On her way out, she set the stack of books on the corner of Fauna's bed so she could reach them, and waved a little before shutting the door.

As Rhiannon left, Fauna grabbed the pages they had turned into games and folded them in half, before slipping them into the blank pages of her journal. A wave of exhaustion hit her after all their antics, so she set the journal aside and got cozy in bed for a little nap before dinner.

The earthy deep brown walls of her father's cabin were the first red flag. They hadn't been that color in a very long time. The stale scent of tobacco and cooking fat transported Fauna back to a very specific time in her life. Unable to move, Fauna stared at each trinket on the shelf and each piece of her life hung on the walls. Little snippets of her former life taunted her. A well-worn knit bear with fraying paws sat in the corner of the room. Little smears of fingerprints stained her window from where she'd drawn designs in the glass while the morning dew evaporated.

A stack of books lay precariously on her little bed, only a single jolt away from toppling over. Fauna was sure that if she scurried under her bed, she would find the well-hidden pages where she'd begun to pen snippets of her writing.

She missed it—missed her quiet life in her silo. But, she also had begun to *like* the people around her. Just a little bit. A very little bit. In the startling quiet of the empty cabin, Fauna felt as if she was trespassing on her own property.

A gentle rapping on the door got Fauna's attention. She pressed an ear to the wood and tried to hold her breath to hear even clearer. A muffled voice, too disjointed to recognize, came from the other side.

"I can't understand you," Fauna said, face still pressed against the door. She reached for the door handle and steadied herself before opening it slowly.

The woman from her prior dream, still wearing the same dress, smiled at her from the doorway. Behind her, not a single soul seemed to be roaming the village. Fauna stepped back and ushered her inside. It was disarming to see someone else in her little space, considering Fauna herself didn't even venture into the cabin in her later years.

The woman greeted her with a sunny smile and held out her hands again. Fauna took them and waited for a greeting. When one did not come, she initiated it.

"Hello."

"Just pretend."

Fauna was genuinely lost. Why would this woman keep telling her that? What did it mean? Was she quoting something important? It didn't make any sense.

"Makes what easier?" Fauna's frustrated tears pooled in her eyes.

"All of it." The woman motioned around the room. "Makes it all easier."

"You were in my dreams before. Why are you here? Are you real? Am I real? Why can I talk? How did we get here?"

"Just pretend."

The woman's docile demeanor slipped for a moment as heartbreak shone through her eyes. She took a deep breath as if she was going to speak an entire monologue, but instead exhaled slowly. She let go of Fauna's hands and instead cupped Fauna's face, gently rubbing her thumb over her cheekbone and placing a sweet kiss on her forehead. When she stepped back, she had tears in her reddened eyes and a tremble in her lip.

"It makes it easier. Much easier."

When Fauna woke, she inhaled too deeply and began to cough. It burned less than it had before before but her throat was still terribly raw. She grabbed her journal to try and write down her dream, but only remembered the feeling of dread that had followed her into the waking world. Something had happened in her dream and it was incredibly annoying to not be able to remember it. Was her father's cabin involved? All she could recall was someone knocking on the door.

The sound of someone opening the door got Fauna's attention. Had someone been knocking in real life too? Rhiannon entered with her normal cart of food and stacks of plates. She looked quite troubled as if something was weighing on her mind. But, Fauna was still so skittish when it came to people that she didn't know how to ask about it. So, instead, she silently ate and waited for her friend to say anything about her mood.

When they were finished, Rhiannon slipped a small plate of pastries out of the bottom of the cart and presented them to Fauna with a small smile. Fauna gladly took one and ate the whole thing in two large bites. A fruity flavor—plum perhaps? It must have taken quite a while to locate the ingredients as plums were not common in their area. Little flakes fell onto her lap and Rhiannon made a show of brushing them onto the floor.

Together they sat quietly, chewing on the pastries as the night drew on. It was still a wonderful interaction, just a stark difference from the giggles earlier. But, Rhiannon didn't offer up any information and Fauna was just fine sharing some silence along with the baked treats.

Rhiannon checked in with her once, to make sure that Fauna still wanted her to stay, which she did. So she disappeared with the dishes and came back with a pillow and a small pocket watch. She snuggled into the other half of Fauna's large bed with a book that looked dreadfully boring and didn't speak the rest of the night. Fauna, now convinced something was wrong, chose to open her journal and try to write down her feelings.

But... they wouldn't come. So many feelings writhing and slithering around her mind and yet not a single word to describe them would appear for her. So, she gave up and just began chronicling her day with Rhiannon. At some point, she fell asleep with her pen still in her hand.

The next morning, Fauna woke alone but noticed the room had been tidied. Rhiannon must have done it while she slept. Of course, she *was* technically a maid, but having someone tidy after her did not sit well with Fauna.

She had too much pride to admit that she needed to use the bathroom and that Rhiannon's absence might be an issue. Could she make it by crawling to the bathroom? Could it get that dire?

"Hiya!" a voice came from the other side of the room. "I'm here instead of Rhiannon. She had something to do."

Wearing only an oversized striped sweater and very thick socks, Scarlet appeared in the doorway with a coy smile and crinkle in her nose that gave her the look of a mischievous child. "She was burned by someone in the kitchen this morning so I sneakily told her that I would help you. No one is supposed to know about you, but I lied and said the librarian told me!"

They had a librarian? Of course they did.

Fauna pointed to the bathroom and smiled hopefully at Scarlet.

"Oh. You need to use that. Of course, you do." The youngest daughter panicked. "How do you normally get there?"

Unable to find her notebook, Fauna huffed quietly in frustration before making a rocking motion with her arms. *"Carry,"* she mouthed, hoping to get her point across.

"Oh," Scarlet blanched. "Well, you see, I'm very small and I don't have much in the way of muscles. So, maybe I should go find Rhiannon after all? You can't even walk a little bit? Not even three little steps?"

Fauna flushed crimson, more embarrassed than she had ever been in her life. To rely on someone to take her somewhere as close as the bathroom was humiliating. But the pressure on her bladder was becoming *very* uncomfortable.

"Be right back!" Scarlet dashed away, curls bouncing and feet slipping on the wood the entire way. "Oh gosh, oh gosh!"

Determined and more than a little pissed off, Fauna swiveled and slid her legs off of the bed. The second her feet touched the ground, she tried to flex her toes and found that she could not. With a push, she tried her best to stand and was successful for a moment or two. After she tried to right herself, her knees caved in and hit the floor *hard*.

Disorientated, Fauna dug her nails into the floor and pulled herself the smallest of bits. Slowly, she inched her way across the room, nearly weeping when a rug scratched mercilessly at the skin that was exposed when her nightgown rode up. When she finally cleared the rug, Fauna sighed in relief at the cold hardwood on the fresh burns. Her biceps quivered at having to pull herself along the floor. While she grew up on a farm, she had never once used her upper body in such a way. The muscles in the back of her arms threatened to cramp as she heaved one hand over the other.

"Hey!" Rhiannon called from behind her. When hands grabbed Fauna's body, she slapped them away with a grunt and kept pulling herself out of spite. She was *tired* of being so dependent on them. She was angry at everyone and everything for putting her through everything. She didn't want help, she wanted to pee without having to ask permission.

Her entire body hurt and she was beginning to feel nauseous, but Fauna kept pulling until she was able to reach over and push the bathroom door open. The light from the high window illuminated her way and the moment her fingers gripped the divots between the tiles of the floor, she began to shake. The tessellation of the tiles below her fingers became her roadmap as she dragged her dead weight across the room. When her fingers finally touched the chilled porcelain of the toilet, she raised her eyebrows and praised herself internally.

Perhaps she wasn't as dependent as she thought. Take *that!*

"Please, let me help," Rhiannon cried from the door frame. Fauna flipped herself onto her back and grunted when her legs didn't go with her. She sat there, half twisted with a stabbing pain in her bladder that made her nearly vomit.

Frustrated, Fauna relaxed and waved Rhiannon over with a flippant hand gesture. When she felt arms grab her by her armpits, she huffed and let herself be guided. Rhiannon's little gasping sobs made Fauna nearly cry herself.

"I'm sorry. I'm so sorry," Rhiannon said quietly into Fauna's ear as she gently helped her tug the dress up above her hips. "I wasn't here when you woke up. Please don't be mad."

Too angry and embarrassed, Fauna chose the silent treatment. Well, an even *more* silent treatment.

"Are you hungry?" Rhiannon whispered with a watery tone. "I can bring breakfast. Or sweets. Or coffee. Anything."

Fauna did nothing but stare straight ahead. She wanted privacy but loathed that she could not have it.

"Is she broken?" Scarlet cried from the doorway. "I *liked* her! I wanted to write with her! I want to help!"

"No." Rhiannon shooed her away. "Just upset. Go downstairs to the kitchen. I'll come find you later."

"I left my book for her," Scarlet whispered. "If she still wants to read it."

"I'll let her know," Rhiannon assured the girl, even though Fauna was directly next to her.

Fauna let her head fall back and plunk angrily against the tile wall.

She missed Aphrodite. She missed the big rocking chair. She missed her silo and she missed her books.

She missed having a say in *anything*.

Rhiannon left her alone for a moment to do what she needed to do, but it didn't make Fauna feel less defeated. What if Rhiannon took an hour to come back? Fauna did not have the strength to get herself into bed, and sitting on the toilet all night was not an option.

Thankfully, Rhiannon appeared only a few minutes later. She guided Fauna back to the bed and made one last apology before shutting the door. Now that her adrenaline had faded, Fauna's embarrassment faded to shame. She didn't mean to be so harsh to the people who were only trying to help. But, she had no other way to express herself, and that was something she would never be able to get past.

Rhiannon showed up again around lunchtime with a bandaged arm and a sad smile. After apologizing almost twenty times, Fauna gently told her to stop speaking and sit down. Food was eaten and books cracked open once more.

Much like the previous days, they spent the rest of the day reading quietly together and did the same after dinner. Rhiannon, who seemed to be in a much better mood, ran a bath and washed Fauna's hair. Being touched still made her stiffen in fear for a few seconds before she would relax, but her reactions were softening more and more by the day. She hoped one day a hug would be second nature to her. She had only started to bond with four of the women in Castle Verity, but it was enough for her.

Rhiannon stayed the night again, this time taking her own time to bathe and change clothes. Before they fell asleep, they talked using Fauna's journal, scribbling little notes back and forth until they both were fighting to stay awake. The fact that Rhiannon would turn to writing her own words down to level their communication was absolutely flooring to Fauna. To be met halfway was so touching.

Who knew all it took was a near-fatal injury and copious amount of recuperation to make her first friends?

Bea stopped in for a moment when Rhiannon was bathing and snuck a single tiny pastry onto a plate in her room. Fauna smiled devilishly and popped the whole thing into her mouth before the eldest sister took the plate back with a "shh" motion and a wink.

Thumbing through her journal, Fauna realized that it had begun to fill up quite a bit. Seeing proof of her friendship was strange... part of her thought that one day she would wake up and realize it was all a dream. Still, it was nice to look back even to a few weeks ago and realize how far she had come.

Later that night, Rhiannon and Fauna were lying in bed together "talking" about some of the gossip from the castle.

And she got caught changing the chore rotation! That girl loves doing dishes so much that her hands are always like prunes. But no one likes cleaning the cellar. It's a wretched job. They were wondering why she'd been off the roster for cellar duty for so many weeks! She got herself a pen and rewrote it behind everyone's backs so they took her shifts! Even learned Lady Aphrodite's handwriting!

What will be done to her?

She'll be forced to clean the cellar for a week and will probably be in charge of tending to the baths. That job is scary enough.

Why so?

Twenty women sharing the same bathing quarters can be stressful.

It can?

Haven't you had to share your things?

No. I've never shared anything with anyone. I lived with my father until I was a teenager and then I moved into my own little place.

You were on your own?

Yes.

I'm sorry. At least you aren't alone anymore.

True. Thank you for being my friend.

Ten

Buttery sunlight assaulted Fauna's eyes the next morning. She grimaced at the harsh awakening and pulled the blankets over her head. When someone squeezed her foot through the blankets, she groaned and whined petulantly.

"I brought a gift, Fauna. Are you still wanting to hide now?" A deep voice made her heart beat quickly. Lady Aphrodite!

Fauna smiled under the blankets and shyly brought the edge down to reveal her face. Missing someone was a strange concept, but she had truly not seen Lady Aphrodite in a long time! How long, she wasn't certain, but it had been ages!

The Lady was dressed rather casually in slacks and a sleeveless blouse with loafers on her feet. Even in common clothes, she was intimidating. Her long sandy hair was loose but still placed intently. She wore no makeup, which meant her natural freckles were very much on display. Her entire body seemed less tense. The ensemble made Fauna's lips turn up in a delicate smile that nothing could dash away.

Her book, the very same one that had been ripped from her grasp before she had been strung up, was placed in her lap. It smelled lightly of oil and smoke but that didn't bother Fauna one bit. She touched the slightly charred cover gently, her fingers tentatively tracing the design on the spine as the familiar wave of joy crashed over her. The damage to the book was not as severe as she had anticipated—only some of the background on the cover had been burned off. The rest of the damage could likely be wiped away with great care.

She flicked her gaze up to Aphrodite, who was staring at her with a tender look of affection. "I sent some workers to the village to see if they could find it. I wanted you to be able to finish your book."

Fauna nodded quickly, a smile still stuck to her face. She blushed and reached for her notebook. When she opened it to show Aphrodite the conversations between her and Rhiannon, the Lady looked quite pleased.

"I knew you two would be good friends!" she clapped her hands together and grabbed the rocking chair, sliding it over to the bed. "Now, tell me all about your adventures while I've been absent."

Fauna wrote quickly, flipping past her conversations with the girls. They still hadn't been told about her and she didn't want anyone to get in trouble. She scribbled quickly without any pain in her hand and told Aphrodite about taking a bath and Rhiannon's borrowed books. She left out the dramatics with Scarlet, but there was quite enough to talk about already.

"You've changed since I was last here," Aphrodite noted, crossing her legs and leaning forward with her elbow on her knee. "Calmer. A little less tentative. Yes?"

It's because I found a friend! Rhiannon is a joy! She's my first friend. I feel very taken care of. She brought me books. She hugged me three times and I did not turn away.

"You're learning. That's okay. You have all the time in the world. You can't completely evolve in just a few weeks."

I haven't had a lot of interactions with other people. I can't think of the last time I even spoke to anyone willingly before coming here.

"Ever?" Aphrodite seemed surprised. "That's so sad. All those years, you went without one single conversation that you *wanted* to have. No wonder you were so scared. I supposed I could have handled our introduction a little better."

I don't remember much. Just voices and being carried here.

"Those were my daughter's voices," Aphrodite replied. "We don't have a lot of exciting things happening around here, so they were very curious. I told them you died from your wounds—you don't need them in here just yet. Some day you will formally meet them. They'll forgive me for lying."

Fauna smiled at the idea of having all three Verity women in her room and reading together. Rhiannon too. It was becoming more and more difficult to keep the necessary secrets straight.

A very pronounced clearing of a throat startled Fauna out of her daydream. While she was off in another world, Aphrodite had taken her customary seat in the rocking chair.

"You're like a skittish kitten. It's darling."

Fauna wanted to be upset at being compared to a kitten, but the warm look Aphrodite had made her rethink her words. Instead, Fauna reached out for a hug and was joyful when Aphrodite stood and leaned over to return it. The embrace lasted only a few seconds but after the Lady pulled away and sat back down, Fauna still felt wrapped in a warm and glowing blanket of safety.

"So precious." Aphrodite sat back in her chair and closed her eyes. "I had such a stressful business trip and your light and energy have chased all those things away. I cannot wait until your voice heals and we can have many conversations over a nice dinner and wine. I rarely have adult company, it will be nice to have someone to simply chat with."

Being seen as desirable company was strange. No one had ever wanted to speak to her before. The irony of her wanting to converse for the first time whilst being forced to be silent was not lost on her either. Perhaps she could see a silver lining—there were fewer opportunities to say something silly if she couldn't say anything at all!

Aphrodite abandoned the rocking chair to gaze out the window and into the garden. Fauna watched the woman with unabashed curiosity. The way her loafers shone in the sun, the sharp creases in her tailored slacks, the gentle edges of her body under the blouse, and the way the ends of her hair curled just so. Her shoulders were relaxed and her posture quite casual. All-in-all, Lady Aphrodite Verity was seemingly perfect.

"I can feel you looking," Aphrodite chuckled. "Don't worry, I don't mind. You're curious because you've been hidden away from people, not because you're a sneaky little thing. I can't imagine never seeing the outside world, let alone choosing not to be a part of it. We'll get you up and socializing soon, I promise. There is much to see here and many people you will get on with."

Fauna's ears burned with humiliation. She did not like getting caught staring.

"Don't be embarrassed, Little Fauna of the Forest." Aphrodite opened her arms again. "You're eager to learn, never be ashamed of that. I'm here to help you heal—from more than a fire. You're welcome to stay here as long as you would like. I cannot wait to see you come into yourself."

She was right, after all. Fauna had watched girls and boys from afar, wondering just how they knew exactly when to touch a shoulder or when it was okay to grab someone's hand. Even well into her adulthood, watching couples on the street perplexed her. Was there an urge in their minds? The books made it seem so simple, so natural. "Second nature" didn't exist for someone like her. Things were coming a little bit easier to her, but it was hardly natural.

"Come, sit in the chair with me. Your little maid has been given the day off and sent to the village to have fun. It's just us up here. Shall I read you a book?"

Fauna smiled as Aphrodite stood and pushed the chair closer so Fauna could transfer herself into it. She wished she were facing the window, but being next to Aphrodite was enough.

"Your skin looks just about healed." Aphrodite sat down on the bed with her knees touching Fauna's. "Soon we can work on your walking."

In response to that, Fauna held out her hands and tried to make a fist. Her progress was noticeable, but not enough to make her happy. She'd graduated to the second-to-smallest pen barrel, but her penmanship was another story. It wasn't that she was terrible at writing, it was that her thoughts came faster than she could write them down!

"My hands hurt me too sometimes," Aphrodite admitted, bringing up her hand and moving it around. She raised her fingers to dance in front of Fauna's face. "When I was younger, I did nothing but lay in my bed with sickness. My bones started to hurt me in a way I had never experienced. Soon my knees and wrists could barely move, and I needed help just standing up. Thankfully, due to a doctor, I was able to get much better after a while."

Fauna grazed her fingertips over Aphrodite's knuckles before looking up to see if she was in pain. When she wasn't, Fauna played with the soft pads of Aphrodite's hands. It felt strangely intimate but not more than playful.

After that, Aphrodite settled into Fauna's spot on the bed and began to read aloud from one of the books. Fauna didn't have the heart to tell her that she'd already read that chapter, so instead she laid back in the rocking chair and closed her eyes.

The gentle timbre of Aphrodite reading helped lull Fauna into a sleepy haze. Extremely comfortable, Fauna didn't even flinch when Lady Aphrodite stopped reading. She was technically awake but far too cozy to do anything other than listen.

"I miss reading to my girls," Aphrodite shut the book quietly. The sound made Fauna open her eyes to see Aphrodite getting ready to stand. "Perhaps I will sneak into their rooms tonight before they sleep, and ask if they would like a story for nostalgia's sake." A gentle silence filled the gap in the one-sided conversation. "I think that's the dinner bell. Where did the time go? I should be off for a bit. I'll have your food up here soon if that is alright?"

When Fauna nodded, Aphrodite grabbed her under the armpits and lifted her back into the bed. Next, the rocking chair was put back and then Aphrodite bent down to bid Fauna goodnight.

"I am so proud of you."

As Aphrodite left, Fauna thought back to before she'd come to the castle. She refused to even make eye contact with half of the village and now she was having conversations with hugs and touches! There was also a voice in the back of her head that begged her to sit and think about the future, but she did not listen. Fauna had been to the edge of life and still made it back. Occasionally, she still craved the dark silence that she had taken safety in for so long. But, little by little, the sunshine was starting to feel rather nice.

Eleven

After the soothing morning with the Lady, Fauna dozed on and off until the afternoon. She woke to a warm room and a beating sun high over the castle. Aphrodite sat in her rocking chair, facing the window and humming a tune as she sketched in a large book. She looked back to Fauna and smiled before turning back around. Had she stayed the entire time? Didn't she say goodbye for the day? Regardless, Fauna now felt compelled to work on something as well. She ruffled around the drawers next to her bed until she found her journal and pens. On a clean page, she began to write.

I am Fauna.

It did look much better than earlier attempts. Perhaps her hands were finally healing. Now, if only her legs could do the same. And her voice. However, that mattered less, given how quiet she normally was.

I am Fauna, that much I know.

My legs look healed but I still can't feel them. My throat no longer hurts, but sounds won't come out. I'm starting to think I will be doomed here forever. I have made a friend though. Well, a few, I think. I think it will take quite a while for me to fully believe that I didn't just make all of it up. I had no idea real people could like me. I want to know more about Lady Aphrodite, but she seems closed off to everyone. Something happened in this castle and everyone tiptoes around it. It makes me nervous. But, overall I'm fine. I'm cared for and fed. I'll get to bathe on my own soon. My only worry is that the days are slipping away and blending in a way that I am a little surprised by. But who could I tell? Would anyone believe me? Does time move this quickly for normal people? Three hours passes so slowly but three weeks have rushed by! I used to count the sunsets but then I started sleeping through them. I supposed I could use the seasons to look, but from the bed I cannot see more than the sky. Perhaps I will use the leaves to tell time.

Sometimes I wish I could only converse with trees. I believe they would be enigmatic listeners.

As Fauna ended the puzzling entry, she realized that she was more confused than before. Being alone was all she had ever craved—until now. Now she wanted to gallivant around the gardens with Rhiannon or learn to write poetry with Scarlet. Aphrodite had an art studio—she wanted to see that too! And the *library*! Oh, she had heard such wonderful things about the libraries in the castle. That's where she would go first!

Aphrodite was a rollicking puzzle with her soothing yet authoritative tone. The fondness with which she spoke of her daughters brought up complicated feelings in Fauna's heart. Would her mother have spoken about her in the same way if she had survived? Would she have been able to sit and watch the night sky with her mother, the same as the Verity daughters? Aphrodite didn't feel like a mother to Fauna, but there was a certain kinship there. She had no idea how old Aphrodite Verity was, but visually she seemed to be no more than a decade older than Fauna. They weren't exactly equals and Fauna was too broken to even begin to think about love. Where did Fauna fit in the castle though? Surely her desire for personal space would drive everyone off. But, when it came down to it, Fauna just wanted her choices back.

Who had she become? Playing with someone's hair and staring at freckles. Fauna found herself entranced by pretty eyes and what jewelry people chose in the morning. No longer was she *afraid* of people. She'd begun to find them... less intimidating and more interesting than before.

Flying under the radar for one's entire life was a privilege of sorts. Now, under scrutiny—if one could call it that—Fauna realized that her actions and words (silent as they were) mattered. People were listening to her! People cared.

As she contemplated her place amongst the community of the castle, Fauna found herself staring aimlessly at the painting on the ceiling. It had begun to give her comfort. It was so complex and intricately painted that she figured that it would be years before she would be able to take it all in. She wanted to ask about it, even if no one else acknowledged it at all.

Was she planning on spending years tucked into a bed with only books and maids for friends?

Well, no, but if her future was her maid and the deceptively complex family of women who were all growing on Fauna like moss on aging trees, then it wasn't the worst outcome. Just... not the best one either.

As if she sensed Fauna's internal panic over her long-term plans, Aphrodite stood from her chair and set the sketchbook down. She walked over to Fauna, still silent, and touched her shoulder gently before leaving the room.

Desperate to see what the woman had been sketching, Fauna scooted down the bed as far as she could until she leaned over to look. Unfortunately, it wasn't enough and the drawing remained a mystery.

Frustrated, Fauna scooted backward until she was able to sit back in her spot. Irrationally irritated, she grabbed a book off of the stack that Rhiannon had brought and cracked it open. Soon her anger faded as she let her mind be carried off into a land of make-believe.

"Reading again?" Aphrodite asked gently as she walked back into the room with a plate of snacks and a glass of water. "I love how much you enjoy reading. It's fun to be transported elsewhere for a little while."

Fauna accepted the snacks and water and set them down to grab her notebook.

It's a children's book, but I still enjoy it.

"Would you like to read together? You would have to be in my lap, if that is okay?" Aphrodite held out her hands and waited for Fauna's nod before lifting her and carrying her over to the rocking chair in front of the window. When they got settled, Fauna closed her eyes and let her head fall to the side to rest against Aphrodite's shoulder. Soon, she was breathing deeply and enjoying the sunshine on her face. As humiliating as it was to sit like a sullen child in the woman's lap, something about the comfortable position healed a little part of Fauna's heart that had been an open wound her entire life. Never had someone simply held her like that. Thirty-five years and it only took being nearly burnt alive to kickstart her *actual* healing.

The day mulled on with snacks and more books but very little conversation. Eventually, Fauna and Aphrodite's time together ended with Fauna half asleep in the bath as Aphrodite rubbed small circles over her back as the water soothed her fingers. Her hands ached in a new way. Fauna had written quite a bit in her journal and held a large, heavily bound book in her lap for a few hours. She hadn't realized how much it would test her hand strength until it fell into her lap and her fingers began to cramp!

With her cheek pressed to the cool porcelain, she sighed dramatically and enjoyed the warm water on her skin. When she began to prune, Aphrodite helped her up onto the rim of the bath and into a robe before carrying her to the seldomly used writing desk in her room.

"Some fresh sheets would be nice, yes? I'll grab some and tell my girls goodnight before I head back up. Would you like your journal?"

Fauna nodded and took her supplies gratefully. She saw the place where she'd left off earlier and began to finish her entry.

I don't know who I am anymore. I am Fauna, that much is true. I am still reading as much as I can, but their worlds no longer feel like my only solace. They feel… temporary. The silo doesn't feel like home anymore either. The castle does, but I wonder how long everyone's good graces will last. It almost seems too perfect, yet I don't want to question it at all, as that would be rude. Am I still welcome? Sometimes I wonder if I died and if this is my afterlife.

As she wrote, Aphrodite appeared in her peripherals a few times as she tended to the sheets and refreshed the room. When Fauna shut her journal and put it away with the pens, her hand lingered over the thickest pen she'd used when she first came to the castle. It was a nice reminder of how far she *had* come, instead of lamenting over how far she had to go. When she shut the drawer, Fauna found herself with a renewed sense of spirit.

Aphrodite approached her with her arms open, to which Fauna responded by opening hers as well. Together they scooted her to the bed with much more finesse than before.

Aphrodite tucked her in and made sure her feet were covered. "I'll send Rhiannon up in the morning. Goodnight, Fauna. Sweetest of dreams."

The next few weeks were equally as wonderful. The Lady visited when she could, usually early in the morning or late in the night. A few times, Fauna swore she heard someone rustling in her room as she slept but she assumed it was Rhiannon swapping out her laundry or one of the daughters leaving a little trinket in her bedside drawer—their new favorite hobby. They would make little poems or drawings and stick them in there for her to find. In return, she began leaving them little lines of stories or crudely drawn things of her own.

As she spent more time with Rhiannon, she developed a wonderful friendship with the girl. Slowly, they worked on Fauna's penmanship—something that frustrated her to no end. Before her accident, she would write with pristine hairlines and confident strokes, whereas now she could barely scrawl a grisly paragraph that seemingly only she could read. Her journal pages were filled with whimsy and wonder alongside mournful rage and defeated melancholy.

The girls still visited her, though they always came alone. They reasoned that if Aphrodite noticed both of them missing, she would panic. If one was available, they could distract her until the other sister left.

While they came alone, both sisters liked to talk about how much they loved spending time with each other. It was strange how they spoke so often of each other, but had no stories from recent times. Didn't they all live in the same castle? There was a certain joy in the air when one of them would laugh or tell funny stories about their lives in the castle. Fauna's favorites were the antics of the staff that the girls only knew through the gossip pipeline. That, alongside Rhiannon's insight, laid out a very detailed map of the staff and their lives.

Most nights when Aphrodite was home, they watched the night sky together while Aphrodite told Fauna all about her day. On the days when Aphrodite was busy, she would send a handwritten note to Fauna with her breakfast. Occasionally, Fauna would send a note back with Rhiannon—but she was so embarrassed by her handwriting and no words on earth seemed fitting to give the Lady! She'd already avoided showing Aphrodite the letters she had written in her first few weeks in the castle and the Lady had been kind enough not to bother her about them. They'd even been ripped out of her journal and hidden in her writing desk.

One night, so far into her stay that Fauna had forgotten how long she'd been there, Rhiannon was changing her bedding while Fauna lounged in the bathtub. They had dropped some scented powder in the water and it made the whole room smell like she was walking in a garden!

"Hey! I have to take off early tonight if that's okay?" Rhiannon popped her head in. "Lady Aphrodite is on her way right now to bring you dinner. Will you be safe alone for a few minutes?"

Fauna smiled and waved to her friend, making a mental note for tomorrow to ask where she was off to. Was it a date? Either way, she was over the moon to see her friend smiling so widely.

"Goodnight, and *be good*!" Rhiannon said coyly with an arched brow. She backed out of the bathroom without another word and left Fauna *very* confused. Was Rhiannon implying something between her and Lady Aphrodite? That didn't make any sense. Lady Aphrodite was her caretaker and someone who treated her with respect. Besides, a woman of her sort needed someone who could provide, entertain, and care for her family.

Fauna could do none of those things.

Her dreams were her security blanket, her safe place to explore her mind. When she'd first come to the castle, her sanctuary was barren—desecrated by nightmares of brimstone and pain. But, as time passed and the pain lessened, the enchanting comfort of her mind bloomed once more.

So, when dreams of running through the garden and dancing under the sky began to replace those, Fauna assumed it was natural. Well, as natural as any of it could be, considering her past. She felt a bit like the damsels in some of her favorite books, only she had already been saved or stashed away in a prison by a supreme ruler. Unless the Matron knew that Fauna was tucked away in the castle. The cruel woman was probably too busy ruling the village with fear and torture to even know that Fauna existed at all.

"Having fun?" Aphrodite asked as she watched from the doorway, startling Fauna out of her reverie."I'm sorry if I frightened you!"

Aphrodite leaned down so she could rest her arms against the rim of the bath. "You were just smiling and staring off into the distance and it was too cute."

Fauna, placated by the compliment but also still quite embarrassed, tried to pull herself together. She flicked a cluster of bubbles onto the floor and refused to look up at Aphrodite.

"Would you like me to stay or come back in a bit?"

Fauna waved to the chair Rhiannon had informally claimed and wordlessly invited her to stay. Aphrodite slipped off her shoes and set them somewhere out of sight. Fauna found herself quite surprised to see her place three towels on the floor to sit on.

Aphrodite spread her arms over the rim of the tub as she overlapped her hands. Soon her chin sat on her hands and she gazed at Fauna with a look of such fondness, that it nearly made her stop breathing.

"Are you okay now?" Aphrodite's eyes crinkled in delight. "Or are you still startled?"

Aphrodite's face was so close to hers, that she could smell the tobacco and peppermint on her breath. She'd never looked at another person so closely. Truth be told, the proximity and intensity of her look were a little unnerving.

"I am only joking," Aphrodite sat back and pointed to Fauna's arm. "You're healing nicely."

Fauna tried but couldn't hold eye contact long before staring at her knees again. Something in the air was shifting slowly and she strangely wasn't afraid at all. It was nice to be known and well-liked, even if she didn't have much to compare it to. Something was about to happen and it seemed like a positive thing. She looked where Aphrodite pointed and realized that her burns had healed. There were little white lines where the skin had been exposed far too soon, but it didn't matter. It was leagues better than when she had arrived.

"Have you ever been in love?"

Fauna was blindsided by the question. She looked at Aprhodite to see if she was joking and when she was not, Fauna shook her head. Wasn't it obvious by now that Fauna was deliberately reclusive?

"Why do you ask?" Fauna, mouthed to Aphrodite, who had gotten better at reading lips if it was just a short sentence.

"Haven't you wondered?"

"It makes no sense to me."

That made Aphrodite laugh. "Nothing about love makes sense, and it's different for everyone. Some people love freely and commit to nothing while there are people who love only once their entire lives. Some people love everyone, but not enough to broach intimacy... and some have forsaken love altogether."

"And which are you, Lady Aphrodite?" Fauna eyed Aphrodite playfully.

"I love people," Aphrodite began. "But sometimes people don't understand the love we give to them. It's as if we speak different languages. That's where the problems arise. If you love but don't know how to show it, then no one knows it's there. They begin to think that you're incapable of it when, truth be told, you're just trying your best and no one sees it."

Fauna sensed that there was a deeper meaning to Aphrodite's words, but did not know what it was. It was nice to have Aphrodite open up a bit. At least she had that.

"All right, let's get you in bed," Aphrodite said quietly. "Thank you for listening and thank you for being here. I would like to think that we are all better because you are in our lives."

Twelve

When summer said its last goodbye to gently usher in autumn, Fauna barely noticed, partially because her concept of time had been thrown about so much. There was no point in trying to reorient herself. The other reason was that she was simply enjoying herself. Her basic needs were met and she was slowly opening up to the people of the castle. The only reason she had any idea about how much time had passed was because Rhiannon mentioned that the seasons were ready to change for the second time since she'd been bed-bound in Castle Verity.

Rhiannon, who still tended to her with care and love, had newly found herself in a relationship with one of the castle groundskeepers. Though the maid always promised to bring her new beau up to the tallest tower on the top floor, she never made good on the promise. But, Fauna understood that this was for her safety. Trusting was not something she did easily, and even if the staff had begun to unwrap the layers that Fauna had wound herself in, it was still frightening to be close to these people at all.

Aphrodite's visits were also becoming further and further apart, though she stayed for much longer when she did arrive. As predicted, Fauna held a rapt curiosity about the woman but did not pursue anything. If anything, she took comfort from slowly learning to be near someone at all. From a skittish raggedy street cat to a docile domestic, Fauna had gotten *comfortable*—which was no small feat.

She continued writing little fictional paragraphs about grand heroic loves inside her journal, though as time passed, they tapered off to mere sentences. Something about the confinement of her room just drained the creativity out of her over time. The idea of exploring feelings between her characters just seemed daunting. Besides, how could she *truly* know the ins and outs of love if she had not experienced it? Fauna was extremely behind the curve on that front. She was still acclimatizing to being hugged. And even then, her only interactions with affection had been with the castlefolk. How could she write beautiful romances with daring adventures from the dark and dank walls of her silo? Would being confined to a single room help with that? How could she describe people when most of her life was spent purposefully avoiding them at all costs? Never mind that she had *no* idea how to even begin to talk about intimacy.

The books had never talked about *that* problem. Every princess in the books automatically *knew* it all: how to kiss, how to seduce, or how to use their wiles to subvert expectations and save the day. Unfortunately, that was not how life worked. But the women in stories weren't human, they were fictional. That was the part that hurt Fauna on a deeply personal level. Who was supposed to teach her about the rest? She had been alive for more than thirty years and not a single soul had stepped up to advocate for her. The resentment of her neglect had recently risen to the surface like fat in a stew—and Fauna was hell-bent on avoiding it for as long as she could.

No one taught her anything—it had always been books. How to cook, how to clean, how to hunt, how to even groom herself; every lesson she had ever learned had been researched and studied by her. But now she faced a dilemma that she had truly never prepared for. How was she supposed to feel? How was she supposed to act? There was no blueprint to memorize. Was there another soul in the entire world who could tell her what to do?

She was in such a strange situation that she knew there were no others in her predicament. Was she a prisoner? No. But sometimes it felt as if she was in purgatory, waiting for a judgment. The whirlwind of dread was so aggressive in her thoughts that Fauna didn't even notice that someone had opened her door.

"Hi." Rhiannon strolled through the door and brought a hamper full of laundry with her. "You fold, I'll put it away?"

Fauna, thankful that her spiral had been interrupted, nodded and grimaced at the pain that radiated from her legs. Either they'd missed one of her massages or something had scratched her somewhere. Aphrodite would be in later, so perhaps she could ask for a bit of comfort while the woman helped her strengthen her legs.

Just like every other day, Rhiannon went on and on about her boyfriend. Fauna didn't mind the conversation but she struggled internally with how much she missed outdoors. Guilt weighed heavily on her bones though. Didn't she *hate* the outdoors? Especially after the maniacs in the village tried to roast her alive? But… it looked so beautiful from the window.

Bit by bit, the laundry fell into her lap and she folded them all, nice and tidy. It was strange how much more attention she paid to a single task when it was one of the most excitingly dull highlights of her day.

"So, he held my hand and we sat under the tree while eating sandwiches. It was so cute! Oh, you would love him. His skin is like this really pretty color that the leaves turn in the late autumn and his eyes are so brown. Like, I think they're made of magic because they're so pretty!" Rhiannon was nearly vibrating with excitement. "Are you even listening?" Rhiannon pouted, though it was clearly a joke. "I was getting to the good part!"

"Where he talked about how to plant carrots?"

Rhiannon, who now never had a problem knowing what Fauna was silently saying, threw her head back and laughed so enthusiastically that her curls bounced back and forth jovially.

"That was *one* time and he was nervous!" Rhiannon spoke in between breathy giggles. "It was cute!"

"You think everything he does is cute."

"Because it *is*!" Rhiannon dropped the rest of the laundry on the bed and flung herself dramatically across the duvet. "Don't you even have crushes? Or little twinkles in your heart when you think about someone."

"I don't think about people. The only ones that matter were in my books."

"That's what you say for everything. Have you never experienced something before reading about it?"

Fauna shook her head, feeling very embarrassed. She truly hadn't. And in that moment, the reality of that statement landed heavy on her mind.

"I'm afraid."

"Of what?" Rhiannon put a comforting hand on Fauna's leg and affectionately rubbed her thumb back and forth over her kneecap.

"Of it being wrong. What if I'm wrong? What if it's bad? What if it's not real? I should have been a wife by now, I think."

"There is no wrong, only different. Do you think being a wife will make you happy?" Rhiannon asked quietly. "Because all of those questions are valid ones, but you might just have to try some of them on your own, without reading about them."

"I didn't used to think that those things would make me happy, but now all I can think about is walking around the grounds with the sun on my face. I want Aphrodite's daughters to like me, I want to be part of

their family because I never felt like part of my own. I hate that they get to see her every day and I rot to death in this room. Am I disgusting?"

"That's... that's..." Rhiannon's voice wobbled. "That's so sad. I don't think you are disgusting! You're family to me, at least. I do love you a whole bunch. I promise I'll never stop coming here every day, even if you don't need me anymore. You're my best and only friend!"

"Stop," Fauna mouthed through her tears, chuckling to break the tension. Laughing while crying was *not* something familiar to her, but it was better than being so very sad.

"No joke! You're so important to me! You were the first person to call me pretty—ever!"

"Really?" Fauna was quite surprised at that, so surprised that her sniffles stopped and the heaves in her chest quelled immediately.

"Yes!" Rhiannon squeezed her knee before sitting up. "Who do you think gave me enough confidence to find a boyfriend!"

Fauna leaned her head against her shoulder, much calmer now that Rhiannon had given her a little pep talk. Perhaps she had just been alone too long and had gotten lost in her head. Though, that hadn't been a problem when she was in the village.

"Thank you," Fauna mouthed to Rhiannon, who just smiled devilishly and grabbed Fauna's notebook.

"Okay, okay, now let's play hangman until it's time for dinner. You always have the best words. Who even knew 'envisaging' was even a word? Maybe I should read more books. Or better yet, when your voice comes back, *you* can read me every darned book in this castle. That sounds like a bundle of fun."

Thirteen

I am Fauna.

I am torn between two planes of existence. One half of me longs to be free from this room, to roam the castle giggling with the sisters and reading all the books in the library. I want to sit on the corner of a desk while Aphrodite does paperwork. I want to explore the garden with the girls. I want to meet Rhiannon's boyfriend. Could I take a bath on my own? Without any help? I've heard there's a lake somewhere on the property... could I swim?

But the other half of me is content. I'm alone and tucked away, which is what I've always wanted. I'm banished to the shadows and I should be happy. I always avoided people like the plague and I took solace in being my only form of support. But... things are changing, I'm afraid.

Why is Aphrodite barely around anymore? She has this way of making you feel like you're the only person alive when she's speaking to you. I'm too old to want it, but I want her to read me stories at night. I like hearing her voice. It makes me feel safe. I never thought I would like being cared for, but here I am.

Does she know that her daughters visit me? That we write poetry together and talk about art? That they call me a friend? Who would have thought that I could make friends and like them?

It doesn't matter anyway. Aphrodite asked me to write her letters and then never asked about them again. Is any of this even real? I feel as if

I don't exist. But I do. I can see and touch and smell. If I was dead, that wouldn't be possible... right?

After an emotional bout of journaling and a nap from sheer emotional exhaustion, Fauna woke to a balmy room coated in the soft pastel light of the setting sun. Aphrodite sat in the rocking chair, lost in thought while staring out the window. She wasn't coiffed as she normally was when she was heading out for business, which was strange enough to see.

"I can feel you staring, Fauna." Aphrodite's voice was jarringly cold. "We need to talk."

Fauna waited patiently while Aphrodite stood from the chair and began to pace around the room. Her uncertain steps in no particular direction were extremely offputting. Something was *very* wrong with Aphrodite but Fauna could not begin to guess what was bothering her. Her hair was the same dusky blonde, only instead of perfect waves it looked a bit mussed. Her dress fit her well, per usual, but it still looked rumpled, as if it was grabbed off the floor. When she turned to Fauna, she seemed to be genuinely exhausted.

"Do you remember how you got here?"

Fauna shook her head. What she *did* remember seemed too farfetched to even be real and to admit that to anyone would make her look silly. What kind of bird is so large that it could fly someone like her to safety? She was a full-sized adult, not a tiny child. Birds that large only existed in books—and as much as Fauna wished some days, she was *not* in a book.

"So you don't remember *anything?*"

Fauna's breath caught in her throat, sending her into a silent coughing fit. Aphrodite's distant tone was unpleasant and triggered something deep in Fauna's mind and she began to panic. Why did it seem like she was being asked a question when everyone already knew the answer? Aphrodite still loomed over her expectantly and was seemingly growing more and more impatient. She looked around the room with an almost paranoid intensity. Was something going wrong in the castle?

Fauna grabbed at the blankets and pulled them up to her neck. Her breaths came in disjointed bunches and did not fill her lungs at all. She looked up, silently begging Aphrodite to drop the subject, but it seemed luck was not on her side.

"I need to keep you hidden up here to keep you safe. The Matron *cannot* know that you are here. She isn't as bad as everyone makes her seem—she has her reasonings for things. But you are new and time-consuming. What happens if you need help and we cannot offer it? What happens if you die up here and none of us know? Do you know how badly that would hurt Rhiannon or me?"

Aphrodite turned and began pacing once more. She tapped at her chin while she walked, each step in perfect time with her fingers. She had never done that before either.

"I want to share something with you, sweet, sweet Fauna," Aphrodite saying her name in such a way sent an uncomfortable shiver down her spine. "I won't leave you, ever. You know that right?

It took quite a bit of effort, but Fauna managed a very slight and hopefully convincing nod. Up until about five minutes ago, she believed it. Now, there was something heavy in the air around them. Oh, Fauna wanted nothing more than one of the girls or Rhiannon to come into the room.

"I've thought about you since the moment you appeared at the door of my castle," Aphrodite sang sweetly—a jostling change from moments prior. "At first, I figured you'd been injured by the animals of the forest, but when I saw the type and severity of those injuries, I knew that something else had happened. Something intentional. I do have to wonder if the Matron was involved at all. She *always* wanted to save the quiet ones—the ones with no backbone or fire in their blood. Which are you?"

Fauna's heart began to beat wildly. Didn't Aphrodite *just* say that the Matron couldn't know about her? But now she was asking about her blood? Fauna had spent most of her life asserting herself against the idiots of the village, she certainly *did* have a backbone. And her blood was fine!

"If it was her, I should thank her. Do you know how good it feels to be able to connect with someone after all of these lonely years? There isn't anyone close to my age around, and chatting with overemotional teenagers is daunting on the best of the days. Would the Matron get involved with some ragamuffin from the village? Did she bring you to me? Am I hiding a secret everyone already knows?"

Fauna hid her hands under the blankets to not show her trembling to Aphrodite. While being afraid wasn't something she did often, it still made her feel extremely weak compared to the brooding woman in front of her. She never once realized that by being bedbound, she was a sitting target.

Aphrodite made her way to the door. She narrowed her eyes at Fauna and studied her in a very exposing way.

"I have many things to ponder and even more to investigate. You're a mystery, Little Fauna of the Forest. An enigma of sorts. I want to know everything about you—everything that you're willing to tell."

Later that night, Rhiannon appeared in her doorway with dinner and a new stack of books. Fauna, who had been sleeping, but had woken just before the door clicked shut, stayed supine and hoped to catch a peek of what the maid would do while she was asleep. She played it cool, just in case Rhiannon had also inherited Aphrodite's strange mood. Pretending to be asleep seemed to be the best and safest option.

At first, Rhiannon wandered just past the foot of the bed. Based on her noises, she had set the tray of food on the writing desk and had begun putting books in the drawers for later. Even with her eyes closed, she could still imagine the maid's movements. They were slowly becoming friends, but being close to someone so often made it easier to read their body language.

Rhiannon began to hum a quiet tune that was unfamiliar to Fauna. It wasn't unheard of for the maid to sing as she worked, but after the unsettling interaction she'd had with Aphrodite, Fauna was a little on edge.

"Are you awake?" Rhiannon whispered as Fauna felt the bed dip. "I brought dinner and some more books."

Fauna debated on whether or not she wanted to engage with another person after the strange visit with Aphrodite but decided that she did enjoy time spent with her friend. She raised her hand in the air for a moment before slowly sliding herself up the bed and getting her bearings.

"Hey." Rhiannon smiled softly at her. "I heard Lady Aphrodite *cursing* in the hallway earlier. *Cursing!* She hates that! What happened?"

Fauna shrugged and tried her best not to let her emotions show. Had she done something to upset Aphrodite? Or had she been upset long before seeing Fauna? Either way, she didn't like the idea of Aphrodite being so upset. Perhaps, if Fauna saw her later, she would ask what was wrong.

"Anyway, the staff is on edge because she yelled at them, so I only have fruit and bread for dinner. I'm sure you don't mind. It was the easiest thing for me to grab quickly."

As they ate, Fauna noticed that Rhiannon kept checking the door anxiously. A casual glance made sense—she had explained Aphrodite's mood earlier. When she thought Fauna wasn't looking, Rhiannon would do a visual sweep of the room, and when the dishes were put back onto the tray, she checked the windows. When she turned around, she caught Fauna eyeing her and deflated.

"I'm nervous today, I don't know why. Something feels off, but I can't explain what. I might just need a good night's sleep. It's been a hard week in the castle." Rhiannon said quietly before zooming into the bathroom to wash her hands. She brought a damp cloth back out and let Fauna wipe the sticky remnants of dinner off her fingers before tossing it into a hamper.

When Rhiannon turned back to her, Fauna patted the pillow next to her, which made Rhiannon smile. "You want me to sit and read with you?"

Fauna just hit the pillow a little harder and pulled the blanket back a bit. Rhiannon rolled her eyes good-naturedly and sat on the exposed sheets.

"Okay, just for a little bit. I kind of wanted to start one of the books that I brought you, but I thought it was polite to let you read it first. However, I think I'll help myself to it tonight."

Fourteen

As she slept, Fauna found herself unable to shake loose the feeling of something being off. Not enough to be obvious—more like a painting that didn't quite hang right or ill-fitting clothes. Yes, Aphrodite and Rhiannon had been a little out of character, but even that seemed pretty circumstantial. But, the discomfort lasted well into her sleep and tickled the back of her mind like she was trying to remember something long buried. Deeper and deeper she fell into a slumber as her breathing evened out and her body relaxed.

While her eyes were closed, she felt a pair of lips gently touch the space behind her ear. It made her shiver at first but Fauna quickly calmed down when it was someone telling her a secret.

"Just pretend."

Fauna opened her eyes quickly and gasped as she stared back at the familiar woman in her dreams. This time she wore a white wedding dress and a smile that was so genuine and pure that it made Fauna tear up. Her hair, which had previously been long and flowing, sat in a beautiful updo with little flowers woven into it. The light in her eyes brought out a secret joy that Fauna did not even know the world was capable of. A gentle aura permeated the air around them, immediately placating Fauna's unease from earlier. Now, properly calmed and on the cusp of happiness, Fauna was able to return the smile and even reach out for a simple touch.

The woman beamed as she extended her hand as well. The pair stood in the middle of a deserted dance floor holding hands and staring at each other.

"I had to pretend that I didn't see it coming. You have seen it too, you just haven't had time to realize it. You did a wonderful job of pretending. I'm so proud of you. You'll see it soon, I promise. It will make sense."

"See what?" Fauna jumped when she heard her voice. It had been so long since she'd spoken aloud that it seemed unfamiliar to her. "What should I see?"

"The end is near," the woman took her hands back and reached out to gently cup Fauna's cheeks. "You've done a very good job pretending. It will all be over soon. Then you can *dance!*"

With that, she leaned in and pressed a kiss to Fauna's forehead. Before pulling away, the woman looked around as if checking their surroundings, and leaned back in to whisper something to her.

"Never let her silence you," the woman said so quietly that Fauna almost missed it. "Just pretend. And then...*don't.*"

. . .

. . .

. . .

. . .

. . .

..

..

..

..

.

.

.

.

.

..

..

..

..

..

...

...

...

"Mother!"

The scream woke Fauna, who shot up in bed and slapped the corner of the bedside table so hard that it jammed one of her fingers and made her gasp in pain. Bolts of agony flew through her veins, pumped even faster by her racing heart. Her breaths were staggered and heavy. She pressed her lips together and fought her body's urge to gulp down the air. What was happening?

"Mother!" another bloodcurdling scream, very familiar to Fauna, came from far inside the castle. Scared and unprepared, she rustled around the bed to find her discarded nightgown and cried out when she saw it crumpled on the floor. Panic rose in her chest and bile began to creep up the back of her throat. Where was Aphrodite? Had she already left to see the Matron? Fauna desperately tried to remember what the woman had said the night before.

"Bea!" Aphrodite's voice cried out, broken and feral. It echoed off the hallways and thundered throughout the castle so violently that Fauna wondered if the glass panes would shatter.

Another desperate shriek froze Fauna's blood. It almost sounded like... a bird's call. Without a single thought in her head except for that bone-chilling yell, she leaped off the bed, desperate to aid Aphrodite in whatever was happening. The agony of Aphrodite's cries and the terror in the screaming had Fauna ready to panic.

The moment her toes touched the carpeted floor, her legs bent incorrectly and she slammed her chin down on her knee, nearly biting off the tip of her tongue. She collapsed into a pile of limbs on the carpet, her elbows crying out where they had been burnt on the area rug in the fall.

Blood, thick and tangy, filled her mouth and made her choke. She coughed and began to cry when it spilled out of her mouth, down her neck, and onto her chest. A loud crash far outside her door caused her to jump, which led her to try to find her gown on the floor frantically. Her tongue ached and the underside of her chin throbbed painfully. The darkness seemed to be heavier down below, but a sliver of light shone under the door frame and illuminated the floor just enough for her to find the bottom of her gown.

She shimmied it on as best as she could and tried to get up on all fours. When her legs refused to move, she screamed in frustration and beat her fists against the floor as hard as she could. The overwhelming silence that had filled the castle after Aphrodite's cries was broken by pitiful slaps of Fauna's scarred hands against the bare floor. She choked once more on the blood in her mouth and began to heave desperately.

Nostrils flared and shoulders trembling, Fauna began to drag herself across her room and to her door. Memories of Scarlet taunting her while she crawled to the bathroom played in her mind like a vision from another timeline. The rug burned her forearms as she pulled with all her might. Inch by inch she scooted across the room until she collapsed in front of her door, a pile of sweaty and bloodied limbs. Her whole body ached and she could no longer tell what was blood from her injured mouth or sweat from exertion.

"Stay away from my girls!" Aphrodite's voice bellowed through the castle. "Don't touch them!"

Two loud blasts, piercing and deafening, rang out through the castle, which motivated Fauna to heave herself up to grab the handle of her door. Her fingers slipped off twice, leaving a blood trail along the golden handle. With a choking sob, she tried one more time and succeeded. She flung the door open to a moonlit hallway and managed to drag herself through the door frame. The very instant her arms felt the hardwood hallway floor, she felt a palpable change in herself. Suddenly, there was a soul-crushing pain in her body, but not in a specific place. She felt as if she was fighting her way out of a vacuum and sorrowfully losing.

As she dragged herself through the doorway, her knee caught against an upturned bit of floorboard and her body immediately went rigid with pain. Bright white flashes of agony ripped through Fauna's body, nearly breaking her like a poultry wishbone. She sobbed as she finally escaped through the frame and was able to scoot her lower extremities into a comfortable position. A tingling sensation, almost like an itch she couldn't find, started in her toes and began to rise along her legs.

What was happening?

"You will pay for this!" Aphrodite's voice was feral, unhinged. A roar, louder than any animal Fauna had ever heard, shook the walls and sent artwork crashing down. A light fixture began to creak above her so Fauna moved into the fetal position as she prepared to be crushed. The sounds of frames splintering as they fell from the walls crashed all around her. The chandelier in the hallway shook and tumbled, landing so close to Fauna's head that for a few moments she could only hear twinkles of glass shattering. Bits of it landed on her face and thankfully missed her eyes. She blew out a breath and hissed when pieces of glass fell from her lips and onto the ground.

Her vision began to tunnel as a roaring ache began in the back of her head. So much had just happened and she didn't understand one bit of it.

An explosion outside of the castle made flames rise so high that the tips of them could be seen from windows that Fauna didn't even know existed until that very moment. The temperature in the castle began to drop quickly, making Fauna's body quiver and her muscles cramp. She wrapped her arms around herself and tried to tuck her knees into her arms. As the sun rose, Fauna realized that the pain she felt was coming from her legs. Had she damaged them further falling off the bed? Little pinpricks of electric pain clouded her judgment but Fauna was focused solely on helping her friends.

As the castle hallways brightened, she saw a doorway at the end of the hallway. Pretty pinks and purples began to filter through the windows, wrapping the castle in a delicate naive light that made the chaos ensuing that much more pronounced. As the hallway came into focus, Fauna saw a banister amongst the rubble, guiding her towards the stairwell. Feeling trickled back into her legs, as if she'd fallen asleep on them. It wasn't quite painful, but more of a persistent discomfort.

Unable to ignore the cries of pain from Aphrodite, Fauna began to drag herself through the small bits of broken crystal that littered the floor. They pierced her skin and tore at her body as she dragged herself down the hall. Her arms already ached with bone-deep fatigue and the pinpricks of pain as she raked her body over the floor only served as a means of staying focused.

She sniffed back the tears, her panic already triggered way too intensely to calm down. Soon, she arrived at the top of the stairs, boneless and exhausted. Her stomach threatened to expel the food still left in it. A shrill slam against one of the windows made her scream. A great black bird, larger than anything she'd ever seen, had exploded against the outside window in a grotesque display of bloody offal and slid down the pane. Feathers and sinew dripped down as Fauna gave in and vomited down her front.

Something was *very* wrong.

Another bird slammed against the window in a bloody lump. It made Fauna startle again as she began to cry. She curled into a ball at the top of the stairs, covered in a soiled gown and bleeding in little rivulets down her body. Her body ached from her teeth to her toes. She looked to the window again and screamed when the Matron's face peered back at her for the briefest of seconds.

The sound of her own scream made Fauna jump, which sent her pitching forward and down the staircase head-first. Unbridled fear shot through her body as she realized finally that she could move her legs and hear her voice. Her errant hands tried to grab at the rungs of the railing as she rolled down the stairs. The first landing came quickly as she hit the carpeted area with a sickening crunch of bone.

Her bloody palm slipped against one of the stairs and caused her to slide further than she meant to. Almost immediately she was careening down the second flight of stairs, the very same ones that Aphrodite had brought her up so many months ago. She put her hands over the back of her head and hoped that she would at least live to see Aphrodite one last time. The wooden steps pounded into her back as she continued to roll so violently that she could not gather her bearings.

When she collided with the bottom of the stairs, she heard a sickening crack and screamed when one of her fingers bent all the way back. She began to hyperventilate and felt reality start to fade from her mind.

Aphrodite.

Where was Aphrodite?

"Aphrodite!"

The sound of a yell distracted her from her broken finger, it took a moment for Fauna to realize that it was *her* voice. *She* was yelling.

But she *could* speak?

"Ahhh," a strangled voice moaned from across the room.

Fauna, too sore and stunned to move much, looked across to where the sound was and gasped when she saw the Matron, bloody and barely alive. Her sneer was long gone, leaving only a face whiter than oleander, covered in sickly black oily blood. Her mouth was open, but the only thing Fauna could focus on was the blackened eyes of the pitiful ruler. Had she always had those?

"Your pathetic mother would be so proud. You told me *many* things all tucked away like a little lamb," she whispered hoarsely, blood and black sludge coating her teeth. "It was so easy. You're very friendly."

"What?" Fauna rasped, her voice foreign to her. Was the Matron speaking to *her*?

"It's too late for your mother." The Matron's eyes closed as oil began to drip from under her eyelids. "Poor little deviant. Your father would be so disappointed that he gave so much, just for you to fail. Sleep tight, Little Fauna of the Forest."

With that, the Matron's body began to sink in on itself and her skin turned a mottled grey. Almost immediately, she was nothing more than a pile of oily black feathers. The pool of black blood grew larger and larger until it almost touched Fauna's fingers.

Just as the Matron appeared, she was gone. Behind her oily corpse pile, was Aphrodite, dressed in an outfit Fauna had never seen. Behind her were her daughters, staring at her horrified. What had she done to them? Were they hurt? Where was Rhiannon?

"Aphrodite, girls. You're alright," Fauna heaved a sigh of relief. Her body trembled and began to convulse as her limbs moved without cause. She was going to die. Between the trauma of falling down the stairs and how weak her body felt, Fauna had nothing left to give.

Something wiggled in her stomach and pressed its way up her throat. Ready to vomit, Fauna tried to push herself up but failed when her broken finger sent shockwaves of pain up her arms. A vignette began to form on the outside of her vision as she reached out for her friends with her unbroken hand.

Why did Aphrodite look so confused?

Why did the girls look at her like that?

"Mother?" Bea asked, her fingers curling around Aphrodite's dress.

Aphrodite kept her gaze *heavily* trained on Fauna but answered her daughter.

"Yes?"

"Who is she?"

Fifteen

Who is she?

Who is *she*?

W
h
o
is

s

h
e
?

.

.

.

..

..

..

..

...

..

..

..

..

.

.

.

"Is she awake?"

"Should we eat her?"

"Has she been here this whole time?"

"Girls, *please*. We've had quite a day. Go lock up and I'll send the groundskeeper to patch the holes so you don't freeze tonight."

"Yes, Mother."

Cold fingertips touched her cheek. It started as a gentle probe but quickly became excruciating when the fingers moved downwards to her jaw. A jolt of pain radiated through Fauna's teeth, making her extremely disoriented. She moved her hands to swat at whoever was causing her pain and cried out when her broken finger hit the floor. For a moment, Fauna couldn't tell what direction she was facing or if she was even lying down. The first few times she opened her eyes the world was so blurry that she nearly vomited a second time. After a few moments, she tried again and found that she was lying on a very cold hardwood floor. Fauna blinked, the world around her was fuzzy, unfocused. Flickering lights and a smattering of noise blaring around her made her surroundings blur together as she fought and failed to remain conscious.

The bright sun boring into her eyes was what finally woke Fauna up. She tried to rub at them, but right before she made contact, she gasped at the sight. There was no tugging pain, no stretch of the marred skin. She tried to flex her fingers in her good hand—a nervous habit she'd picked up whilst bedbound for so long—and found that even the small bones in her hand hurt. She admired the skin around her knuckles and how clear it looked. She'd nearly forgotten what her normal hands looked like.

The room she was in felt different from the one before. The decor was muted and sensible—the extreme opposite of the ornate room she had spent her time in. Fauna took in her surroundings and realized that she was lying on a table surrounded by a meal that had been interrupted.

Her index finger had been taped to the one next to it, and there were little cuts from the glass, but the rest of her skin was decidedly *not* scarred. Her hands were healed? How had *that* happened?

"So you are alive after all. Well then, who, might I ask, are you?" Aphrodite demanded. Fauna flicked her eyes upward and saw an imposing figure, who looked at her with a chilling fury that she'd never seen before. The person in front of her felt like a stranger, not the same woman she had been bonding with upstairs.

Fauna panicked, unsure how to even begin.

Aphrodite, looking identical to the woman Fauna knew but dressed up in extreme impatience, leaned over and peered directly into her eyes. "I asked you a question."

"F-F-Fauna?" Fauna replied with a terrified stutter. "You don't know me?"

"I don't know you." Aphrodite agreed with pursed lips and skepticism. "But you seem to know me."

Fauna's heart dropped so violently, that she felt about to faint. "N-n-n-no."

"No, what? You don't know me? Tell me or I'll throw you out the window myself. You don't want to try me, woman. I've had enough action today and you are only adding to my ire."

"S-she," Fauna bit down hard to stop her trembling chin, which caused one of her teeth to crack. She spat part of it out in her hand and gagged at the site. "The Matron?" she felt drool and blood spill from her mouth. It dripped down her chin and onto her neck. She began to choke before trying to sit up. "She's gone?"

"Well, she is dead. So, unless you have something to tell me about that, I have no time to waste on you. How did you get in here?"

"I've been up there," Fauna's arm shook as she pointed upstairs. "Healing. Months. I talked to *you*. You helped me heal. There was a rocking chair? The window. The girls? Rhiannon?"

"The rocking chair? The girls? Upstairs?" Aphrodite's expression softened, but only a little bit. "Why would you be in there? That room is locked for a reason. My castle is extremely well guarded and anyone with an ounce of intelligence would know not to trespass, especially upstairs of all places. I should throw you in the cellar but I find myself too exhausted at this point. Don't make me regret it."

"No! Aphrodite!" Fauna cried though the ache in her mouth was slowly returning. "I swear! I have been healing! I couldn't talk or walk! I heard yelling! I thought you were hurt!"

The confession made Aphrodite pause curiously. She narrowed her gaze at Fauna and looked her up and down before taking a dramatically long breath. A long pause, only accompanied by Fauna's labored breathing, weighed heavily over the room.

"Go on," Aphrodite demanded with a displeased expression. She walked over and kneeled over Fauna. "What did she do to you? I'm still not convinced."

Fauna pushed herself up onto her elbows, still in shock but no longer trembling. She winced when her freshly bruised arms pressed against the wooden table, but did not cry out. Instead, she took a deep breath and tried to summarize her last few months. "I was burned. I was getting better. I could almost walk again. We were going to maybe look at the library."

"You can walk now," Aphrodite said incredulously, pointing at Fauna's legs. "You walked in here. Granted you were dead weight against me but you still walked. Burned how?"

"The villagers burned me alive. I was injured. But I couldn't walk or talk." Fauna pushed herself the rest of the way up and hiked up her gown. All she saw was pale skin with soft hair instead of scarred flesh that ached. Little tiny cuts from her crawl down the hallway lined her shins and knees, but there was not much blood. There *was* an egg-sized bruise on her knee, which reminded her of falling down the stairs trying to save the family she had come to love.

Aphrodite's face did not move. She simply blinked once and seemed to wait for a further explanation that Fauna did not have.

"I can show you where I stayed! I need you to help me." Fauna pleaded desperately with more bloody drool running down her chin. She wiped her mouth before reaching out again with shaky hands.

"Don't touch me," Aphrodite hissed. "I will cut off your hands and feed them to my staff. You need a bath and to stop crying like a child."

"I'm sorry," Fauna felt herself falling back on old habits. That was why ever trusting a single soul was her greatest mistake. "I was starting to feel loved. The girls loved me! You might have too! I was finally making friends."

"I doubt it," Aphrodite snarled, putting her hands in her pockets and motioning to the walls with her head. "You're in my study for now. But, you reek of sweat and other unsavory things. I will let you bathe in the employee baths and give you *one* meal. Then you may present your case to me. I don't generally partake in *senseless* murder, but your explanation is lacking in some critical areas."

"I'm not used to standing anymore. I'm kind of dizzy. " Fauna tried to lean back on her elbows, but winced at the pain and fell back down against the table with a hollow *crack!* The room swam before her eyes before it faded completely.

"Obviously," Aphrodite muttered.

When she woke once more, Fauna found herself on the same uncomfortable table as before. She tentatively touched the side of her head and winced when she felt a very painful knot. Perhaps her legs and voice had returned to her but they weren't making existence any less painful in this moment.

"You stink, but I want to know what you're talking about," Aphrodite grumbled from somewhere in the distance. "So, you will show me and then let whatever staff that isn't mysteriously missing clean you up. I'm impatient and my castle is in desperate need of repair after the day we've had."

"Thank you," Fauna whispered, tears hanging precariously from her eyelashes. "I'm so lost."

"You can pretend it's for you, but it's because you're suddenly the star of this sorrowful day and I don't want you to smell like a hovel when I question you. If this ends up being a ruse, you will die painfully," Aphrodite sighed. "Get up."

Fauna swung her legs over the table she was lying on. She looked around and groaned when her vision lagged and nausea built in her stomach again. The room was spinning—when was the last time she'd eaten?

"Well?" Aphrodite demanded, holding out her hand. The cold demeanor of the woman she had grown quite attached to was a shock to her system.

"I don't know what's happening," Fauna set her bare feet down and cried out when she felt the cold floor slam against her feet. "I haven't felt my legs in months. I haven't been able to speak in months. I wrote everything down. I need my journal. What is happening? What did she do to me?"

"Show me," Aphrodite demanded as she walked out of the room. "Come."

Fauna nodded and pushed against the table for some momentum. Her legs trembled after so long without use, but she was determined not to fall again. It was strange to not feel the pull of healing skin or the scabs on her ankles

"I can walk," Fauna admitted. "I'm not hurt, except for my finger and the cuts and bruises. Where did my scars go? This is so… strange!"

"I feel a headache coming on," Aphrodite pinched the bridge of her nose. "Let's hurry before my temper gets the best of me. I'll admit, you've piqued my curiosity now."

"If the journal is still up here, it will help," Fauna assured Aphrodite. Hopefully, her pathetic demeanor would add merit to her story.

Slowly, Fauna crept past the remains of a puddle of her blood. Someone had made an effort to clean the bulk of it, but smears of it were still spread across the wooden paneling on the floor.

She stepped on the first stair and used all of her strength to clutch the railing. She repeated the process with the second step. By the time she'd gotten to the fifth, Aphrodite was impatiently tapping her foot against the floor at the top of the stairs. After a few seconds, Aphrodite went back down, grabbed Fauna under her arms, and walked up the rest of the stairs backward while taking most of Fauna's weight.

"There's glass down there, be careful," Fauna muttered, holding up her shredded arms once Aphrodite let go of them. "That was from a chandelier."

"I knew I smelled blood up here," Aphrodite said. "I had forgotten about that, I was a bit busy, killing that damned woman."

"The Matron?" Fauna muttered as the spot where her tooth had fallen out began to ache. "She called me a deviant."

That got a short laugh out of the woman. "Why would she, of all people, do that?"

"I don't bow to her," Fauna spat blood onto the floor. "I bow to no one. I haven't worshipped her in all my years. My mother despised her and subsequently so do I."

"So I see," Aphrodite narrowed her eyes as she navigated the hallway. "If you have lied, you'll be out in the cold to fend for yourself. I'll admit it's too far-fetched to be a lie, but I'm still curious as to how you got here."

"It's too disturbing to be false," Fauna admitted. "I can't even begin to explain it. I haven't processed it. I still don't recognize my voice anymore. I haven't spoken in so long, I don't even know how long I've been here."

"How did you communicate?"

Fauna led her to the door and motioned for her to go in first.

"I wrote it all down."

Aphrodite looked at her with obvious distrust. "I'm supposed to believe that?"

Fauna simply shrugged and walked into the room. As soon as her toes touched the wooden floor, she collapsed and tried to yell. Her knees buckled and she slammed to the floor with a pathetic silent whine.

"What are you doing?" Aphrodite demanded as Fauna's skin began to warp and shine with the familiar scars she was used to seeing. The woman stomped toward her and pushed at her body with a shoe before pushing again with more force.

Fauna held out her arms and began to cry. Aphrodite knelt and grabbed one of Fauna's hands to examine. She moved Fauna's fingers and inspected every rough patch of scarring.

"What happened to you?"

Fauna tried to speak but was met with the all-too-familiar wheeze. Aphrodite wrapped a hand around Fauna's neck but did not squeeze.

"Speak!"

Fauna used all her energy to scream in Aphrodite's face, but nothing came out. With a dissatisfied *thump!* Aphrodite dropped Fauna's hand and walked directly out of the room. When the door shut behind her, Fauna began to sob.

She had no energy and a taste of freedom. Utterly defeated and barely alive, Fauna dragged herself across the floor until she collapsed in front of the rocking chair and cried herself to sleep.

Sixteen

When Fauna woke up a second time, she was still clothed in her nightclothes and tucked into a strange bed. It felt achingly similar to the bed she'd gotten accustomed to, only this one was in a *very* different room. Large, floor-to-ceiling windows let in the most potent golden-hour sunbeams. It would have been a nice, tranquil moment, had she not been run through the emotional gamut. Her body ached and her muscles cried out with fatigue before she was even able to move.

"Are you awake?" a gentle voice called out. "I'm here to clean your wounds."

"Rhiannon?" Fauna sat up quickly and looked over to see her best friend. Well, kind of her best friend. Reality set in, causing her excitement to plummet. "Are you real?"

"I'm real. But, uh… I don't know you. That's not a problem, though! I think?" Rhiannon stumbled over her words and bit her lip nervously. "I don't know what's happening, but you seemed *really* out of it when Lady Aphrodite brought you here. You looked *dead*."

"You were my best friend," Fauna whispered, trying her best not to cry in front of a familiar stranger. "I think the Matron played a very cruel trick on me. You were my best friend."

"Oh." Rhiannon kicked awkwardly at the edge of the bed. "The Matron is dead, just so you know. It's not like anyone is sad about it though. She was pretty awful."

"My mother hated her," Fauna admitted. "My father- *oh!*"

Rhiannon rushed forward, bright orange curls bouncing against her cheeks. "Everything okay?"

When her hand touched Fauna's shoulder, Fauna felt the tears start to come. It was all so familiar in the most heartbreaking way. However, she wasn't in any place to refuse the comfort.

"She said that my father would be disappointed." Fauna inhaled sharply. "I don't even want to know what that could mean. All I know is that I *hate* her."

"She's dead now, so you're free to hate her all you want," Rhiannon offered. "Not like she can come back from the dead. Oh... maybe she can. That's a *terrible* thought." She chuckled absently.

"Where's Aphrodite?" Fauna adjusted her position under the blankets and realized that laying in a bed with the full feeling of her legs was a very foreign sensation.

"In her office—I'm supposed to get you cleaned up and take you to her as soon as I can. But, you looked so feeble and sad that I had to stop and ask. I do have one question though, if you're willing to answer it."

Out of habit, Fauna searched the blankets for her notebook before realizing she could speak. When she nodded, Rhiannon sat gently on the side of the bed and looked at her intently.

"What happened? How did you know the Verity family? I only know what I heard being whispered around the halls and castle gossip is dreadful for accuracy."

"I... was burned at the stake," Fauna began, wringing her uninjured hands. "And a raven saved me, I think. That does *not* sound possible, but I promise you that's exactly what I remember."

"The Matron controlled the birds. I'm blaming her regardless," Rhiannon said. "I knew that much from having to clean the castle grounds after she visited!"

"Bones?" Fauna suggested. "Carcasses?"

Rhiannon shook her head sadly. "Mostly a lot of bird poop on everything. But anyway, go ahead."

"I ended up at the castle and Aphrodite carried me to a room where I recuperated for a very long time." Fauna didn't have the heart or energy to explain it all. "And now I'm here. I think."

"I know this castle like the back of my hand," Rhiannon assured her. "There is no way you were here. Are you sure you didn't sneak in from the village? I won't tell anyone! It's just very unlikely that you would have been somewhere without anyone knowing."

"I was in a room with windows that overlooked a garden," Fauna offered. "It has a big painting on the ceiling?"

Rhiannon's face paled as her eyes widened. "No."

Fauna blinked in confusion. "Yes? I tried to show Aphrodite, but she left before I could explain very much. Perhaps when you take me to her I could explain myself better."

"*Lady* Aphrodite," Rhiannon gently warned her. "Don't be too familiar with her, it's disrespectful. You're still a stranger to us."

Shame flooded Fauna's cheeks. She was dreadfully out of her element. "I'm sorry, I'll remember. It was so just *real* up there. I can tell you the color of her outfits and all the conversations that we had. I spent nights just gossiping about the kitchen staff with you."

Rhiannon shot her a sympathetic frown. "But that wasn't me."

Suddenly an idea struck Fauna. "I'm not dead, am I?"

Rhiannon's somber demeanor broke as she smiled softly, her rosy cheeks as round as cherries. "No, you are not dead. I can assure you that."

"What is real?" Fauna's body suddenly felt *very* heavy. "It felt so *real* up there. I can't believe she was able to do that! And I'm just *here!* I can't even trust my mind. Why would she even do that?"

"The Matron was an awful woman," Rhiannon said softly as she rummaged around her things for her supplies. "Be careful what you say about her to the Lady—she's *very* sensitive about the Matron. I don't even know the full details and none of the staff does either. None of us were around when things were really bad. We just know that it's an extremely sore subject."

"Are you all new here?" Fauna asked, clearly confused. "You weren't around?"

"Not quite." Rhiannon suddenly looked like she'd been caught in a lie. "Perhaps that is a conversation for later. You've already had so much happen and I might not be the best person to explain *that* story."

Fauna decided to let it slide. "My thoughts are jumbled and my perception of reality is skewed. You were my only friend up there and we became so close. You were dating one of the groundskeepers. I don't even know how old I am. How stupid is that?"

"Who was I dating?" Rhiannon asked, as she plugged the top of the bottle with the rag and tipped it over. "And I don't think it's stupid. A little overzealous on the Matron's end, but that's just in character for the old bird, God desecrate her soul."

"I don't remember his name, if you—well *other* you even said it at all," Fauna sighed. "Sorry, my head is very confusing right now. It's probably in one of my journals. We talked about everything under the sun. You were my first friend. My only friend."

"I was?" Rhiannon asked as she warily eyed the cuts on Fauna's arms. "I don't have many friends around here. I don't really trust you, but if the Lady thinks you're important enough to sleep in a guest bed, then I guess you're all right. Forgive me, the culture here isn't good for making friends. I'm a little much for some people."

"You and I would talk about books," Fauna smiled as she remembered all the books she had read. "I could grab my journal once I've shown the Lady the room. I think I'll be mentally recovering for a little while. Would it be okay if I asked you for recommendations at some point?"

"You like books?" Rhiannon's voice perked up. "That's pretty nice. Of course you can ask me about books. Hold still, okay?"

Fauna smiled even though her cuts stung. "Do you read often?"

"Every day." The maid smiled shyly with a blush across her freckles. "I like getting lost in them. I play pretend with my mind."

"I do too," Fauna admitted. "For so long, I was determined to die alone. I don't even mean that as something sad. I enjoyed silence—darkness felt like home. People were just distractions and relationships just got in the way of my books. Their worlds were so much better than mine! Oh, how I longed to be a prince, taming dragons and marrying princesses. Imagine my broken heart when I realized I couldn't be one."

"You want to marry a princess?" Rhiannon repeated back to her with a wry smile. "That's very cute. Perhaps we *could* learn to be friends again."

"Perhaps we could." Fauna stuck her hand out, though it was strange to see it simply cut and not burned to a crisp. "I'm Fauna, nice to meet you."

That earned a small chuckle and an eye roll from the maid. She curtseyed and offered up her hand as well.

"Rhiannon, lowest in the chain of command and your new friend. A pleasure to make your acquaintance. Just mind your manners and tell me all about your favorite books and perhaps we'll get along as well as you imagined."

"Thank you." Fauna's body relaxed. "I'm so lost and confused. I appreciate your effort to trust me. I didn't realize how much I needed a friend until I didn't have one."

"Me too," Rhiannon admitted as she stood from the bed. "Me too."

Fauna stood in front of the large wooden door, more frightened than she had ever been in her whole life. Lady Aphrodite Verity's reputation was extremely worrisome, especially after seeing (or rather, hearing) her defending her children.

Before Fauna could gather her bearings, the door swung open and a woman with short black hair and a square face peeked her head out.

"You the woman from the stairs?"

Fauna nodded.

"She's ready for you."

With that, the door opened further and Fauna was ushered in. Lady Aphrodite, clad in a plain dress and looking much cleaner and more coiffed than earlier, sat behind a desk and stared at Fauna with a stony curiosity. The person who let her in disappeared behind another door, leaving the two women alone in silence.

"Sit."

As Fauna took a seat across from the woman, she dipped her head and waited to be addressed. She wasn't exactly sure what had happened, but it had deeply affected the residents and she decidedly did not want to make it worse.

"Who are you?" Aphrodite's voice was eerily calm. "Do not lie."

"Fauna. I… I am Fauna. That much I do know."

"And you appear here, on the worst day this castle has seen in a century. Why is that?"

Fauna shook her head. "I don't know! All I remember is being burnt alive in my village and being transported to the castle by a raven."

Aphrodite did not show a single sign of emotion. "What did the raven look like?"

"Black, beady eyes," Fauna—still unused to the sound of her own voice—whispered. "Black wings that I *think* had blue underneath. It grabbed me by my shoulders and flew me away from the fires. It dropped me in front of the castle and flew away. I was in so much pain that I don't remember much."

Aphrodite eyed her, clearly wanting Fauna to continue.

"I was carried up the stairs, but my eyes were closed. I thought I knew what happened, but I was clearly very wrong. I was then put in a bed and cared for. I know that much for certain."

"Cared for by me?" Aphrodite raised an eyebrow.

"I... suppose so. And Rhiannon. And the girls."

"Don't speak of my daughters," Aphrodite said low and slow. "They have seen enough today."

Fauna nodded once, panic in her veins. Aphrodite was *terrifying*... but not in the way she expected.

"Why would the Matron recognize you?"

"I truly have no idea," Fauna begged. "My Mother refused to worship her, but she died decades ago."

"And your father?"

"Died twenty or so years back—he loved the Matron, however. Had a shrine and attended every gathering he could."

"And you?"

"I don't like the Matron," Fauna admitted, though she held back on any more intense criticism. "I didn't go to anything or listen to her. I read books in secrecy. I never cause problems. I never really *did* anything except mind my business."

"Why should I trust you?" Aphrodite eventually asked as she leaned back in her chair and crossed her legs. "Prove that you aren't lying."

"I had no voice when I was up there. You saw that! There's something wrong with that room." Fauna pointed upstairs. "I was able to write down all of my experiences. I had a journal up there. Sometimes I fell asleep looking at the painting on the ceiling. Did you paint it?"

"Yes," Aphrodite said calmly. "But that still doesn't answer all of my questions."

"Are you one of the women in the painting? Who is the other one? The one with the ruined face?"

Aphrodite's entire demeanor shifted. Her eyes narrowed and a snarl began to form on her lips.

"Gelon! Take our guest to the baths. I have some investigating and do not wish to be disturbed. You, Fauna? Meet me back here after dinner. We still have much to discuss and you smell disgusting."

After some time, Fauna was gently guided to an enormous bath that felt more like a pool. It was a little disappointing to know that the scents from the upstairs room weren't real. She figured it was a blessing in disguise—smelling like her fake self was just salt in her emotional wounds.

Rhiannon sat with her back to the bath, turned away from Fauna, flipping through the pages of her book and sighing every so often.

It was cute to see her so enveloped in something. Occasionally she would chew her lip or gasp. Fauna had never truly read with anyone before she'd been transported to the castle and while her time in the room was not real, it *did* prepare her for sharing spaces with other people.

"This story is heartbreaking." Rhiannon shook her head while she flipped a page. "I'll let you read it when I'm done."

"I would like that," Fauna smiled shyly to herself. "I still think it's weird that the Matron sent me books to read, even in my room. Why would she do that?"

"That is strange." Rhiannon kept turning her pages. "Did they all have a theme?"

"Death," Fauna realized and laughed, though she didn't find the situation very funny. "My Mother was vehemently against the Matron. She openly defied her and refused to even address her by her title. I barely knew my mother, but my father told me a lot of stories about her when I was a child."

"Woah, the Matron didn't kill her instantly?" Rhiannon slid her bookmark into her book and turned slightly. "That seems a little bit odd. She's not exactly known for her patience when it comes to disobedience."

"Well, she did die when I was born," Fauna told her. "My father always said she was killed in childbirth, but he never quite knew *why*. I know it happens sometimes, but he would never speak of it. I just assumed he was too heartbroken to talk about it. He hated winter because of it."

"That's quite suspicious." Rhiannon set her book down. "Do you need someone to talk to? I'm not the best at listening, but I have been told that I'm easy to speak to."

Fauna shook her head. "No, I'll just write in my journal later, if we end up finding it. It's easier for me to work through things that way. I hope that part of my time up there wasn't fake as well. That would surely make me seem like a liar. I don't even want to know what Lady Aphrodite would do to me if that happened."

"Well, if it's not, I can find you another one. Just know that I'm here to listen. Lady Aphrodite insisted that I bandage your wounds—the castle staff is weird about blood and open wounds. It might seem like overkill, but I promise it's for the best."

"Is it bad to say I'm used to that?" Fauna grumbled, remembering her first few weeks in the room. "I was wrapped in bandages and smeared with all kinds of creams for what seemed like ages. I forgot what my skin looked like for a while."

"Not bad, just unusual." Rhiannon scrunched her nose in the most precious way and turned around fully. "Ready to get out?"

Fauna nodded as she lifted herself out of the bath and wrapped herself in the fluffy robe that Rhiannon had hung. As the maid began tending to her arms, the feeling of bandages being wrapped around her, triggered an avalanche of emotions from her initial stay in her prison above.

Each stretch of the fabric made her shiver and each pull against her skin made her jump. Simply existing was terrifying, especially now. So many memories flew through her mind and sadly none of them were real. Well, they were real... kind of. It was dreadfully confusing.

After she was dried and dressed, she followed the maid to the kitchen where she ate whatever scraps were leftover from the staff's dinner. When she was finally full, she asked for directions on how to get back to the Lady's room and bumped into a daughter along the way.

"I'm sorry, Bea!" Fauna hissed when she felt herself bounce off the girl. A solid hand shot out and gripped her bandages painfully.

"How'd you know my name?" the girl narrowed her eyes.

"I... don't have a very believable explanation," Fauna said while trying to wiggle out of her grasp. "But it has to do with the Matron. I'm sorry!"

"Liar," Bea replied simply. "Why should I trust you? I hadn't even heard of you until you fell down the stairs and yet you seem to be way too familiar with me. I don't like it and I don't like you."

"I was really fond of you and your sister," Fauna tried not to show her frustration. "I thought I had found friends and family. Turns out I was kept in some kind of illusion."

"Well we aren't your family and neither is my mother. I hope she throws you in the cellar," Bea spat as she walked away. "Leave us alone."

"The upstairs version of you told me all sorts of things. You told me you would take me to the gardens when I got better! I'm not lying." Fauna, defeated and dreadfully tired, kept walking towards Lady Aphrodite's wing of the castle until she felt a cold hand wrap around her neck.

"Listen, I don't know *who* you think you are. But, if you try to make this whole ordeal about you, I will kill you myself," Bea growled and her eyes turned *yellow*. "Leave my mother alone."

"Make *what* about me?" Fauna cried out, coughing as Bea threw her backward. She hit the ground and her bandaged skin made a terrible noise against the hardwood floor as she skidded.

"Talk to my mother," Bea snarled, her eyes now back to normal. "Don't let me see you again."

"I heard you scream for your mother," Fauna groaned as she stood. "And then I heard her cries and I jumped out of bed but I *forgot* that I couldn't walk. I crawled to the door while bleeding because I wanted to see you all, in case anything happened. I fell down the stairs hoping that I would at least be able to see if the people that I loved as if they were my own family were okay. They were the only people I had known for ages. I don't know how long I was up there! I don't even know how old I am! Imagine waking up and hearing your family crying but then realizing they weren't even real and nothing is real and everyone hates you and you have nothing and no one!"

Bea did not respond, but the look of fury in her eyes faded to a stern discontent.

"And now it's gone. All of it. Everything," Fauna cried as she began to back away. "I don't know what I did to deserve any of this. I never wanted friends or family but here I am hurting without them and they *weren't even real*!"

Before she could hear anything else, Fauna stopped backing up and changed direction to dash past Bea. Her hips ached and her bare feet slapped angrily against the floor. She navigated past the debris left over from the fight and gulped down stale air as she made it to the stairs. If she turned left, she would head to Aphrodite's office. If she went up the stairs, she could die happily in her illusion. But, she wouldn't be alone. She would be dooming herself to death regardless—Lady Aphrodite would be furious that Fauna decided to make her wait longer, but Fauna craved the comfort of the prison she'd been kept in for so long.

"I want it back!" she screamed as she ran past where she'd landed as she fell down the stairs. One by one, her bruised legs carried her back up the staircase. How ironic that she'd craved the ability to walk again, just to scorn it merely a few hours later. Her broken finger was purple when she unclenched her hands and pushed against the hauntingly familiar door with everything she had. "I want to go back! Take me back!"

The door opened slowly and Fauna stumbled in, falling immediately to her knees and sobbing silently into the floor. Her tears leaked into the rug beneath her face as she yelled without sound into the void. She would give her voice and her legs just to be back in her comfortable realm. Her bandages disappeared to reveal scarred flesh along her arms once more. Her curse to bear, so long as she had her family back.

Creak.

Creak.

Fauna whipped her head up to see Lady Aphrodite, sitting in the rocking chair and gazing out of the window at the damask night. She rocked back and forth, a cigarette in a long holder in one hand and a wine glass in the other. Her posture was relaxed, but still noticeably different from the fake Aphrodite that Fauna had gotten so comfortable with. This was the real woman. And she was clearly not okay.

Desperate to reclaim her life, Fauna dragged herself with open wounds on her burnt arms and useless legs until she was beside the woman. When she looked up, she saw that tear trails marked her cheeks. This wasn't her Aphrodite, this wasn't her life anymore. She had to admit that harsh truth. Aphrodite's face was so relaxed to the point that had she not blinked, Fauna would have assumed she was asleep. Or dead.

Fauna raised her scarred hand and tapped the chair, her chest filling with dread. Aphrodite looked down at her with a broken expression. She nodded knowingly and set her vices gently on the table next to her. When she turned back around, the same dissociative expression ghosted across Aphrodite's face. Before Fauna could find a way to ask if she was okay without her voice, Aphrodite's expression shifted to one of egregiously false content. Her lips turned up in a defeated smile while her entire body remained unmoving. When she spoke, Fauna jumped, startled.

"In your world, your reality—I'm not sure what to call it—did I sit in this chair?" her voice was small, petite. "Did I read to you, show you the stars? Tell you everything would be all right?"

Fauna simply nodded even though the explanations were too complicated to explain in a second. Was it love? Was it finally feeling safe? Was it friendship? She'd never know. How did Aphrodite know all of that?

Aphrodite turned back to the night sky and looked at the moon. A palpable sadness hung around her, weighing her down and giving her a downtrodden posture. She wasn't crying or moaning, as though she was down in the dumps, but more like a bone-chilling agony that weighed like a heavy anchor on her heart. She seemed so tired, so unwilling to fight any longer, that Fauna just wanted to do anything she asked, just to take some melancholy away. The fear she'd invoked earlier was gone and replaced with a defeated sorrow. Seeing someone so intimidating and powerful be reduced to merely a sad woman in a chair was extremely unsettling.

Aphrodite nodded before scooting over to the very edge of the large rocking chair. "We can pretend. Just for tonight. We can make it easier, just pretend. It always helps."

For a moment, Fauna was immobilized. The visitor from her dreams had said the same thing about pretending and that it made things easier. Before she could even think about what that could mean, a pair of strong arms lifted her from the floor and set her in her lap. It was strange to be nearly the same size as Aphrodite; in the old reality, or whatever it was, Fauna felt small and powerless lying in her bed with everyone standing over her. But now, Aphrodite and Fauna were of equal size, sitting in a rocking chair. Aphrodite wrapped her arms around Fauna's waist and loosely clasped their hands. It didn't seem romantic at all. In fact, Aphrodite didn't even look at Fauna. Instead, she continued to gaze out the window and into the garden. When Fauna turned her head to gauge just how Aphrodite was faring, she felt her heart sink.

Upon closer inspection, Aphrodite's eyes revealed a hint of defeat. Fauna had no idea what this woman or her family had gone through, but if it had anything to do with the Matron, it was most certainly awful. Aphrodite bowed her head and let her hair form a blonde curtain between her and Fauna. Understanding the wordless request, Fauna moved her attention to look out the window as well.

When Fauna was finally able to relax, she finally let all of her sadness go. Silent sobs robbed her of the sounds of relief, but it was just added to the pile of things that had been stolen from her. She grabbed desperately at Aphrodite's hand and wrapped her scarred ones around it. To her surprise, Aphrodite simply let it happen. Almost as if she was taking the same amount of comfort in return.

"Just for tonight," Aphrodite's voice cracked and tapered off as she stared aimlessly into the pearlescent light in the sky. Using a single foot, Aphrodite rocked them both in the chair. "We can pretend."

Fauna knew that very moment that she would never look out of that window again. The room would crumble and the door would be locked. She gazed out onto the garden and vowed to visit it sometime soon, should she be allowed to.

From her mother's death to her father's emotionless and silent parenting… every single person who was in charge of loving Fauna had been torn from her life. Now, she felt the sting of loneliness in a castle full of people. People who barely knew her and already hated her.

But regardless of her plight, she was not the only one in pain. And if Aphrodite was willing to at least be cordial and let her stay, she could at least offer the woman some compassion. Perhaps, later on, they could even regain the semblance of the comfort Fauna remembered. She briefly considered writing her story down, but what kind of person would believe such a tragic tale?

She surely wouldn't have.

Seventeen

When the moon rose high in the sky and the wind whistled through the chilled trees, Fauna slowly woke to Aphrodite's quiet sobs. She was still wrapped in Aphrodite's arms, but the woman was not looking at her at all.

"I'm sorry, but I have to destroy this room." Aphrodite kept her gaze focused on the garden outside. "We can talk later, but this room just needs to be *gone*."

Fauna tried to speak and when she could not, she motioned wildly towards the dresser at the end of the room.

"You would like to take some things?" Aphrodite guessed.

Fauna nodded gratefully but pointed to her legs.

"Show me what you need." Aphrodite gently moved out from under Fauna and let her sit back on the rocking chair.

Fauna tried her best to imitate someone opening a book and writing in it. Aphrodite seemed to understand and set off with a silent nod. As she wandered the room, Aphrodite's fingers grazed the small stack of books that Fauna had accumulated during her stay. Fauna wanted to ask for some of the trinkets she had acquired but also wondered if she should even keep things from people who did not technically exist. For all she knew, they would disappear as soon as she left the room.

She glanced back to Aphrodite, who had stopped to look at the painting on the ceiling. Aphrodite's face remained passive, but the rhythmic squeeze of her hand at her side gave away just how affected she was. Dreadfully curious but emotionally exhausted, Fauna swallowed the urge to get Aphrodite's attention and just simply let the woman stare at the ceiling.

Feeling as if she was intruding on a personal moment, Fauna readjusted herself in the rocking chair and stared out into the deeply calm night sky. The room, while being the source of so much torment, did have a gorgeous view. Perhaps that's why the garden was placed below.

The sound of a sharp but desolate wail startled Fauna so violently that she choked on her air and began to silently sputter.

"What a pompous *tyrant!*" Aphrodite cried out. For a moment, her facade broke and her face crumpled. But before even a moment had passed, her composure was back in place. Without another word, Aphrodite grabbed the notebook and satchel of writing utensils and tossed them into Fauna's lap.

"We will destroy the room together. If you speak the truth, she has hurt you as well. You may stay here tonight if you wish. Take a few days to heal. I will have you dealt with soon enough. Just don't get into anything that doesn't belong to you."

And with that, Aphrodite turned on her heel and left, not even bothering to shut the door as she left.

The tidal wave of grief slammed into Fauna's chest and did not crest. Now alone in her prison, she was faced with a very perplexing dilemma. Should she sleep in the bed one last time and gaze at the ceiling? Should she crawl back to the hallway and ask Rhiannon to help her find a bed? Should she tell Aphrodite to destroy her too?

How could she choose? Building a relationship with the Verity women seemed daunting and too difficult to do all over again. But Rhiannon was in the castle and so were the small things she'd missed, like hot food and sunshine. She could walk and talk, that was true. But where would she walk and to who would she talk?

"Fauna?" a careful whisper came from the doorway, where a very solemn-looking Rhiannon stood holding a pile of linen.

Fauna began to cry quietly. Was this the real Rhiannon? It had to be, right? The Matron was dead so wouldn't her illusions be as well?

"I brought you a gown to wear to bed." Rhiannon looked around the room with wide eyes. "It looks so normal in here. I thought it would be much different."

Fauna pointed to the ceiling and raised an eyebrow, hoping Rhiannon would understand her question.

"Oh that's *beautiful*," Rhiannon gushed as she set the linens on the bed. "Lady Verity painted that herself, many years ago. I've never seen it—only heard about it from the staff. I don't know *how* she managed to paint it. A ladder maybe? Did she stand on the bed? Oh, I suppose that could move. Wow, I could stare at that for ages."

Fauna pointed to the woman across from Aphrodite in the painting and looked back at Rhiannon.

"That's… someone who used to live here," Rhiannon said softly. "Not my story to tell, sorry."

Fauna nodded, still quite curious about it all. Instead, she slid off of the rocking chair with a silent farewell to the view and began to crawl towards the bed. Rhiannon began to rush over, but Fauna waved her away.

"Going to spend a last night here?" Rhiannon asked kindly. "I would offer to stay, but this room creeps me out."

Fauna hoisted herself up into the bed and grabbed the plain nightdress Rhiannon had set down. She looked up at the painting one last time and nodded.

"Okay, I'll leave you here then. Come find me in the morning when you wake. I'll be in the common room waiting for you, okay?"

Fauna nodded and mouthed a thanks before Rhiannon left and closed the door. She laid back and stared at the ceiling, trying her best to imagine what the painting had looked like while it was being painted. Had Aphrodite planned it methodically? Did someone pose for it? Perhaps it was impulsive. Fauna had little experience painting so she had no idea how the process worked.

She fell asleep that night thinking of her time in the room and lamenting the process of restarting all the progress she had made. Was it worth it? Should she have let Aphrodite kill her?

The painting on the ceiling looked... different. But in her dream state, Fauna couldn't quite figure out how. She closed her eyes, willing herself to wake, but when she opened them she was *very* surprised to see the woman in the painting simply gone. When she sat up, she noticed someone in the rocking chair.

"Grief is strange, isn't it?" her dream visitor spoke from the chair. "It changes us—makes us do things that we would never even dream of."

Fauna took a deep breath and tested out her voice. "Like what?"

The woman stopped rocking and abandoned her chair to sit on the edge of Fauna's bed. She crossed her legs casually and leaned back against the bed on her elbows. Her dress sat primly around her legs, looking dreadfully out of place in such a somber room.

"It makes us mean, makes us cold," she admitted. Her face stayed assuring and carried a wisdom that made Fauna feel very safe. She could trust this person, she just *knew* it. "It makes us lash out, instead of asking for help. We make rash decisions. And then we have to pretend that it's okay... until it's not."

"Who are you?" Fauna asked.

"I am the sum of everyone who has ever loved me, same as you." The woman smiled brightly. "My love is the moon and I am the sun, and together we ushered little stars into existence."

Not exactly sure what that meant, Fauna still felt a ping in her heart over the poetic words. "Your love is the moon. The moon is a person?"

"Damask and dark, but the brightest and purest of lights you can find." The woman closed her eyes and turned her face towards the moonbeam. "I am the sun that protects the garden—I am the afternoon warmth after the bitter chill of the night. I am half of the day, but I am no longer. I need you to be the sun. Can you be the sun?"

"I need to be the sun?" Fauna was confused, to say the least.

The woman nodded and slid further up the bed to sit beside Fauna. She gently pushed on Fauna's shoulder to make her lie back and joined Fauna lying down in the bed. Where any other person would have been an unwanted intrusion, Fauna felt the need to open her arms and offer this stranger an embrace. The mysterious dream visitor snuggled next to Fauna and laid her head on Fauna's chest. Something about the woman helped calm the storm in Fauna's heart. There was no flinch, no desperate urge to make herself small and tucked away.

The dream visitor reached for Fauna's hands and turned them over, brushing a thumb over the scars and patches that had appeared once more.

"You pretended and it got easier. Now you don't need to. You both pretended. You can be the sun now."

"I am Fauna, I am not the sun," Fauna whispered and looked down at their hands. Never in her life had she been handled so gently. Even in the room, she had not felt skin so soft and a smile so tender.

"You are the sun that has risen against all odds." The woman smiled so happily that Fauna began to tear up. "Even when grief has obscured you. I am so proud of you."

"Grief?"

The woman moved to cup Fauna's cheeks and placed the sweetest of kisses on her forehead before sliding off of the bed. "Yours and others. You will soon learn. But you are safe now. The Matron is dead and we are all better for it."

"You know of the Matron?" Fauna's comfort was shaken.

The woman sighed heavily.

"I have never hated a single soul in my life," the woman's voice began to drift away. "Until I met her."

Fauna felt the woman begin to fade. She reached out again, desperate for her comforting touch one more. She had no idea who the woman was, just that she wanted her to stay.

"Goodbye, sweet Fauna," the woman sang softly as she disappeared into nothing. "Hopefully we'll meet again. I like you quite a bit."

"Get up," a voice called from far away. It was not kind but also held no malice. Fauna waited a moment until she heard the command once more but louder.

Slowly, she blinked awake and noticed that the sun was already quite high in the sky—so high that a singular beam had maneuvered between the curtains of the large window and had been warming her exposed feet.

"You need to get up," Scarlet said once more. "Mother is not in a good mood and she's been extra hard to track down. I need you awake in case she tells me to bring you to her."

Fauna nodded, still on edge from her dream, and slid off the bed and onto the floor. Before she could scoot to the door, the youngest daughter gasped quietly.

"I thought you were lying," Scarlet admitted. "Bea said you were probably lying for attention, but you wouldn't do *that* if you were lying… right?"

Fauna shook her head and managed to slide herself over the doorway and into the hallway. She scooted to sit against the wall to catch her breath. Her bare legs reminded her that she was no longer under the control of the room and that she chose to spend a final night there. It was still strange to see her legs uncovered and without any scars. The night dress came to her mid-thigh but it was still much shorter than what she normally wore—not to mention that most of her time in the room had been spent under a blanket. The bandages on her arms were mussed to the point of being useless, but her skin seemed mostly healed anyway.

"Breakfast was hours ago, sleepyhead," Scarlet said from the doorway. She handed over the journal before walking down the hallway. "But Rhiannon seems to already have a soft spot for you, so she saved you some biscuits. I'm supposed to take you there."

"Would you be willing to get me a dress from the dresser in that room?" Fauna asked tentatively.

Scarlet shook her head. "There's nothing in the drawers. The only thing around is that journal of yours. Everything else is empty. It's fading, like ink in the sun."

"So that was fake too?" Fauna was astonished. "I can still feel the textures and see the patterns in my mind. How could she do that?"

"If there was one thing I knew about the Matron, it was that she was always capable of things worse than you could imagine," Scarlet warned her. "I have personal experience in that. Come. Let's go to Rhiannon. If that's her shirt, she must have something else you could wear."

Fauna nodded and let herself be led around the twists, turns, and stairs of the castle until they arrived at a very plain-looking dormitory. Scarlet knocked on one of the doors and stood back to wait.

"Oh!" Rhiannon's welcoming face appeared at the door. "I was wondering if you had gotten lost. Thank you for the slightly rumpled delivery, Scarlet. You can go back to writing and snooping around the castle now."

"Thank you!" Scarlet rolled her eyes before looking dramatically at Fauna. "I hate being the youngest sometimes. I have to do whatever no one else wants to do. Someone has to learn the dirty secrets of this place."

"You're also the most dramatic," Rhiannon said knowingly as she opened the door wider. "Typical youngest."

"You're so mean to me!" Scarlet snickered and began walking away. "Bye!"

Fauna looked at Rhiannon and back to Scarlet's retreating figure. "Are you friends?"

"Well, I work here, so technically she's my employer," Rhiannon explained. "But she's known me my whole life. It's easier to get along and like each other, than the alternative. She's coping rather well, but I suppose that's what feeling safe can do to someone."

That stopped Fauna mid-step. "How old is she?"

Rhiannon laughed nervously. "I don't honestly know. Older than she seems. I wouldn't ask her though. You know, she's pretty sensitive about that."

"She looks like she's barely sixteen!" Fauna admitted wide-eyed. "But also she looks a little... timeless? Does that make sense?"

"Nope," Rhiannon laughed as she shook her head. "But so long as you believe it, I do too. But, you're here for clothes and some breakfast, yes?"

Fauna had forgotten that she was in a long shirt and not much else. "Please."

"And we'll find you some shoes," Rhiannon assured her.

"I just realized that I never brushed my teeth in that room," Fauna admitted as she sat gently on a rigid wooden chair in the corner. "How did I not realize that? I only saw the bathroom a handful of times."

"Well, based on your description of the whole ordeal, I would assume you were more focused on other things?"

"I suppose," Fauna admitted. "It feels like I had no time at all, but when I was in it... it felt like time wasn't moving or even real at all. I wonder if the sun and the moon were even real."

"I hope so," Rhiannon muttered as she dug into her drawers. "That part of the castle has a great view."

"Was I in the highest room?" Fauna wondered. "I've only seen the castle from a distance in the village. It always seemed like it was so tall that it went into the clouds."

"There is one room at the very top of each wing," Rhiannon explained. "The atelier, Lady Aphrodite's painting room, the reading room, the room you were in, and a guard room. No one is allowed in any of them. You were in an old bedroom, but it had been locked for a *very* long time. The Matron must have known that no one ever goes in there if that's where she hid you."

"I just wonder how I didn't starve to death," Fauna wondered aloud. "But also, do I actually want to know at all?"

"That's a good point," Rhiannon agreed as she pulled out a shapeless black dress, which looked like more of an oversized shirt. "This isn't the prettiest and I'm fairly certain it was once a bedsheet, but it will work."

Fauna's smile was large and powerful. It looked so similar to the one she'd worn until she was burned!

"It's perfect!"

After a slightly stale and crumbly breakfast filled with an almost comfortable silence, Rhiannon informed Fauna that Lady Aphrodite was busy until later in the afternoon. Fauna was permitted to roam the castle if Rhiannon kept her in line and told her not to wander into any of the castle's private rooms. So, when Rhiannon asked Fauna what she wanted to do with her spare time, Fauna nearly scared her with her eagerness.

She wanted to see the library.

When Rhiannon asked her *which* library, Fauna nearly wept with joy. She'd forgotten about the multiple libraries! What a wonderful thing to have. Together, the pair decided on the common one on the ground floor, which was available to anyone inside the castle.

"*How* many are there?" Fauna asked again as she tried her best not to slip on the floors in her newly socked feet.

"Four-ish." Rhiannon held up her hand and ticked each finger as she listed them. "There's one for the whole castle. We call it the common library. The girls have their own, but they aren't private per se; it's just polite to wait to be invited. Lady Aphrodite has one, but it doubles over as her office and no one is generally permitted there without explicit permission. Don't even try, Gelon will tell on you and she doesn't take any excuses. I've heard rumors of a room in one of the wings that was used as a secret book stash, but it's been filled in and no one will talk about it, so I'm not sure if that counts."

"This castle has a lot of secrets." Fauna sighed.

"Grief makes you do strange things," Rhiannon agreed as they walked.

That stopped Fauna in her tracks. She skidded a bit on the freshly polished floor and had to grab onto the railing next to her.

"Someone else said that to me," Fauna realized as she steadied herself. "I just don't remember who."

Rhiannon gave her a confused look and pointed in the general direction of the library. "Like, that exact phrase?"

Fauna thought back and tried to remember more but struggled. "I think it was in a dream that I had. But I only remember a woman saying that grief makes people do strange things."

Rhiannon did not reply but did maintain a lingering eye contact that made Fauna a little uncomfortable. She didn't know this version of her friend at all and was already worrying that she would be too forward or casual with anyone in the castle. So, instead of pushing the subject, Fauna was quiet for the rest of their walk.

When she eventually pushed open the double doors to the library, the smell of books wrapped itself around Fauna and squeezed her tightly. It was a quaint room, much bigger than her bedroom but still smaller than she'd expected. Floor-to-ceiling shelves filled with mismatched books of all widths and heights lined the walls, adding a quaint but comfortable atmosphere to it all.

Fauna walked to one of the walls and ran her fingers over the various spines of the books. Upon closer inspection, she realized that all of the titles were in many different languages that she didn't understand.

"How many languages does Lady Aphrodite speak?" Fauna wondered aloud.

"Well, I have no idea," Rhiannon began as she made her way over. "She's led an interesting life with many tales to tell. Back in the castle's prime, there were always books left on tables and lessons going on at all times. The girls would ask a thousand questions a day, and someone always found the answer to them all."

"In its prime?"

Rhiannon looked around the room as if she expected someone to barge in and motioned towards some of the chairs stashed in the corner. Once they had settled in, Rhiannon took a few deep breaths before beginning the conversation.

"What would you do if someone you loved as family hurt you so badly that it extinguished every single light you have inside yourself?"

"I… I don't know," Fauna whispered, unsure if the questions were rhetorical. "Is that what happened to Lady Aphrodite?"

"The Matron did something so vile to the Verity family, that I don't even dare say it aloud within these walls," Rhiannon informed her. "I don't even think I know all of the details. It's just something we don't talk about."

Was that why everyone was so cold? Fauna had tried to prove that she meant no harm, and yet everyone so far except Rhiannon had been incredibly closed off.

"The Matron can rot in hell," Fauna muttered.

"I don't think they want her even there," Rhiannon admitted. "My knowledge of her is limited—most of what I know is hearsay or maid's stories, but the bits I do know are awful. Every time the Matron would surprise the Verity family, it took them ages to get over it. I only saw a few visits, considering I'm one of the youngest here, but it was very bad each time she left. Not a shred of humanity in that one."

"Lady Aphrodite seems to be quite protective," Fauna noticed. "Especially when it involves her daughters."

"She would do anything for them," Rhiannon agreed. "*Anything.* And that's not an exaggeration."

After their heavy conversation, both girls split up in the library and began to search for books. There were little golden signs engraved on the shelves that reminded them that no books were to leave the library. That in itself didn't bother Fauna too badly, very rarely did she need to stop reading to do something else. There was a certain sense of completion that came from reading a book in one sitting.

When the sun finally began its descent, Rhiannon took off to help the staff prepare dinner. Fauna had been given very detailed instructions on how to get to the maid's hall to eat and bathe once the food was done. It made sense to bathe after eating, so Fauna spent the rest of her library time snuggled in a chair sideways with her feet dangling in front of the fireplace. For all the trauma she'd endured in the last few days, reading by the fire was one glimmer of happiness that she was very happy to have.

Later in the evening, after a very quick and humbling bath amongst the other maids, Fauna nestled herself into the empty bed across from Rhiannon. When she'd asked her friend why it was empty, Rhiannon shyly admitted that no one spoke to her and that she wasn't very well-liked by the others. It was nice to be able to feel bed linens now that her bandages had been removed and her skin was allowed to breathe for the first time in… a very long time. Instead of talking to each other, Fauna chose instead to write in her journal until she fell asleep.

I am Fauna.

That's all that I know right now.

I have my journal. I have a place to sleep, I have meals, and I have freedom… sort of. Does this count as freedom? I still feel as if the entire castle is hiding something from me, but I don't know what. Before all of this, I would have loved the isolation. But… now it feels damning. Am I destined to be alone in life? Why would the Matron show me what having friends is like, just to take it away? Could someone genuinely be that cruel?

Never mind that I'm terrified. What evil shrouds that room I was in? What was I pretending for? Does the Matron have an island of corpses? Why did she mention my father? Will I ever get to be close to the Verity family again? So far, only Rhiannon speaks to me. I think she's just as lonely as I am.

There are so many things to process and feel. I'm not ready for any of them. Why do I feel like a child again? Shouldn't I have learned all these things by now?

How do I look at these people, this little family I thought that I had made, and pretend that it's okay?

I need space. I need books.

I need to sit in the library again.

I need to be alone.

Eighteen

The castle seemed much more peaceful during the night. The moon sat pristinely atop the skyline, looking sagely through the windows as Fauna ambled down the hallway. She stopped to peek out at the clouds and found herself swept away by the view. Standing on her tiptoes like an excited child, Fauna pressed herself so close to the glass that little fog clouds appeared where she breathed. It was strange to see the world from above. For so long she'd simply existed in her little barren silo, unwilling to do anything but read and sleep. But now she wanted to do things. She wanted to make friends, she wanted to frolic in the gardens, and she wanted to talk to people.

It was almost as if she had been slowly rotting away in her village, just waiting for death. However, now she was *excited* to live. There were so many things within Castle Verity alone that she could eventually explore. Had a near-death experience been the catalyst for her to start living truly?

She walked through the castle for a fair bit of the night, just peeking out of windows and admiring the decor, but she stopped outside the main library when she passed it. Rhiannon hadn't said much in the way of rules, only that there were beasts in the woods that were dangerous in the night and to not sneak where she didn't belong. Lady Aphrodite was supposed to have sent for her, but she never ended up doing so. Fauna had woken after only an hour or two of sleeping and decided that she would explore but not go too far. She wanted to learn about the castle on her terms and with an open mind, not the presumed lies she had been told by whoever or whatever was controlling the illusions upstairs, nor the rumors from villagers who had never even seen it.

The library floor was surprisingly cold on her bare feet. Rhiannon had given her more socks before bed, but Fauna didn't want to chance slipping and knocking down some of the ornate decor that lined the castle. Instead, she gauged the softness of the hallway runners with her toes and tried to avoid any pointy stray bits of glass left over from the castle brawl. Once Fauna was sure she wasn't going to be caught in the library, she walked to a random shelf and picked the first book that caught her eye before she cozied up in one of the chairs from earlier.

The book itself was science-related. It had something to do with gravity that was far beyond her scope of knowledge, but it felt nice to read again. Even if most of the words made no sense to her, the familiarity was comforting. The Matron could take everything from her, including her autonomy and her voice, but she could never take her mind.

"An interesting choice," a voice called quietly from the doorway. Fauna jumped a bit before looking up and seeing the eldest Verity daughter.

"I think it's too smart for me to understand," Fauna admitted quietly with a smile. "But I couldn't sleep and it's too dark to read in Rhiannon's room. I get nervous when I can't see the moon."

"This library *does* have the best lighting," Bea admitted, pointing to a large window that went from floor to ceiling—a style that seemed to be quite popular in the castle. "Even on days when it's too hot to burn the fire, the moon lights up this room well enough to read all night. Mother used to turn a blind eye when Scarlet and I would sneak in here to read."

"For some reason, I can't picture you two as children," Fauna said tentatively. "No offense. You seem young, but also not?"

Bea looked apprehensively around before making her way deeper into the library. She took the seat next to Fauna and looked at her hands for a long pause. Eventually, she took a decisive breath and looked up at Fauna.

"We weren't children in the way that you're thinking," Bea said very carefully as if she was picking each word individually. "We were younger, but our 'childhoods' weren't normal at all."

"How so?" Fauna knew what an atypical childhood felt like, but something about the way Bea spoke indicated that perhaps Fauna could not at all relate to whatever Bea was speaking about.

"Well," Bea began, nervously clenching and relaxing her hands over and over again. "Aphrodite isn't my real mother, for starters. Scarlet isn't my actual sister… well not by blood. But, we're sisters. There is no debate over that."

Fauna kept quiet, surprised that Bea would be so forthcoming with such information. Not long ago she had been very threatening.

"Before you ask, none of this is a secret." Bea seemed to know what Fauna was thinking. "Scarlet and Mother seem to believe your story and I trust their judgment. It's just that no one cares to ask before they make assumptions and it's been so busy around here that I don't want any misinformation happening."

"I did that. I assumed a lot," Fauna admitted. "When I was much younger, I assumed that this castle was filled with murder and diabolical evil. But, all I have seen is kindness. Well, except for what the Matron did to me. You're right for being so protective. I understand."

Bea nodded a few times and they fell into an easy quiet. After a few minutes, the tension seemed to fade and she regarded Fauna carefully.

"So what exactly did the Matron do to you? You don't look too hurt. Your finger will heal and so those cuts already look better. All I was told was that the Matron did something to you and you appeared when she died. You scared my mother, which scared me. I'm not going to apologize for being careful."

"I understand." Fauna slid back into the chair and crossed her legs. "I'm still a little confused about what happened. All I know for sure is that I was burned at the stake and was saved at the last minute. Then I ended up bedbound in a room upstairs until I heard you yell for your mother."

Bea raised her eyebrows. "Why did the village want to hurt you?"

Fauna took a deep breath before preparing a story that she could already tell she would be repeating many times in the future.

"They caught me reading. Reading isn't necessarily forbidden, but books from outside the village are."

"You can't have books" Bea half-laughed and half-scoffed. "Quaint. All that over a book?"

Fauna wanted to laugh but found none in her chest. "I don't think Matron cared that I read books. She stuck me in that room for some unknown reason. That room ended up being my prison for… I'm not sure how long. Time didn't feel real there. But, I was slowly brought back to health even though my legs did not work and I had no voice."

"That was why you were so surprised when you could walk." Bea nodded as she began to understand. "I wondered why you were so confused that we didn't recognize you. I thought you were faking so we didn't kill you."

"That, and I was realizing that I had been duped in a very malicious way," Fauna admitted with a lump of emotion in her throat. As she continued, her voice began to crack. "I thought that I had begun to change, to make friends. I used to be *very* against anyone knowing me. I barely spoke at all."

"What brought you down the stairs?" Bea sat back and crossed her legs primly. "Other than gravity?"

Fauna laughed at that one. "Well, you yelled, and then I heard Lady Aphrodite yell for someone not to touch you. I didn't even think; I just jumped off the bed and crawled to the door. When I crossed the threshold, I knew I felt different, but I was so preoccupied with finding you all that I didn't stop to think about what that could mean."

"She was fighting with the Matron," Bea said softly. "I hated when they fought. The Matron was a cruel woman, and Mother took the brunt of it so we didn't have to. She won't show it, but Mother is hurting quite a bit over it."

Fauna felt her heart twinge, even if she barely knew the people involved. "Did they fight a lot?"

Bea's eyes glistened with tears. She tried to hide them, but when she turned to the side, Fauna noticed the watery gleam from the light of the fireplace. At that moment, the woman who seemed to have wisdom beyond her years looked more like a scared little girl than Fauna had ever seen before.

"She hurt us. *Badly*," Bea whispered before she cut herself off. Her breathing began to get louder and deeper until she took a very large breath and exhaled slowly. "She took something from us that left us all scarred and bitter. I used to dance. I used to dance and sing in the gardens! I think back to the girl who wore yellow dresses and made up songs about frogs, and I wonder what happened to her."

Fauna wanted to comfort the eldest daughter but did not quite know how. Everything she knew to say came from books and those didn't cover such a scenario!

Bea threw her hands in the air. "And now? Now I don't see the purpose of anything. I don't want to die... as if I could anyway. But, everyone is so *sad* here all of the time. I'm so *sad*. I don't even know why I'm telling you all of this. You're a stranger to me. But, I suppose if the Matron hurt you too, we have something in common. "

"I just don't know *why*," Fauna whispered. "I don't know why she was so focused on my parents. My mother died years ago and my father is gone as well."

"Maybe my mother will help you understand. She knew the Matron better than any of us." Bea exhaled a shuddering breath. "She's been hurt the worst of all of us. It's not my story to tell, you understand. But, you're probably best off not knowing."

"Your mother sat with me," Fauna admitted. "The night that everything with the Matron happened. I had a moment of weakness and took off for that prison cell of a room. When I got up the stairs and fell into the room, I noticed she was in the rocking chair. I don't know how I knew it was the real Aphrodite and not the fake one, but I just felt it in my bones. She sat with me in that rocking chair and told me that we could pretend everything was fine, just for that night."

"Just pretend," Bea repeated in a tone eerily similar to her mother. "It makes it easier."

"Someone said that to me!" Fauna's eyes widened. "In my dreams."

Bea made a noise that was half whine, half sob. She swiped at her eyes angrily and refused to make eye contact. For a minute she only sniffled and gazed off in the distance, almost as if she was lost in thought.

"I wish I had dreams, but I don't have them anymore," Bea admitted as she sat up from her chair. "You should go to bed, it's getting late. Mother will likely want to speak to you first thing in the morning, and I've said way more than I anticipated tonight."

Before Fauna could even respond, Bea turned and walked briskly out of the room and did not look back. As she rounded the corner and disappeared, Fauna sat back in the chair and gazed into the smoldering fireplace. What had just happened? Would Lady Aphrodite help her find out why she was the Matron's target? What had the Matron done to the Verity family to cause such heartbreak? There were so many questions in her mind that Fauna simply laid her head in her arms and fell asleep staring at the fireplace.

The next morning, Fauna set off to explore the castle with socked feet and another of Rhiannon's old dresses as her entire outfit. She knew that Lady Aphrodite meant to talk with her, but from the whispers she heard amongst the people in the castle as she walked, things were stressful. She'd fallen asleep in the library and managed to sneak into Rhiannon's room right after she had left to do her daily duties. Breakfast would have to be missed, but that was her fault for sleeping elsewhere.

The castle itself was a maze of stairs and turns, but Rhiannon had assured her that so long as she could see the common area of the castle behind her, she was on the right track. Four of the hallways went to each separate wing, and only one went toward the maid's quarters and common areas. The final wing was locked and was not allowed to be accessed. It was nice to at least know she couldn't wander someplace private. Even the library was easy to find amongst the dormitories.

As she walked through the rest of the common areas of the castle, she noticed puddles of dried blood and scratches up and down the walls. They shredded the wallpaper and left deep gouges in the wood behind it. Loose sheets of wallpaper bent over passively, asking to be ripped down. Broken windows were secured with cheesecloth and nails, which took the bite out of the cold but still made Fauna shiver from the draft.

A grand staircase appeared as she exited a side door and made her way into the main hall of the first floor of the castle. Finally, after so many days of solitude and recuperating privately, Fauna found herself in the middle of the hubbub.

"Get those boards!" Gelon called from the center of it all. Whereas she'd looked somber when Fauna had met her prior, she now seemed fairly amicable. "Grab those damned dead birds and burn them! Where are the rest of the maids? Find them too!"

Maids in working clothes and sensible boots carried planks across the room. More workers hauled away wreckage in wheelbarrows. It was strange to see maids in the castle doing jobs that were normally reserved for men.

"Watch it!" a warm hand pulled her backward as a train of maids with boards made their way past.

"S-sorry," Fauna nervously spoke. "I'm new here."

"Aren't we all." the maid rolled her eyes. "Okay, where are you trying to go?"

"I was supposed to find Lady Aphrodite this morning, but I don't know where she is and I don't remember how to get to her office."

"Good luck with that," the woman chuckled while her eyes still roamed the room. "She's impossible to track down on *normal* days and these last few have been pretty chaotic."

"Okay." Fauna was suddenly overwhelmed by the amount of noise and people around her. She wrapped the shirt around her body and walked back through the door she had come through.

"Oh, hello," a familiar voice called to her. Fauna turned around and squinted down the corridor into a small room. The person's face was obscured but the haphazard pile of curls gave her away.

"Scarlet?" Fauna asked. "Is that you?"

"Sure is. It's your lucky day. I've been looking for you. Mother is asking for you. Did you find Rhiannon for breakfast?"

"I fell asleep in the library," Fauna admitted. "I was waiting for her to be gone so I could explore and let her do her work without me bothering you all."

"Oh, you liked the library?" Scarlet looked conflicted for a moment but eventually softened. "Do you like poems?"

Fauna remembered that the Scarlet in her room upstairs had talked extensively about poetry. Perhaps that part of the illusion had been true.

"I do. Do you write them?" Fauna tried her best to seem as if she knew nothing about the girl.

Scarlet's face lit up—a stark difference from her melancholic sister, and she held out a hand. "I do! Come! I'll take you to Mother soon, but you *need* to see my library! Don't let me forget to take you there, though. I get lost easily."

"Don't you live here?"

Scarlet laughed at that. "Yes, but I get lost frequently. Well, not physically but mentally *distracted*. I have a lot of thoughts in my head at once and sometimes they are hard to wade through, so I get a little confused. Anyway, let's *go!*"

Well, Fauna had little else to do that day, so she took Scarlet's hand and was surprised at how *cold* she was. The surprise quickly passed though as the bouncy girl led her down halls and into her wing, all the while speaking of inspirations and little phrases of poems that she liked.

When they arrived at a plum and, well... *scarlet* door, Fauna was quite surprised to see how quickly the girl had dropped her defenses. Bea had nearly pushed her into the fire before opening up and Scarlet seemed only to pretend to be cautious around her.

"So what type of poems do you like?" Scarlet asked, with a smile so large that it was all Fauna could look at.

"I don't know that much about poetry," Fauna admitted. "I envy anyone who can write them, though. I liked reading the few poetry books I could get my hands on."

Scarlet blushed a little at the subtle compliment. "It's not as hard as it looks! You think of how you want to describe something and then you add extra words to it!"

With that, she pushed the door open and revealed a small but very maximalist room. It wasn't *messy* per se. It was more of an organized chaos that seemed to only be decipherable by its organizer. Little piles of books stacked haphazardly on tables while pieces of paper with errant sentences littered the floor. Off to the right was a well-kempt four-poster bed that faced off against an extremely disorganized closet.

"I like to sit in the window and look at the stars." Scarlet wrinkled her nose with joy, which made her look very much like a child. "Sometimes, Mother will sit with me while I practice reading my writing."

"Who do you perform for?" Fauna was genuinely curious. "Could I hear one?"

"The staff, usually," Scarlet laughed like twinkling lights. "They tolerate me. I've always wanted to go into town or to one of the nights when amateurs perform. But, I'm not allowed past the gates usually, and the only person willing to go with me isn't here anymore."

"The performers at the taverns aren't very good, if that helps," Fauna offered. "I would love to listen to one if you want."

Scarlet blushed. "Well, I have one that I've been working on. It's about the fight the Matron and mother had. But, it's not finished and I haven't polished it yet. Maybe another time?"

Fauna smiled at the girl and nodded slowly. "Of course. You know where to find me."

"Would you like to borrow one?" Scarlet motioned to a few shelves with well-worn books. "I'm just very excited to share this with someone. Mother said to be careful because you're a stranger, but if the Matron didn't like you, that usually means you're a good person."

"What's this one?" Fauna pointed to a plum-colored book with lavender and pastel pink embroidered flowers along the spine. "*Spirits in the Garden*?"

"Oh," Scarlet looked away as if she was trying not to react too obviously. "I wrote that a long time ago when I was very sad. Have you seen the garden here? It's quite large."

"I have not," Fauna admitted. "Only through the window in the room, so I wasn't even sure that it was real."

Scarlet reached for the book and set it gently on a table to her left. "Perhaps Rhiannon will take you out to see the gardens. They're beautiful and it's a shame that no one goes to visit them very often."

"That sounds lovely."

With that, Scarlet nodded towards the door and held out her hand again. "Come, I will lead you to Mother. If she gets cross about how long we took, tell her that I got lost and distracted you with poems. She'll understand."

Fauna nodded with a smile as she was led back out of Scarlet's space and past the common area, into a wing on the opposite side of the castle. Opulent green and gold decor led the way as they approached a heavy wooden door. Scarlet rapped against it twice and waited.

"Come."

"That's your cue," the youngest daughter assured her. "Come find me if you ever want to write or read together."

"Thank you, Scarlet." Fauna smiled and turned towards the door. "Here goes nothing."

Nineteen

"Hello, Fauna."

The simple greeting was enough to make her nervous; hearing Aphrodite greet her with such heavy insignificance was unsettling. It was similar to the way Aphrodite had been right before Fauna escaped, though lacking the maliciousness.

Fauna bowed her head slightly. "Lady Aphrodite."

"I apologize for my hasty departure the other night." Aphrodite stood and adjusted her dress. She stepped out and around her large desk and sat gingerly on the corner. "It was an unexpected moment of weakness. One that I am not proud of."

"I wasn't exactly at my best either," Fauna reminded her. "All of this is quite confusing. I apologize if I have made things complicated here."

Aphrodite chuckled softly. "You did, yes, but it wasn't your choice. Would you join me for a walk? I have a room to show you, that might explain some things to you. Perhaps we could clear some of the air between us."

"Sure," Fauna agreed tentatively. "I would like that. I'm at a loss for what's happened and I genuinely do not mean to harm anyone."

"Have you had breakfast?" Aphrodite looked her up and down. "Why are you only in socks?"

"I have nothing else," Fauna explained. "All of the items I had in that room upstairs weren't real. Rhiannon has been kind enough to lend me some things."

"Understood," Aphrodite leaned over, grabbed a very expensive-looking pen off her desk, and scribbled a note hastily on a large calendar on her desk. "I'll have that rectified. Our seamstress has gone missing, so it could take a little bit of time though. For now, if Rhiannon is willing to share her clothing, it is much appreciated."

"I have no money," Fauna held out her hands. "But I can sew and I'm pretty strong if you need a helping hand around here."

Aphrodite smiled only the tiniest bit. "That won't be necessary, but the offer is appreciated. Come, let me ask you things as we walk."

Fauna nervously tucked the gray streak of her hair behind her ear and walked into the hallway. Aphrodite joined quickly and locked the door behind them. She began to walk and only a flick of the wrist at her side beckoned Fauna to follow her.

"So, tell me. What do you know of the Matron?" Aphrodite's tone was neutral, but Fauna knew they had a storied history together, so she tried to choose her words wisely.

"Well, I told you that my mother hated her," Fauna explained. "And my father was *obsessive* in his devotion to her. We had a photo of the Matron hanging over the mantle and he attended the gatherings up until he could no longer walk on his own."

"And he stayed married to your mother?" Aphrodite sounded impressed. "It takes quite a love to overcome differences that vast."

"I've wondered about that most of my life," Fauna explained as she followed Aphrodite up, down, and around a shrouded wing. "She died when I was born. My father spoke of her fondly for most of my life, but eventually, as I got older and began to take on more of her qualities, he refused to speak to me at all. I think when he died, we had not spoken to each other for years."

"The Matron said something curious to you as she died," Aphrodite mentioned. "That your father would be disappointed and it was too late for your mother. Any idea what that could mean?"

Fauna shook her head. "I do not. That whole interaction is fuzzy in my mind. I hit my head pretty hard on the way down. My father only told me that my mother died immediately following my birth. He kept a photo of her beside his bed, but it vanished over the years. Everything of hers seemed to vanish eventually. It was like she stopped existing as time went on."

"Are you familiar with the Matron's island in the sky?" Aphrodite asked as they turned a final corner.

"Hurmehovi?" Fauna suggested. "I've heard the villagers speaking of it. Only that it's where she keeps her army of undead soldiers and a prison for the worst offenders."

"That is partially true. There is no army or prison, but it is an entire expanse on the tallest mountain—so tall that it reaches beyond the clouds. I need to venture there, for personal reasons. You see, she took something from me, something extremely dear to me, and I need to remedy that now that she is gone. I cannot let anyone go with me, for reasons that are too complicated to explain, but would you like me to look into any leads about what she said?"

"I would appreciate it," Fauna admitted. "Though part of me just wants to leave it all behind. Is that normal?"

"I wouldn't know," Aphrodite let out a deeply soft laugh. "I am nowhere near normal. All I am willing to share with you right now is that the Matron loved nothing but devotion, and would do anything in her power to amass as many followers as she could. She used to call them her 'army of follow-things.'"

Fauna waited patiently for Aphrodite to unlock the door in front of them.

"I'm sure, by now, you've realized that I am not related to my daughters by blood." Aphrodite began the conversation as she opened the door. Inside was a very dark room, illuminated by one lonely window with the curtains drawn. Inside looked to be a very large velvet couch and an easel. "We are family, that much is not a question. We are bound together forever."

"Forever?" Fauna repeated a little apprehensively.

Aphrodite nodded slowly. "Sit. I have much to explain and very little time to do so."

Fauna took a seat on the large couch and noticed that the wooden frame had quite a bit of dust over it. How long had the room been locked?

"Before I tell you things, I need to know that you will promise to keep calm. My girls are my entire world and I will do anything to protect them. But, they would also do anything to protect me. I am not threatening you, but I am laying it all out on the table. We, as a family, have been hurt quite a bit and the Matron's death is bringing up a lot of feelings we had long since buried."

Fauna agreed silently with a tepid nod and waited for the explanation.

"This is my atelier. Are you familiar with those?"

When Fauna shook her head, Aphrodite stood and walked over to a large shelf covered by a sheet.

Aphrodite lifted the sheet to show many canvases stacked upon each other and a very organized set of painting supplies.

"It's my painting room—my solace away from the world. I keep memories of my life here. All the paintings are covered to avoid exposure to the sun and to avoid me having to see them constantly. It's been quite a span since I have painted and many of these depict my worst moments in time. Some are highlights, but even those make my heart ache. Perhaps someday I will pull the curtains down and explain it all to you. We do not have the time today and to be honest, I am not ready."

"That would be nice, but please take your time," Fauna assured her, even though she was unsure if it was working. She knew she was a stranger to Aphrodite, but it seemed that the woman trusted her a bit more now that things had somewhat settled.

"So, my girls came to me because of the Matron," Aphrodite began as she sat on a stool in front of her easel. "The Matron knew how deeply I wanted to be a mother, but that it was not possible for me."

"I'm sorry for that," Fauna spoke gently. Even if she did not desire children, she did know what it felt like to crave something she could not have.

"I made peace with it long ago," Aphrodite explained with a wave. "I was focused on maintaining the castle and restoring it after it had been abandoned for a few hundred years. But the Matron is… sort of a mother to me. She birthed me, but not physically. I held a parental love for her—as complicated as our relationship was. She gave me life and could just as easily have taken it away."

Fauna's heart began to *pound*. There had been many clues littered amongst her time in the castle that pointed to something other-worldly, but she had been able to explain those away as illusions or even just a mistake. Fauna nodded slowly, unsure if speaking was appropriate… or what she would even say.

"When I was a girl, I was sickly, fragile. My body could barely tolerate a change in seasons without weeks of sickness. As I got older, I was coddled and sheltered. I believe that I spent an entire year shrouded by darkness because the doctors were grasping at straws and told my parents the sun was poisoning me."

Fauna looked at the woman. Really *looked*. A strong stature, eyes the color of fresh honeycomb, and a figure that many would be envious of. How could the woman in front of her have been such a sick child?

Aphrodite's demure expression softened as she continued her story.

"My parents died midwinter when I was sixteen. Before they passed, they sent for a doctor of blood medicine. No one had ever heard of such a thing, but they were desperate for someone to care for me when they were no longer around. A woman arrived the day we buried them. Not more than an hour after the funeral, she was poking and prodding me with needles and tubes. Very rarely did she speak, but when she did, it was so soft that I barely could make out her words. And just as the sickness began to fatally spread through me… it was gone. I tried asking the doctor what sorcery she had done, but each time she shook her head and said she would visit the next year to check on me."

"Did she?" Fauna finally sat back into the cushions and crossed one leg over the other.

Aphrodite nodded. "She did. Like clockwork. As soon as the winter's chill thawed to a muddy paste, she would arrive at my door and do the same things. I became comfortable with her, but she never once divulged anything. I was naive to think she was looking out for me. This routine happened every year until I turned thirty-five—the age my parents were when they died. That year, she came with suitcases and made it quite clear that she would be staying."

Fauna listened quietly, stunned that Aphrodite would be so forthcoming with her about her life. Just a few days ago, she'd threatened to kill her. Bea had done the same. Nevertheless, Fauna was always willing to listen.

Aphrodite smiled sadly and looked downwards toward her feet. "I knew something was wrong, but I was a lonely child who'd grown into a lonely adult. I had been kept away from society for so long that I didn't know how to speak to people. I was afraid of them and afraid of getting sick again. So I loved the attention from her, even if she gave very little in return. When I laid down for a routine set of pricks and pokes, I didn't expect to black out. But I did."

Fauna's eyes widened.

"I woke three days later with a craving so ferocious that it burned from my throat to my belly. I felt stronger and more assured. The only issue was that nagging urge for something that I couldn't pinpoint until the doctor came to my room with a glass of wine. Suddenly, the scent of everything was overpowering. Her perfume, the wine, the breeze outside. I was thrown into a sensory overload. I couldn't complete a single thought, I was just so hungry and thirsty that it was all I could think of."

Aphrodite waited a moment before she continued.

"A blood doctor. Ha! She was more of a blood *demon*. She changed me, *groomed* me into being the perfect specimen for her trials. She wanted to see if she could heal a curse that *she* inflicted on me. The sad part? She never did. I am not healed and I will never know a life of peace because of it."

It suddenly hit Fauna so suddenly that she forgot to quiet herself. "Vampirism."

Aphrodite, while clearly surprised that Fauna would offer up such a preposterous idea, did not do much other than quirk an eyebrow.

"Correct," Aphrodite admitted. "I had been changed, forever. The wine that had smelled so sweet? Gently bled from the doctor herself. Had I known that would have bound me to her for so long, I would have smashed the glass and tried my best to navigate my life alone. But I drank it down eagerly, and then another. I fell into a sated stupor and slept soundly for the first time in my entire life."

"You sleep?" Fauna asked, quite surprised. "I've never read about vampires that sleep. Can you be in the sun?"

Aphrodite laughed, a harsh bark of a thing. "If you think that any book on vampires has been written by someone who knew one, that's a large mistake. Listen to me. The people in my castle are kind and not all of them are afflicted. Some are your standard human beings, just in need of shelter and employment. We aren't malicious beings and very few of us chose the life we were given. Try to remember that, okay?"

"How do you survive?" Fauna wondered aloud. "I wonder if that's where your castle's reputation came from."

Aphrodite nodded in agreement. "That's a possibility. Years before you—probably even before your grandparents were born—we had a deal with the village. People would have some of their blood taken by some of the mortals in this castle and, in turn, they were paid for their donations. Livestock that died naturally were sold to us and we would let the people with normal diets use the rest of the animal. It was a peaceful exchange and it helped the village's economy. People who normally could not provide for their families suddenly found themselves able. And my daughters could live without harming anyone."

"Could you do that again?" Fauna offered, trying her best not to visibly react to Aphrodite's story. Never in her life did she think she would come into contact with vampires, let alone peaceful ones. Most books painted them as lascivious creatures that went on murderous sprees when they were bored.

It took Aphrodite a moment to answer. She gazed towards a grime-coated window that looked as if it hadn't seen a good cleaning since the turn of the century. Finally, she shook her head, blonde waves sliding back and forth over her shoulders.

"Not anymore," Aphrodite admitted. "I don't know if this castle will ever know peace again."

Fauna started to ask why, but Aphrodite raised a hand gently. "I need some time. More than I had anticipated. Ask Rhiannon to show you around the castle grounds instead. It is a nice day, and you look like you need some sun. Have a picnic in the garden. Tell her I said it was fine."

Fauna nodded and rose to leave. As she passed through the doorway, she turned back to see Aphrodite gently peel back a sheet that covered a canvas. Slowly, a portrait of a woman, dressed in white and swathed with a cloud of butterflies appeared. She looked familiar, but Fauna couldn't quite place *why*. Aphrodite's actions stopped as she took a shuddering breath and looked back over her shoulder.

"Please go," Aphrodite whispered pitifully. "Please."

Fauna gasped and turned on her heel to quickly make her way back towards the center of the castle. As she walked the long hallways, she thought back to the portrait. It was beautiful! Did that woman have anything to do with the reason there was such a cloud over the castle? Everyone seemed so downtrodden, even after the Matron was gone.

She spotted Rhiannon leaning against the railing at the bottom of the stairs and waved at her friend.

"Good afternoon! I'm supposed to ask you to show me around the grounds! Lady Aphrodite mentioned a picnic in the garden."

Rhiannon's eyebrows rose with joy and she smiled. "Oh, that's wonderful! I don't get to enjoy the outdoors nearly as much as I want to and it's such a beautiful day out. Our gardener works so hard to care for it. If she insists that you go see it, I think that means she trusts you. Perhaps this is the beginning of a healing era for us all?"

Fauna nearly lept with joy. "I've never been on a picnic before and the gardens sound wonderful. Should I meet you there?"

Rhiannon scrunched her nose most adorably. "Nah, I can pack a basket in just a few minutes and I don't want you getting lost in this big old castle. We can also stop by my room and get you something more appropriate for heading outside. Being barefoot in the grass is fun, but not very safe. Your socks will muddy and I don't want you to fall!"

Fauna laughed at that. "Safety, yes. The number one priority in the castle."

Rhiannon shot her an amused look. "More than you think!"

After a quick stop in the kitchen and a few introductions to the staff, Fauna and Rhiannon stepped out the side door of the kitchen into the expansive yard. Clad in a *very* pretty simple black dress and holding a *very* heavy basket, Fauna found herself swaying with joy as the pair walked in silence. Never in her entire life thus far did Fauna think she would enjoy simply existing next to someone.

She watched as Rhiannon closed her eyes and tilted her face to the sky, so Fauna did the same. The sun's warmth on her cheeks made her smile in a way she had not done since she was a little girl. It was strange that, after all the heartbreak and deceit that had happened to her, Fauna felt happier to be alive than ever before.

She heard Rhiannon stop walking, so Fauna stopped as well and opened her eyes. The first thing she saw was Rhiannon looking up at one of the castle's wings with her hand covering her eyes from the sun. She pointed to an ornate-looking stained glass window that hit the high daylight just perfectly. It depicted two hands reaching toward each other in front of a castle's entrance. From so far below, Fauna could not see the colors, but she assumed it was rather pretty.

"That window is how I navigate my way around the confusing castle grounds," Rhiannon explained. "But don't ask Lady Aphrodite about its history."

Fauna frowned. "Why not? It's quite pretty."

"If you're ever allowed in the room it's in, you'll see that it overlooks an area with a small pond. One that you can't see from anywhere else. It's locked away within these gardens and only visible from above. There are sad memories buried in that spot. Painful memories. So painful that Lady Aphrodite had a pond built right over it so no one could ask about it."

Fauna tried to imagine where in the castle that room would be, but couldn't quite picture it. So, she simply nodded that she understood and continued to look at the window in awe.

"Are they reaching for each other?" Fauna asked after a solemn moment. "It's hard to see from down here."

"They are. Forever destined to reach but never touch," Rhiannon whispered glumly. "Come on, let's go look at the gardens."

When Rhiannon had told Fauna that the garden was bigger than it looked, Fauna did not realize how accurate the statement was. From the outside, it looked like a simple gathering of flowers with high walls and trees. But, once they walked inside the enclosure, Fauna was bombarded with colors and textures, so much so that she almost began to feel overwhelmed. Patterns and scents swirled in front of her, making her mind spin with glee. She set the basket down in the grass and turned slowly to commit it all to memory as best as she could.

"Beautiful, isn't it?" Rhiannon said with tears in her eyes. "When the garden was being built, Aphrodite sent workers all over the world to find the seeds. They told her over and over that the flowers wouldn't grow in the weather here, but she didn't listen. She was convinced that with enough love and care, they would grow."

"And it worked?" Fauna asked, gently touching the lavender petals of the flower closest to her face.

"It did." Rhiannon smiled and took a deep breath. "That far wall? It was damaged years ago in a bad storm and the groundskeeper at the time broke his leg trying to save it. So the villagers came and helped rebuild it within two days so none of the flowers would die."

"The same village I am from?" Fauna laughed but was not amused. "The very same ones that tried to burn me alive?"

"Sort of," Rhiannon motioned towards a bench and led Fauna to it. "This was before my time here. Way before. Did you know that this castle used to be considered one of the most important and sought-after places to work in the village?"

Fauna could not contain her disbelief. "I can't picture that for the life of me."

"My grandmother worked here as a seamstress nearly seventy years ago," Rhiannon spoke with palpable pride. "She told me stories for a long time until she passed. You'd be surprised at how much the village changed in as little as fifty years."

"I can only imagine," Fauna admitted. "This place is so beautiful. I feel… protected here in the garden. Is that weird?"

"Not at all," Rhiannon assured her with a very large smile. "I think that was the purpose. We all need to feel safe and that was the reason for all of this. When you're in the garden, the world disappears."

They sat in the shade of a large tree and pulled out their picnic. It was nice to eat in a comfortable silence. As much as Fauna loved her newfound sense of peace in a very strange world, some quiet was still comforting. However, it made it quite easy for her mind to wander.

She thought about the woman in Aphrodite's painting. She looked so happy, so free. But the sorrow with which Aphrodite stared at the painting also sat heavy in Fauna's heart. This Aphrodite was new to her, but she could still spot the longing on her face.

"I have a question, but I'm not sure if I'm allowed to ask," Fauna broke the silence as she swallowed the last of her food.

Rhiannon, freshly jolted out of her concentration, simply shrugged. "Not much is off limits at this point. If I'm not mistaken, you've finally been told their... ahem... sanguine secret?"

Fauna laughed. "You know what, she *did* tell me that and for some reason, I didn't think too hard about it. But, as I was leaving the atelier, Aphrodite got very sad and was gazing at a portrait of a woman. Is that woman someone important?"

"Oh," Rhiannon groaned as she blew all the air out of her mouth slowly. "That is probably a question that I could answer, but should not. I wasn't here for any of it, so all I know is whispers and the occasional story from some of the staff."

Fauna sighed and felt very defeated. "This feels like something I should know, but no one wants to talk about. I just want to understand why everyone here is so sad all of the time—especially concerning the gardens."

Rhiannon smiled at her sympathetically. "I can't tell you, I'm so sorry. But, if you go into Lady Aphrodite's office, you'll find a woman working there named Gelon. She's in charge of chronicling the castle's history. There's a book she uses to write down all the things that have happened, and I'm sure that you would be allowed to read it if Lady Aphrodite told us to go to the gardens. Gelon has been here since Lady Aphrodite has and she's the only person you'll ever want to get your information from."

"Do you think she would mind if I paid her a visit?" Fauna wondered. "Was she the one directing the repairs?"

"Yes! She lives with the staff, but is mainly Aphrodite's assistant," Rhiannon explained. "She also was one of the only women in the castle that could write for a long while but that has since changed."

"Maybe I'll go visit her later, before dinner. Am I going to sit with you again? I feel kind of bad not doing anything while everyone works," Fauna admitted. "And the other workers are quiet."

Rhiannon laughed. "I'll let you fold towels while I sort the laundry. Would that make you feel better?"

Fauna laughed out loud and nodded. It felt good to laugh, to just exist without the heavy weight of impending doom. "I used to do that in the room upstairs while I listened to you gossip. So, of course, I would love to do that!"

The rest of the picnic continued pleasantly. Not an overly talkative person, Fauna was perfectly content listening to the *real* Rhiannon tell her all kinds of things about the castle. She spoke so quickly that Fauna gave up trying to remember who was who in the stories but, to be fair, Rhiannon's re-enactment was most of Fauna's entertainment. As the picnic wound down, Rhiannon flopped on her back, curls splayed over the grass like spilled juice, and began to hum.

It looked rather fun, so Fauna did the same. The edges of the clipped grass scratched gently at her bare legs, and the breeze skittered across her cheeks. Never had she simply laid in the grass and existed. It was truly blissful.

Twenty

Fauna wiped her hands on her dress and knocked on the door. She'd been in Aphrodite's office before, but never had she realized there was a second person's desk there. It wasn't until Rhiannon mentioned there was an assistant in Aphrodite's office that Fauna realized she hadn't paid enough attention the first time.

"Fauna, yes?" Gelon looked up and asked as she opened the door. "Come in. My office is to the left."

Fauna nodded and followed her inside before she spoke. "Rhiannon told me that I might find you here to ask about the castle's history. There is supposed to be a book about the story of the garden. Do I need to ask Lady Aphrodite if I could read it?"

"She was one step ahead of you—you already have permission. I just finished writing the entry about the battle between Lady Aphrodite and the Matron this morning. I assume you don't need refreshing on that front, considering you were there. Hell, if you have some spare time soon, I would like to get your version of events. "

Fauna, immediately relieved by the woman's kind demeanor, smiled and pushed out a short breathy laugh as she shook her head. "Sure! It's a bit fuzzy, but I remember some of it."

Gelon winked at her and pointed to a small writing desk next to hers. "Sit right there or by the fireplace, I'll fetch what you need. It's a rather large book, so you'll need to use the desk or your lap to hold it. I reckon it weighs about as much as a piglet, given how much history is in it."

When Gelon turned and began to unlock a drawer in her desk, Fauna wrapped her arms around herself and padded over to the chair that was closest to the fire. On a side table laid a discarded book, face down and bookmarked. Fauna grabbed the paperback and flipped it over. She took in the red cover that featured a man strapped to a table with a pendulum swinging above him.

She opened the first page and saw a personal note in a wonderful script.

My love,

May you always remember that the pendulum cannot swing forever. For one of these days, it will cease and you will know peace.

Feeling as if she'd read something she shouldn't have, Fauna placed the book back down the way she'd found it and tried to forget she had seen it.

"Here you go," Gelon said softly as she handed over a book that seemed to nearly match her in size. How did she manage to carry something so heavy?

Fauna smiled at her and took the book. It was in very good condition considering how old it must have been. The leatherbound cover had yet to fray and not a single golden stitch had broken. The metallic clasp had no tarnish, and the only sign of aging was a single crack in the spine where the book had laid flat for some time.

"You'll want to make sure that none of the pages show signs of wear," Gelon warned her. "Every time even the smallest of tears appears, I have to rewrite the entire page and redo the binding."

Fauna nodded and gently traced the embossed "V" of "Verity" on the cover. "I understand. I treat books very well."

"As you should," Gelon agreed. "Just leave it on the table when you are finished. I will collect it later. See that you leave before sundown. Lady Aphrodite has asked that she be alone this evening, myself included."

Fauna nodded again. "I will."

With that, Gelon nodded and sat at her desk, humming a gentle tune accompanied only by the scratch of her pen tip. Fauna opened the book to a random spot nearly halfway through and began to thumb through the pages, overwhelmed by how much information was documented. Newspaper articles and handwritten accounts were also pasted to the pages and coated to keep them protected.

Aphrodite Verity, soon-to-be Lady and Heiress to the Verity estate arrived at the Castle on a blustery February morning. Her husband, Victor, came two days later by carriage from the north.

Fauna stopped reading. Lady Aphrodite had a husband? That was news to her. Not that it was her business, but it just seemed a little... out of character. She skipped a few pages and stopped at a page that looked like an obituary.

Count Verity was buried in a private ceremony in the forests of Hurmehovi, along with his three siblings and his father. His mother, the Matron, instructed all the bodies to be kept under charmed lock and key, should anyone wish to rob them.

Fauna stopped reading and opened her mouth to ask Gelon a question, but decided to go back a bit to try and find out more on her own. Suddenly there was so much information to take in and Fauna was nearly overwhelmed by the desire to read it all. Thinking she went a bit too far ahead, Fauna went back a few pages to learn a bit more.

Victor Verity is alone no more! The Count of Castle Verity has found a wife in a marriage arranged by his mother, the Matron."

Fauna's eyes widened at the headline of the paper pasted to the page. Lady Aphrodite was married to Matron's son because she had arranged it. Why did no one speak of this? Was *his* death the thing everyone was mourning? Who was the woman in her dreams? The newspaper clipping didn't specify much more than that and there were no photographs in the next few pages. It was an event worth saving, right?

"You look very perplexed." Gelon appeared over her shoulder. "Ah, yes. The Count. He was… not well liked here, by anyone. Not a very easy person to socialize with. Wanted to boast about everything he had ever achieved… which truly wasn't much. His crowning achievement was marrying a woman like Lady Aphrodite and he didn't even do that on his own merits. He wasn't even truly a Count, hence why Lady Aphrodite never used the title of Countess."

"Lady Aphrodite had a husband?" Fauna still was confused. "But why isn't he mentioned anywhere?"

Gelon sighed and took a seat in the chair across from Fauna. She ran a hand through her short hair and looked around the room. She saw the discarded book and sighed softly before turning her mouth into a pensive half-smile.

"Lady Aphrodite came to this castle as an unwed, middle-aged woman," Gelon explained. "And if anyone were to take her seriously, she needed a husband. That's the official reason. What I truly think happened was that the Matron knew her only son was going to die without any heirs and so she paired the two together. There was nothing but animosity between them though. They fought like none other. He would insult her and call her all kinds of wretched things, but she was smarter than he was and never took it seriously. I think that made him more angry than anything else—being outwitted by his wife."

Fauna smirked. "Did they ever learn to get along?"

Gelon shook her head. "Lady Aphrodite wanted nothing to do with him until the Matron showed up with two orphaned little girls. They were both so tired, dirty, and practically feral. It was only then that Aphrodite softened. It was as if the squabbles and spats no longer mattered. Those girls became her whole world. She spent every waking minute caring for them and trying to win their trust."

"What happened to them?" Fauna asked. "What killed their parents?"

Gelon sighed. "The official story is that they were found in the forest wandering after their parents died in the village. Supposedly they had been in the wild for nearly a year before being spotted by the Matron."

"You sound like you don't believe that story," Fauna admitted.

Gelon smirked. "I write what I am told is the truth, but I speak about what I think. I truly think the Matron took those girls and killed their parents in a desperate attempt to quell Lady Aphrodite's distaste for her husband. She knew he wasn't worth his salt, but she needed heirs."

"Did it work?"

Gelon laughed. "Not at all. She immediately took to the girls but ignored her husband all day. They even had separate bedrooms. Soon, he began to sneak out to the village at night."

"Was he also a…"

"Vampire?" Gelon asked with a raised brow. "He was, but he didn't have the same caution that the rest of them did. He would swagger into town with tales of adventure and pompous lies about his wife being lackluster. The widows and singles ate it up, and he loved the attention. But, more than the attention, he liked killing his lovers. He would suck them dry and leave nothing but scraps. The village thought they'd been cursed by the Matron."

Fauna frowned. "How did he die?

Gelon winked. "One of his victims fought back. Cut his head right off his shoulders. Didn't even know he was a vampire, just took it clean off. Good for her."

Fauna tried not to laugh, but the surprise of it all got her. "Is that why everyone here seems so sad? Because he died? It doesn't add up."

Gelon's laughter faded into a sad sigh. She chewed on her cheek for a moment and licked her lips nervously for a few seconds. "No. That's a dreadful story. Read up a bit, closer to when the girls are older," Gelon urged her. "That will explain. I would tell you more, but it brings out a sadness in me that takes weeks to shake. Just… remember that this family is immortal and forever is a very long time. Forever spent *with* people is also forever spent *without* them."

Fauna looked away nervously. "I suppose it is."

With that, Gelon rose and placed a sturdy hand on Fauna's shoulder. "If you are allowed to look at the book, you are allowed to know it all. With that comes a lot of pressure. Just take care to remember that a lot of this staff remembers all of these things that have happened. So, when you speak of it to others, be cautious of how you mention it. I'm going to go to the kitchen to make some tea. I'll bring some for you too."

Fauna watched Gelon leave the room and shut the door gently. She looked down at the book with a strange heaviness in her heart. Whatever she was going to learn in the book was obviously something so dreadful that it ruined a whole village.

After a moment, she opened the book and skimmed the pages as quickly as she could until she caught up to where she'd left off. Instead of newspaper clippings, it started to read like a children's book of sorts. According to the signatures at the bottom of the pages, Bea had begun her portion of the book and was learning how to write. It chronicled day trips with Aphrodite and memories Bea had of growing up. It was so honest, as children usually are, that as she read the book, Fauna could almost picture the memories in her mind. There were things that children remembered that adults did not. Even as a child, Bea was the analytical one, focused on practicality and sustainability. Her entries were very numerical—inventory of stones in her collection or accounts of how often the maids swore. There were also stories of counting the bricks in the walls or learning to play number games with the castle staff.

After a few some time, the handwriting changed again. This time it was Scarlet. Doodles filled the margins, along with fragments of words and phrases to remember. Plots and characters and castle gossip littered the pages with little to no sense. She spoke of adventures in the brook alongside the castle and the animals she discovered. Then the writing began to switch regularly, as if they were taking turns writing down their days. However, the book was so large that their entries took only a few pages at a time.

As Fauna's back began to ache from leaning over the book, she skipped a chunk of pages until she saw a beautiful sketch of a woman looking out the window. Her hair seemed to float in a breeze and her nightdress glowed with the lightest of blues. Her skin was fair, almost the color of the moonbeams that struck her... and in the background was a *very* familiar rocking chair. Aphrodite's signature, lengthy and resplendent, curled around the bottom of it. Fauna had no idea the woman could sketch so well. Underneath it was a paragraph written in what seemed to be in direct response to the drawing above.

The Lady of the Castle was a rose amongst thorns. Eyes the color of a summer storm and a smile that made even the burliest of farmers stop and blush. Her hair, as vibrant as the first leaves of autumn, was rumored by the village children to be where she kept her magic. And while she was indeed magical in her own right, the Lady of the Castle was nothing more than a mere mortal with a smile so warm that not a single soul spoke against her.

She spent her mornings in the garden, singing softly to the flowers so that they might bloom as brightly as they could. Forest creatures, from the smallest insect to the most imposing of bears, would gather at her feet while she sang. Her voice, as gentle as a butterfly's wings and as effortless as a yawn, was so enchanting that even the birds stopped their passing journeys to listen in.

Afternoons were spent visiting her daughters. Sometimes they took tea as they cried into her lap over the neverending woes they seemed to accumulate as teenagers. Other times, she read books to them in front of the fire. They loved this mother so much that not a single day was spent away from her. Even when she traveled to the village, the girls looked out the windows with their foreheads pressed to the glass, waiting for the sight of their second parent once more.

Early evenings were saved for Lady Aphrodite herself. Aphrodite only ever asked two things of her darling wife. One was that she posed in the atelier for the occasional portrait, and the second was to join her for tea in their favorite rocking chair as the moon rose in the sky.

Though she kept to a routine, the Lady of the Castle always made time for anyone who asked kindly for her presence. The village adored her. She treated every person, from pauper to prince, as if they were deeply important, and because of that, her death caused a debilitating sorrow that never quite left the people. Had the villagers known the truth behind it, the Matron's wrath would have ended immediately. But, instead, they prayed to her and asked for the Lady to have a sweet and pleasant afterlife.

The details have been withheld from this account per Lady Aphrodite Verity's request, but the Lady of the Castle's name was to be removed from all records and the details of their lives be sealed. All that is permitted to be penned, was that she loved her wife very much and that the Lady of the Castle chose to die by her morals, rather than turn into something she despised. To utter her name is a crime that all should be frightened of committing. Instead, she is referred to only as 'The Lady.'

It took two weeks from the incident for her to see her final sunrise. The air about the castle was already thick with grief and workers could be seen wiping their eyes and looking worriedly back and forth, waiting for news. The villagers only knew that their kind-hearted hero was dreadfully ill and that she would not recover. Handmade gifts made by children and adults gathered at the castle's doors, and prayers were etched onto every visible surface. But it was all for naught.

On her final day, with cheeks so sunken in a sorrowful grey and eyes filled with a pitiful melancholy, the Lady of the Castle kissed her wife twenty-three times and told her daughters that she loved them nearly triple that. Not a single soul in the village nor castle spoke for an entire week.

As the moon began to rise on the final night, Lady Aphrodite sat with her wife's frail body in their favorite rocking chair and began to sing a song so mournful, that even the stars in the sky dimmed to pay their respects. As she took her last rattling breaths, the Lady of the Castle asked Aphrodite for two promises. One was that her garden would remain free for everyone to work in and take from. There would be no charge for its vegetables and anyone could tend to the flowers. And two, that the castle walls would never know silence or darkness. She urged that they would sing and laugh and dance in the sun, as she herself loved to do.

Soon the castle children turned into adults who had children of their own. There came a whole generation who had not been moved and impacted by the Lady of the Castle. But still, they sang her songs and kissed the budding flowers each morning in her wake. And each evening when Lady Aphrodite sat in her rocking chair while the sun dipped lower *in the sky, she sang the same mournful dirge of a woman whose kindness changed the world. And when the sunlight finally touched the corners of her shadowed room to begin a new day, she stood and did it all again.*

Fauna burst into tears. Not the kind of tears that one could just wipe away. These were thick and warm. The pooled at her chin and eventually dribbled onto her dress. It all made sense. All of it. Why the garden was protected and why the castle seemed to be in perpetual mourning. The Lady of the Castle was the woman in the painting—she had to be. Oh, she wanted to hug every single one of the Verity women. And had the Matron not died under Aphrodite's shoe… Fauna would have risked her only pair of socks to invoke the same wrath.

Still weak from crying, Fauna slid the book onto the table next to her and stood carefully. When she was sure that her legs wouldn't give out, she returned the book to Gelon's desk and headed back to her chair. Before she could sit again, she noticed the discarded book from earlier still on the table across from her and grabbed it. The message inside about the swinging pendulum, which already seemed cryptic, now hurt in a new way. Wanting a reprieve from the sadness, Fauna flipped to the first page and tried her best to decompress from what she'd just read.

Cold fingers grabbed her arms and shook her slightly. When she came to, she realized she was staring into Lady Aphrodite's eyes. Fauna gasped and sat up the best she could, though her body did not like being in such a strange position in the chair. Next to her on the table was a meal, still steaming, and a large glass of water.

"You need to eat," Aphrodite chastised her, though there was no bite in her words. "I can't have you fainting and hurting yourself. This castle is large—you could seriously injure yourself and it could take a while to find you."

"I'm sorry," Fauna grimaced as she tried to move her body back to a good position. "It was very cold and the fire was very warm."

"Are you always to be found amongst the books?" Lady Aphrodite sat back in her chair and crossed her legs. "Eat up."

Seeing no reason to move the tray of food, Fauna adjusted herself and slid a plate into her lap. It warmed her legs, which reminded her of her tender skin when she'd woken up for the first time in the castle so long ago.

"Books are the only family I have ever known," Fauna began in between bites of food. "They're my only experience with the world."

"You know, I was the same way," Aphrodite pointed towards Gelon's desk. "I'm sure you read all about it. For the first two decades of my life, I lived vicariously through other's tales."

Fauna swallowed before answering. "A little. I got to the girl's stories and then the part about the Lady of the Castle."

Aphrodite took a deep and unsettlingly even breath before she nodded slowly and trained her gaze on the fire crackling in the hearth. The flames cast dancing shadows across her face, making her stony expression almost spooky.

"I suppose we've danced around the subject." Aphrodite's voice was uncharacteristically meek and quiet. "Ask your questions. Just… be patient with me. I am no longer well-versed in being vulnerable."

"Are you sure?"

The older woman just looked out the window into the night sky. After a few minutes of silence, she glanced back at her with red-rimmed eyes and a defeated expression.

"Do you see that star—brighter than the rest, and exquisite? The one that makes you feel like it's shining just for you?"

"I do."

"I knew the woman who hung it there."

The silence after the statement hung heavy in the room for quite a long while. Fauna ate as quietly as she could while Aphrodite stared out the window.

Fauna silently finished her food after a bit and set it aside. Aphrodite turned to look at her and waited for the questions to begin.

"Who was she?"

"Would you believe me if I said that she was a woman lost in the woods?" Aphrodite, still facing the fire, closed her eyes and took a moment. "My poor, pitiful husband had just died a year prior, and while his presence was not necessarily missed, I was dreadfully lonely. I loved my girls, but they didn't trust me yet and it hurt me. They wanted their parents and I didn't blame them."

"Did they ever bond with your husband?" Fauna asked.

Aphrodite breathed out in a half-laugh type of way. "Hardly. He never saw them. I barely saw him and that's how everyone liked it. He was terrible to be around and never wanted children."

Fauna was a little confused. "So if the girls are… afflicted now, were they not back then?"

"No," Aphrodite finally opened her eyes and looked directly at Fauna. "They were turned without their consent, just as I was. That story is just as unsettling."

Fauna gasped. "That's awful!"

"When my husband died, the Matron pulled away from us for a few years," Aphrodite explained. "We'd kept our secret from the girls, but I was starting to feel the effects of going without actual sustenance for too long. I had always promised myself that I would only take from the game in the woods. I hated harming animals, but I would rather do that instead of harming a person. I didn't want the girls to think that I was dangerous at all."

"Animals are sufficient?" Fauna was surprised. "I suppose that's fortunate."

Aphrodite readjusted her dress and shot Fauna a look. "It feels a little barbaric if I'm being honest. I would much rather just drink a glass of blood diluted with wine than go hunting. It brings out a side of me that I generally loathe."

Fauna nodded. "I could see why. Tell me more about how you met, if you're willing."

"One night, I was feeling lonely and a little desperate," Aphrodite chuckled. "I put the girls to bed and set out to join in the village's festivities. Winter was on its way, so the people butcher and cure all their meats to prepare for the cold months. I figured that I would chat up some townsfolk and sneak off with a carcass, which is what I tried to do. They did not have any, but I still enjoyed being amongst the people. I did not have the reputation that I do now. They barely recognized me at all."

Fauna sensed there was more to the story, so she stayed quiet, though the vision of the elegant Aphrodite Verity walking around with an animal carcass just felt… wrong.

"I grabbed what I needed and walked back home to the castle. On my way, I heard the whimper of what sounded like a wolf and decided to check it out. I thought that maybe if it was dying, I could take it back and store it in my cellar. When I found it, this woman was leaning over it, with her arms around the wolf, crying softly.

When she looked up at me with the moonbeams reflecting off of her tear-stained cheeks, I was stunned by her beauty. It was like I had forgotten how to speak. She asked if I could help her bury her friend. The wolf had gotten stuck in a trap and had fatally injured itself trying to break free. She had never met the wolf before that, but she viewed all creatures of the world as her friends."

"It seems that they viewed her the same way," Fauna added. "That's what all of the stories make her out to be."

Aphrodite smiled for the first time that Fauna could remember. A single dimple appeared in Aphrodite's right cheek and peaceful reverie washed over her.

"They did," she said with a smile. "I helped her bury her friend and offered her a reprieve in my castle since it was much closer than the village. She stayed with me and took tea in my office and we talked until the girls woke the next morning. I sent her home but asked if she would like to have tea the next day. She agreed."

"What did you talk about the second day?" Fauna leaned forward, eager to hear.

"My failed marriage, the girls, and my need for blood."

Fauna gasped. "That's quite early to tell someone, isn't it?"

"Would it be better that I fall in love with her, just for her to be disgusted by something I could not control?"

"I was talking about your failed marriage."

Aphrodite laughed quietly. "No, you were not."

Fauna smiled but did not admit it aloud. "And how did she respond?"

"She asked if she was in danger and if the girls were in danger. I knew that the moment she cared about the wellbeing of my daughters, that I wanted to fall in love with her."

"You didn't fall in love right then and there?"

"That's not how it works," Aphrodite said kindly and pointed to the books behind her. "These romantic novels paint love as a feeling so powerful that it takes over everything in your mind. But, what love actually is… is the desire to want to spend the rest of your life learning about someone. Wanting to experience all life has to offer, with them by your side."

"And when did the girls meet her?"

"The fourth night that she stayed for tea, I had asked if she would like to spend the night to avoid a snowstorm. That night, the storm raged on and it became very cold. She slept in my bed, but nothing unbecoming happened. Just two women sharing a bed. The girls stumbled in at dawn with their messy hair and morning grumpies and were very surprised to find someone with me. It sounds cliche, but that's how it happened. She talked to them and tickled them before breakfast and they were smitten immediately. They bonded with her and in turn, began to open up to me."

"So you found her in the woods and then fell in love?" Fauna asked, with a hand over her heart. "That's beautiful."

"It was," Aphrodite, still smiling, laughed softly. "I haven't thought about that in quite some time. It does seem so silly that it could happen like that. But, she fell in love right back. Even after I explained that I needed to hunt, she made a plan to gather blood ethically. We had only known each other for the better part of a fortnight, and yet she was willing to help."

"You got married too, right?"

"We did!" Aphrodite smiled with such *joy* that Fauna nearly wept. "I'm not ready for that talk, but I will be eventually."

"Did she ever get angry?" Fauna wondered. "The stories make her out to be happy all of the time."

"Just once, when the girls were turned into vampires in their sleep," Aphrodite admitted. "She got so mad that she laid with her arms around the girls in one bed for an entire day while they slept. No one, not even me, was allowed to come anywhere near them. She yelled at the staff and yelled at me. Never had she ever raised her voice, and she never did it again."

"Is that why they still look like teenagers?" Fauna asked. "I know the girls are much older than they seem. But if they came to you as children, I assume that they had time with you as mortal children."

Aphrodite nodded. "The Matron turned Bea on the night of her 18th birthday and when Scarlet came running at her sister's cries, she was turned as well. I always had a feeling the Matron would do it, so I had prepared myself for it, but... I was not. That should have been the reason that I eventually broke ties with her. She had an emotional hold on me though, and I will carry that forever. If I had, perhaps I would have had many more happy years with a healthy family."

"Is it too soon to ask what happened?" Fauna risked ruining it all to ask the most important question. "I read the book, but it's not very detailed."

"We had forty beautiful years together, and for that, I am so thankful." Aphrodite looked down at her hands. "She was my sun and my sky, the kind of woman that takes your breath away by just existing. She was *good* all the way through and through. Never once did she force my hand at all, but she had voiced her displeasure at how much The Matron asked of me. Whether it was running errands that had me out of the castle for weeks, or saying suspicious things about finding heirs for my girls. I heard over and over about how I deserved better, deserved a peaceful life. But, my wife's words eventually made it to the Matron and if there's one thing that woman hated, it was losing power. Over people, over her village, it didn't matter."

"So the Matron was threatened by your wife?"

Aphrodite nodded. "And just when I had gotten comfortable in my life with my family, the Matron swooped in and turned my wife into the same beast that I was. Only my wife was stronger than I was. She said no."

"Stronger?"

"She refused to feed," Aphrodite's voice cracked when she spoke. "Said she would never harm a living thing or consume any part of it. She held no judgment for her wife and children, but could not do it herself."

"So she didn't eat at all?"

Aphrodite shook her head.

"She starved to death?" Fauna gasped as a lump formed in her throat.

Aphrodite nodded and wiped discreetly at her eyes. "In my arms, in our rocking chair. She kept begging me to pretend that she was perfectly well and that the Matron's curse did not affect us."

"Just pretend!" Fauna remembered. "I heard that in my dreams!"

"In your dreams?" Aphrodite looked bewildered. She fell to her knees and placed her hands on Fauna's thighs, looking upwards with urgency. "What kind of dreams? Please tell me, I haven't had dreams in so long."

"When I was in the room!" Fauna pointed vaguely upstairs. "A woman would come to me and be so kind! She told me that it would be easier if I just pretended! Red hair and the sweetest smile I have ever seen?"

"*It's easier when you pretend,*" Aphrodite whispered with a husky voice. "It's what she told me when she made me wine mixed with blood for the first time. It's also what she told the girls when they were getting used to drinking blood with regular food. She said it a lot to calm us down."

"She danced with me," Fauna whimpered. "And was so gentle! She told me that I would be okay!"

"Then you have experienced her kindness and gentle spirit," Aphrodite sniffed and cleared her throat. "So you understand why her death weighs so heavily on this castle."

"I do!" Fauna began to cry. "Loves like that exist and then they are taken away! Why do we even love if that's all it ends up being!"

"Because happy endings are bittersweet," Aphrodite stood and pointed towards the door. "And rarely come true. But, that is enough for now. I am tired and *you* need to sleep in a proper bed."

Fauna knew that Aphrodite wanted time alone, so she agreed and stood. As she walked past Aphrodite, on a whim, she wrapped her arms around the woman. Aphrodite's dress felt soft and welcoming under her fingers as Fauna rubbed up and down her back. Aphrodite went still for a moment, before relaxing into the hug and squeezing Fauna tightly. Fauna heard the soft sniffles while they were hugging, so she stepped back quickly and bid Aphrodite goodnight before making her way to Rhiannon's room. When she slid into her makeshift bed, the weight of the past few hours hit Fauna hard and she fell asleep almost instantly, but not before wondering if the Lady of the Castle would ever visit her dreams again.

Twenty-One

The next morning found Fauna at a different table for breakfast. This time, instead of maids, she was sitting amongst a family of very familiar strangers. The Verity women valued practicality over gratuitous displays of wealth with their expensive but functional decor. Large windows let in a lot of natural light, while the high ceilings and low-strung lights made it a robustly refreshing room to gather in. Even the high-backed wooden chairs weren't overly decorated, but instead felt sturdy and meant to last for an entire lifetime… and maybe a little longer.

The girls, who were still a bit careful around Fauna, talked to each other but never quite spoke directly *to* her. Aphrodite Verity sat at the end of the table, eyes focused on a stack of papers in her hand and a plate of untouched but very delicious-looking fruits underneath her.

Desperate to ease the tension but pitifully awkward at speaking to others, Fauna took a deep breath and took the plunge.

"So, you eat real food too? If it's not too rude to ask."

Scarlet nodded and raised a finger to pause the conversation while she chewed. "For me, it's like putting a bandage on a gaping wound. It helps a little but doesn't solve much. I think we mostly do it so we can spend time together. That, and it helps me feel a little less… abnormal."

"And food is good," Bea laughed as she shrugged. "The cooks here are *very* talented."

"I mean, they've had a long time to learn from what I gather," Fauna tried to crack a joke. When the girls chuckled quietly, she relaxed into the conversation.

"You're taking this all suspiciously well." Bea eyed her suspiciously. "And not that I don't appreciate it, but I suppose I'm just curious as to *why*. You find out that we aren't quite normal, and that we have to feed on blood to survive, but you just accepted it."

Fauna exhaled softly as she tried to formulate a concise response. "I don't quite know. I think that I just learned it while something much more frightening was happening, so I glossed over it. Also, you have all assured me that no danger will come to me. Well, not at first. That was kind of scary."

"Mother can be very frightening when she wants to be," Scarlet nodded solemnly towards the end of the table, where Aphrodite sat quietly. "Don't make her mad."

"Oh! I don't plan on it," Fauna laughed nervously. "I think that your vampirism is the least shocking thing that's happened to me in the past few... months? Weeks? I don't even know."

"To be fair, we don't know how long it was either," Aphrodite chimed in finally. "I know little about the things happening in the village and I hardly think they would be kind enough to answer any questions we may have. So, to ask how long it's been since you were attacked is not likely to yield any results."

"And I'm not going back there." Fauna was adamant in her decision. "There is nothing for me. Just memories of things—like being set on fire—and a sad little silo with one pillow. I suppose my books are still there, but I assume they burnt those too, eventually. Besides, I kind of like it here. I don't feel unsafe."

"And we don't harm things," Scarlet said with an earnest nod. "Never will. Ever."

"So you're just hungry all of the time?" Fauna asked though she realized a bit too late that it might have been poor timing. "That has to be rather awful."

"No, we just don't like to hurt people," Bea explained in a quiet voice. "We were always taught that we are equals amongst all things. I also don't like violence. We didn't choose this, but we can choose how to manage it. So, we make do however we can."

Fauna thought that over for a moment. There was a lot of wisdom in Bea's words.

"We have a cellar where we have stored enough supplies for us to be sustained for quite a bit longer," Aphrodite explained as she raised her wine glass and set down her papers. "Do not worry about us or yourself. We will not need to restock for many years."

"Mother, when *do* you leave?" Scarlet asked, looking genuinely worried. "I'm going to miss you a lot."

"Tomorrow morning," Aphrodite looked at all three of them. "I will be gone for nearly a month. There is a lot for me to do and I have many things to search for. But I will be safe, do not worry too much about me. In my absence, you can get to know each other more. And you, Fauna, will be able to spread your wings in this castle. I've arranged for you to have a room and some basic clothing and amenities. I'm sure Rhiannon will be able to get you settled a bit more permanently if you're willing to stay here. I suppose that I should have asked, but you seem to be enjoying yourself."

Fauna nodded. "Thank you, Lady Verity, I appreciate it. I like everyone here very much and I have nowhere else to go."

"And you two know the rules," Aphrodite spoke to her children.

Bea smiled sadly. "We do. No trips outside the castle, no hurting each other, and no setting the library on fire."

Fauna quickly looked at the eldest sibling.

Bea snickered. "Just kidding. Well, kind of. It's a long story."

After a long day of helping Rhiannon mend the maid's clothes and talking about their favorite books, Fauna practically fell into her bed after dinner. Aphrodite had been absent from the table due to packing and the girls were glued to her side as she did so. Rhiannon had invited Fauna to the maid's table where she listened to theories about where the missing maids had gone off too. Gelon had popped by towards the end to procure an apple and offer her two cents to the conversation.

From there, Fauna enjoyed a nice bath and eventually made her way to her new room. Even though she had seen it earlier that day, she had not slept in it. It was strange to be away from Rhiannon for the night, but the privacy was great. Fauna's journal and pen set—the only remnants of her time upstairs—laid on a sturdy wooden desk, ready to be written in.

She snagged it before sliding back into bed and opening the cover. Relief filled her when she saw her writing on the pages. Too mentally exhausted to re-read anything she had written, Fauna turned to a fresh page and began a new entry.

I am Fauna.

That has never been up for debate. But the facets of my personality are slowly breaking apart. I yearned for silence, for desolation and isolation amongst my disparaging view of society. And yet, here I am crying over a love between others so divine that it was seemingly born in the books themselves… a love that died alongside the life of this castle. Everyone is so sad and now I understand why. How could someone so… good be taken in such a horrific way?

I'm currently situated in my new room. It looks freshly polished, with nothing on the walls, and now I'm alone again. But I don't like it. Does that make me a hypocrite? Am I a liar? Was I wrong all along? Perhaps. I liked having Rhiannon as a roommate, but I know I will see her tomorrow, so I doubt I will miss her too much.

I can hear the bustle of the castle outside my door—the repairs are almost finished. The noise makes me feel safe… I don't know if I'll ever be able to handle silence again. The Verity history book said that the castle should not know silence at all… but I have yet to hear a single person sing. Is it too painful? Do they sound as dreadful as I do when I sing? Why does it matter? Who cares if we are good? We would be fulfilling a wish.

I see now why Rhiannon told me to stay away from the cellar. Without any context, that would have been terrifying. Wait, did Rhiannon actually tell me that or was it all part of the illusion? Is it wrong to ask? I am dreadfully curious about how it all works. They have large windows that let in beautiful, natural light and they aren't pale like the vampires I've read about. Their teeth seem normal, not that I've looked. Almost everything I've ever read about vampires is wrong. Well, or maybe I just don't understand. Or they aren't normal vampires. Are "normal" vampires even a thing?

I feel as if I will never be able to separate what happened upstairs from the people who live in this castle. But, time will tell I suppose. And considering I might be the youngest person here… time is something we all have. Can I ask how old people are here? I'm almost afraid of the answers that I'll get. I think Rhiannon is mortal, like me—I should ask her. I should also ask her why she thinks no one likes her; everyone I have spoken to speaks quite highly of her.

Regardless, I hope that I sleep well tonight. I wish I could summon the Lady of the Castle—we would have much to talk about. Perhaps she could teach me to paint. What a silly thought.

The next morning went the same as the last, only after breakfast was a teary goodbye from the girls and their mother. Aphrodite, dressed in her outerwear but still impressively put together, handled their cries with maternal calmness and kindness. After bidding the girls farewell, she brought Fauna into a hug—one that was *very* unexpected, and let her go with a gentle pat on her shoulder. As Fauna and Rhiannon walked away, Fauna found herself touching her cheek where a particularly cold button on Aphrodite's jacket had pressed against the skin. She'd grown rather fond of Aphrodite again and little things started to make Fauna smile.

Enjoying the silence, Rhiannon and Fauna walked around the castle, enjoying their people-watching, until Fauna's curiosity got the best of her.

"How old are you?"

"Twenty-three," Rhiannon spoke with a coy tone. "And I'm not lying."

"Are you perpetually that age?" Fauna asked but made it clear she was being humorous.

Rhiannon shook her head. "Nope. I'm that age. The Matron never cared much about the staff being turned at all. We seemed pretty insignificant to her. Most of the ones who were turned here were afflicted because they asked to be."

"Being ignored seems like a blessing and a curse," Fauna admitted. "A little dehumanizing but also the safest option?"

"You're right!" Rhiannon laughed a little. "She never once knew my name but still could pick me out of a crowd because of my hair. Even as a child, she gave me the worst looks. Said I was born out of something foul, blah blah. Regardless, she never did more than scowl at me, so I consider myself lucky."

"Maybe she was jealous of your hair." Fauna reached up slowly and tugged softly on one ringlet before letting it spring back into place. "It is quite pretty."

"I'm glad you think so," Rhiannon laughed. "My mother used to curse over it. I hated baths as a child and never let her comb it, so I ran around with who knows what in my hair until I was twelve!"

"And then boys entered the picture?" Fauna rolled her eyes goodnaturedly.

"Everyone entered the picture!" Rhiannon laughed. "Suddenly, everyone was beautiful and I was an urchin hissing in the corner. Safe to say, Scarlet helped me a lot with my hair after my mom passed. Her hair is more soft and wavy than my tighter curls, but still. It was nice to have someone who understood. And that's how we became friends!"

"You and Scarlet?" Fauna asked as they turned a corner. "Cute. You two are very different, but I feel like differences can make the best of friends."

"We're different enough that we can learn things from each other, but similar enough to know what the other needs. I can tell when she needs someone to listen, and she can tell when I just need reassurance that I'm not the worst person ever."

Fauna stopped walking and turned to her friend. "Why would you think that? You're *wonderful*."

"It's not often that I hear nice things, especially when my back is turned," Rhiannon admitted. "The older maids here don't like me because I was born in another village but raised here. They say I didn't earn my place. I think it's because my mother was very close to Lady Aphrodite when she was alive."

"Your mother was a maid?"

Rhiannon nodded. "She was a personal maid, though Lady Aphrodite didn't treat her like a servant or anything. My mother did all kinds of things around the castle. Sometimes she helped Gelon with writing in the book when her hands were sore. Sometimes she would help tend to the garden. That was my favorite chore. She used to sit me on one of the ceramic benches and task me with removing all the seeds from the sunflowers. It kept me busy for hours, so I didn't get under anyone's feet."

"When did she die?"

"Three years ago," Rhiannon told her. "She went to sleep and just didn't wake up. She's buried in the castle's cemetery right next to my grandmother."

"I'm so sorry that happened. I didn't even know that there was a cemetery here," Fauna admitted. "Do you know where it is?"

"Way out on the edge of the property—it takes almost a full hour to get there and back if you walk. I only go once a year. It's not very extravagant."

Fauna began to walk again. "I understand. Is it only staff buried there?"

"And their families, should they suggest that."

Rhiannon seemed to appreciate that and began to walk again. She looked towards the stairs to the side and pointed. "The staircase leading upstairs is just ahead. It's been a while since you've been up there. Do you want to go again to visit?"

"Not yet," Fauna replied. "I think when I go, it should be Aphrodite and myself. Together we can destroy the room, if she hasn't already. I don't trust myself to be up there alone. What if I get sucked in again?"

"I didn't think of that," Rhiannon admitted. "I doubt she's been in that room at all since you two left it. It's locked up for a reason. That and the room with the pretty window, have been forbidden to visit since I've been alive."

Fauna shook her head and kept walking. "So much history in this castle, and yet so much of it is shrouded within tragedy. Sounds about right for this family."

"It only gets worse, honestly," Rhiannon admitted. "The Verity women are extremely kind and no one seems to know it. Even when some of the maids go back to the village, their husbands tell them that they shouldn't work in such a foul place. But, have you ever seen any cruelty here? No. And you won't! It's all just rumors that spread. But, even if everyone out there has the wrong impression, it means the castle knows peace, which is important too. All it would take is a mob to tear this place apart. Look what they did to you! Just think of what would happen to the family here."

"The last time I checked, this castle was something generally revered by the villagers. I think they'll be safe. And if Aphrodite was willing to kill someone like the Matron for her children, she could keep everyone safe. Thanks for walking with me." Fauna reached out and squeezed Rhiannon's shoulder, hoping that was an appropriate thing to do. Being a friend was much more difficult than the books had made it seem. Perhaps it would become second nature to her in due time.

Rhiannon gently bumped her shoulder into Fauna's as they walked. "Of course, silly!"

"Oh, hello!" Gelon called from her desk. In front of her, a mountain of paperwork was nearly stacked high enough to cover her face. "Here to look at the book again?"

Fauna smiled softly. "Just for a little bit. I want to read a little more. I fell asleep last time and didn't get to finish the section that I was at."

Gelon looked at her with a very knowing look. "It's a tough one, that's for sure. I'll bring it over in a bit. Until then, feel free to get comfortable in one of the chairs. I just stoked the fire, so it should be cozy."

Fauna nodded before heading over to the chair and pulling the hem of her new dress over her knees. Her bumps and bruises from her tumble down the stairs had all but faded, and her broken finger still sat taped ramrod straight against the ones next to it. Thankfully it wasn't on her writing hand. That would have been awful.

It felt strange being in Aphrodite's office without her in the castle, but everyone around had said that she was allowed to be there. The big secret was out and Fauna genuinely wasn't worried about her safety. But based on the way people in the village spoke of the castle, she'd assumed that she would be stuck in some torture chamber. To think that the women of Castle Verity had been some of the kindest people to ever meet her... well, that was a lesson that the books hadn't taught her.

"You know, they seem happier with you around," Gelon said warmly as she leaned over the back of the chair and set the large tome in Fauna's lap. "The air in this castle was so... stale for so long, it was as if everyone had lost the desire to do anything. Even though you had a strange introduction to everyone here, it seems that you've fit right in. And if we're being honest, I'm happy that strange girl has a friend. Rhiannon? She's far too full of life to live and die in this place."

"Can she leave?" Fauna realized she never asked about the terms of their employment.

"Everyone here is free to go as they please," Gelon assured her. "Some of the workers here have families that they see on the weekends. The ones that have no one still venture into the town for whatever tickles their fancy. No one is ever held here against their will, and they never will be."

"That's good to hear," Fauna admitted. "The *rumor* was that this castle is filled with monsters and things that rip you to pieces and shred your soul. I was always taught that the deviant and miscreants ended up here to be fed upon and discarded."

"And yet here we are, a castle filled with people who just want to exist peacefully with each other. Nothing is taken from anyone and everything is earned. In a world run by men competing for senseless titles and money, women silently make sure the world doesn't go to shit."

"So very true," Fauna laughed as she accepted the book. "I'll leave this on your desk when I'm done if that's okay? I'm scared that I'll damage it if I try to maneuver it back how you had it."

Gelon nodded to her and patted her shoulder as she turned back to her desk. Fauna looked down at the large book again and it hit her just how *old* it was. Even the inks inside hadn't faded. Though, she wondered if it would be helpful to have a copy made at some point. When Aphrodite returned, she would ask. She opened the book again and flipped through the pages until she found where she had left off. By the swirls and intricate lines, it seemed to be Aphrodite's personal musings.

How does one fall in love with the sun? Am I the moon, perpetually destined to chase one so beautiful and yet always fall short? Or is my presence needed to keep her moving forward? Am I willing to run and run, just to make sure my lover—the sun—has something to look forward to? I certainly am.

And what happens when the sun dies? Am I supposed to carry the burden of eternal darkness on my own? Is it my turn to carry a lantern over the world, lest the darkness come and never leave? To make sure the sun can rest, I will take this pledge. For I do not love the world, but I love the sun that illuminates it in my wake.

Further down the page, another paragraph of writing made Fauna's heart hurt.

"Do you ever look up at the stars and wonder where they came from? Are they lost souls, wandering in eternity? Perhaps they are little bits of joy, stashed amongst the clouds for only those who fly to see. And as monstrous and mangled as I am, I cannot fly. My wings are clipped and they will never heal.

"There's always one star in the sky that shines brighter than the rest. Do you think that it's the same for all of us? Or does each star pick someone down on this lonely planet to love? Well, the star that shines for me—the one so beautiful and filled with awe and joy?

"I know the woman who hung it there."

Hearing the last line again hit Fauna square in the chest and before she knew it, the tears came and did not stop. Her breaths stuttered in her chest as she tried her best to stay quiet. Whether Aphrodite had written it as a diary entry or simply part of the family's history, it still tore a gaping hole in Fauna's heart. It had been years since it was written, maybe even a century, but the grief still felt fresh. It felt wrong to keep reading, so Fauna shut the book and took a moment to catch her breath.

When Gelon saw Fauna's splotchy face and puffy eyes, she looked at her sympathetically. "I know, I know. It's a hard part to read. Where did you leave off?"

"She hung the star in the sky that Aphrodite loved so much."

Gelon inhaled sharply before turning away. "I had forgotten about that part. Yes, Lady Aphrodite is very talented in many aspects and words are no exception. Have you seen her paintings?"

"I saw one, just for a second though," Fauna admitted. "I saw a lady with butterflies. It was beautiful."

"That is a wonderful one." Gelon's voice trailed off for a moment. "That woman loved to paint. She used to tell us about all the beautiful things in the world, amongst all the chaos. No matter how much death, despair, and debauchery happened around us, the world was still beautiful and Aphrodite wanted to paint it all."

"Why did she stop?" Fauna asked even though she felt as if she already knew the answer.

Gelon sighed and looked away. "The world lost its beauty when she lost her wife. Simply put. It's hard to see anything hopeful in a situation like that."

Familiar with mourning but not exactly how to do it properly, Fauna sat for a moment, trying to put herself in Aphrodite's shoes. To lose someone so important to her and everyone around her must have such a terrible feeling. Grieving a spouse was one thing, but grieving a mother and someone *so* beloved by everyone around? Misery. Pure misery.

After a minute of silence. Gelon gently got her attention by waving her hand. "All done with the book for now? Just leave it there. Will you be back tomorrow?"

Fauna shrugged. "I'm not exactly sure. I don't have structured days yet, so I hesitate to make any plans. I would like to come back though."

"Well if you ever want to be sealed away in a quiet place while Lady Aphrodite is gone, you're always welcome here. You clean up after yourself and you know how to take good care of the books. Just make sure to balance your time! You don't want to get sucked into the library and forget about the rest of your well-deserved new life. Besides, we'll need to talk in-depth so I can chronicle your time above."

"Would you like to borrow my journal?" Fauna offered. "It has letters and games I played with the people upstairs."

Gelon looked shocked at the offer. "Well, if you're okay with that? Sure, drop it by sometime. It won't take me too long."

With that, Fauna agreed and snuggled down into the chair. Lost in the flicker and crackle of the flames, she let herself be carried away by visions of women with butterflies and dancing under the stars.

Twenty-Two

"**I** knew the woman who hung it there."

The line played over and over in Fauna's mind, permeating her waking and sleeping thoughts. It sat heavy in her heart, keeping her tethered to someone else's grief. Even her trips up and down the hallways were spent thinking about the phrase. It became so all-encompassing that the incredible breakfast the next morning didn't grab her attention. It wasn't until Scarlet said her name multiple times and waved a hand in front of her face, that Fauna realized just how out of it she had been.

"So… do you have a boyfriend?" Scarlet asked very loudly. "Hello?"

Fauna's ears burned in embarrassment. "I do not."

Scarlet tilted her head to the side in the most precious gesture. "Girlfriend?"

Fauna shook her head again. "I don't even have a *friend*."

Scarlet looked *offended*. "What are *we* then? Rhiannon? That's rude."

Fauna tripped over her words as she clarified. "I don't know. I thought that I had made friends with you when I was up in that room and I got very attached. But now, you're so familiar but also not. I feel weird knowing so much about you, but about things you never actually told me. It's kind of unfair to you."

"So, tell us about yourself," Bea offered as she swirled her breakfast around her plate. "Make it even. We never get visitors, especially nice ones, so it's nice to have someone new here. Mother seems to like you too. She only threatened you once. That's not too bad, considering what kind of mood she was in."

"How old are you?" Scarlet eyed her. "You look like you're twenty."

"Chubby cheeks and little sunlight," Fauna offered. "I'm thirty-five."

"Oh, well that's still young compared to us." Scarlet motioned to her sister and herself. "I stopped counting ages ago. Numbers are silly, in my opinion."

"Time moves differently when you have an abundance of it," Bea explained. "A week for you is a year for us. We've learned how to pass the time. Otherwise, I would have died of boredom here. Well, metaphorically speaking."

"I have no concept of time right now," Fauna replied. "I only know that it's getting colder at night, which means I've been gone at least a season or two. Or twenty. Sometimes I wonder if I'm even real."

"Gelon said that no one has even mentioned your disappearance," Bea admitted. "Which is strange considering they tried to kill you. But, even then, she spends most of her time corresponding with people about investments and other boring things that she and Mother deal with. The village day-to-day is more of an afterthought. Though, I wonder if they know that the Matron is dead."

"I didn't have much of an impact on the community," Fauna explained. "I got my things in the market, I bought books, and I went back to my home. I didn't speak to anyone, I didn't stop unless I had to. I grew most of my food, and the rest of it was purchased when no one else was around. The people around me knew better than to try to interact with me."

"You didn't talk to anyone?" Scarlet looked at her like she was insane. "Like, there were so many people around you and you didn't even say hello?"

Fauna shook her head. "No. I didn't like them so I didn't even try. I almost forgot that I needed to talk to ask for things. All that got my attention was books. My quiet time was where I found true peace. I didn't need or want anything they had to give me, other than the basics. I raised myself after a certain age when my father stopped speaking to me. So, it's always been just me. I like it that way. "

Fauna watched both of the Verity siblings exchange a wordless look before an awkward silence descended on the table. It was even more unsettling without Lady Aphrodite there to appease any tensions. Somehow she had made them upset, though she couldn't figure out how. Didn't Scarlet just say they were friends?

After a grueling few minutes of uncomfortable silence and very conspicuous pointed looks, Bea set her fork down with a little too much force and looked directly at Fauna.

"Do you want to guess how long it's been since I've spoken to anyone outside of this castle? Go on... *guess*."

Fauna felt herself being set up for a punchline but didn't quite understand if the question was rhetorical or not. There was no way to win, no matter what answer she gave. So, she said the first thing that came to mind.

"A few months?"

"Thirty years," Bea informed her. "Thirty years of never meeting anyone new, never having a casual conversation with someone who didn't know me."

"Twelve for me," Scarlet chimed in. "We used to have deliveries from the local farmers and I was tasked to receive them. So, it was never anything fun or engaging. My last *fun* conversation with a stranger? So far back that I can't even remember."

"And you want to speak to them? I can assure you they aren't that interesting. Most of them can't read or write and they only care about booze and their nightly proclivities." Fauna scrunched up her nose in distaste.

"But that's the thing, you lived there—you *already* knew that. We are stuck in this castle, we don't get to leave if we want," Bea tried to explain. "We see the staff that comes and goes, obviously. But for our safety, we can't venture outside the castle grounds."

"Well, why not?" Fauna waited for the reply.

"Mother said so," Scarlet admitted with wide, frightened eyes. "She told us that the Matron held her to a *very* high standard. And though the Matron is gone, Mother is still frightened of her. She's… lost a lot and we try not to make it worse. You don't even know a sliver of what's happened to her."

"You're afraid of her still?" Fauna asked with genuine interest. "The Matron?"

"She killed our mother. The *other* one," Scarlet said sternly with a wavering voice. "Someone so near and dear to us, that we boarded up an entire wing of the castle. Do you know the pain of someone being torn from your life? Especially someone so kind and altruistic?"

The realization hit Fauna. She did not. She knew grief but had always felt that it was for others and not her. Grief was for those who lost someone dear to them, and although her father had previously been dear to her, her anger over his silence overtook all of it. She wasn't happy her father was dead—not at all. However, there was a lingering resentment over the fact that the one parent she desperately wanted to meet, had died. And the other one wanted nothing to do with her for years.

Bea yelled and slammed her hands on the table. "Do you know what it's like to want so *badly* to speak to people who aren't afraid of you? Do you know what it's like to see the same walls every day for hundreds of years? Do you know the pain of mourning someone relentlessly, when their killer is part of your family and had such an emotional stronghold on your mother that everyone is scared to speak out?"

Fauna was quiet at the outburst. Once again, she did not know the feeling. Properly embarrassed, she swallowed quickly to avoid crying. She did not like it when her friends were upset, especially if they were upset with her.

"At some point, you need to realize that books are made to be entertainment, not a blueprint for life," Scarlet, now much softer, told Fauna. "You have free will and we do not. Don't forget that."

Fauna felt the tears of shame begin to well in her eyes and she looked away. "I'm sorry."

Scarlet shook her head. "No, I am too. I get very nervous with Mother gone and I'm taking it out on you. It's not your fault any of those things happened, and I shouldn't have gotten so hostile."

"I'm also sorry, but you *did* deserve some of that," Bea said with a small smile. "Just a little, though."

Fauna thought for a moment. Perhaps she would try to alleviate the tension instead of wallowing in it. "Would you want to have a picnic in the gardens this afternoon? We could celebrate life instead of mourn it?"

The sisters looked at each other with hopeful expressions. Finally, a smile broke through Scarlet's facade and she brightened. "Please? It's been so long!"

"I would love that." Bea turned to her sister. "We could show her the greenhouse?"

Fauna's jaw dropped. "You have a greenhouse? Why have I never seen it?"

Bea turned to her. "It's on the other side of the gardens! It's a bit of a walk, but we have all the time in the world! Oh, it's so beautiful that you're going to want to move in there and live amongst the plants!"

Fauna laughed. "One question. Do the immortality jokes ever get old?"

"Nope!" The sisters laughed together as they jumped up.

"Meet us at noon in the gardens!" Scarlet shoved the last bit of food in her mouth and turned to run away.

The Verity garden was strangely empty for such a well-tended place. High walls, similar to a maze, boasted pops of vibrant color that made Fauna want to skip and gallivant like a child. A tender breeze blew around them, bending the branches of the trees and dancing over the leaves. A single statue of a weeping angel in a chair sat directly in the middle. Around the statue's feet, concrete animals lay staring up in awe. A single bench, big enough for two to sit and be one with the garden, sat against the angel's back as if the resident was sharing a tender moment under a tree with a friend. Tucked between the stone animals were more flowers, giving the atmosphere a little bit of hope. From afar, Fauna could picture the exact scene it was based on.

A small stone plaque stood out amongst the bricks of the garden floor. Upon it was a very touching epitaph:

Here Lies a Soul Whose Love Inspired Us All

She tended to hearts as tenderly as she did her flowers. Her melody lives on in our hearts and we will never stop singing her song.

Fauna knelt before the plaque and gently brushed away a dirty leaf that had landed on it. For a moment, she simply looked at the words etched into the stone. How could she tell the Lady of the Castle that the castle *had* gone silent? Affectionately, Fauna followed the swirl of the script with a finger, tracing the shapes and dips of the writing.

She looked up and stared at the statue with love in her chest. Was it possible to love someone who had been dead for so many years? Regardless, she had helped form the people that Fauna trusted most in life, so she felt that at least a small moment of appreciation was necessary.

"Is she buried here?" Fauna asked gently.

Bea nodded and smiled at Fauna before gazing at the statue with profound love. It was nice to see her joyous instead of swallowed whole by her grief. "She is the angel."

Fauna took a moment to pay her respects.

"Would you like to sit with me?"

Bea shook her head. "Not yet. But thank you. I'm going to go look around, it's been far too long since I've been here."

Fauna stood from her squat and made sure to avoid the flowers as she walked towards the angel. As she sat down, a gentle hum of emotion began to buzz in her chest. To ground herself, she gently ran her fingernails back and forth on the bench, enjoying the feeling of it on her skin. She closed her eyes and focused on her other senses. The sweet smell of flowers and the breeze on her cheeks. The longer she sat there, the emotion in her chest swelled until fat, hot tears began to dribble down her cheeks.

She *cried*.

Not tears of fear or pain. Not grief over someone else. Just tears that encompassed years of loneliness disguised as willful solitude and the fear of the world. Her anger towards her upbringing had been the scapegoat for all of Fauna's resentment. She wanted to love, hug, kiss, and bond with people. She wanted to shop and bake and go to places. She wanted to learn, she wanted to hold someone's hand. She wanted her mother alive and well.

And so did the Verity daughters. They wanted their mother back too.

Instead of the damning dread that used to fill Fauna's heart, she now felt a sense of belonging. She had something in common with someone. Something more than just a love for books. She sat like that for quite a while, so long that the tears on her cheeks were chilled by the wind and her chest hurt as if she'd run for an hour.

"Come, Fauna!" Scarlet called to her. "There is so much to see!"

With her reverie interrupted, Fauna stood from her perch and vowed to return to the area. She cast the angel a passing glance and felt something indescribable fill her heart. After a gentle pat on the angel's arm, she turned to face the girls that had brought her there.

"Look! Those are the roses she loved so much!" Scarlet pointed with so much excitement that Fauna could *feel* the joy radiating off of her. "Do you remember the day they arrived, Bea?"

"Mother worked tirelessly to have them delivered from the south." Bea turned to Fauna to further explain as she laid out the picnic blanket on a grassy patch. "I remember *you* pricking your finger on them and crying because you had never seen blood before!"

Scarlet's jaw dropped as she seemed to think about it. "I only just remembered that. How weird is that? Now I feel as if it's all that I know. I forgot that I was once that innocent."

Fauna watched the sisters bicker and reminisce with a fondness in her heart. It was wonderful to see them so happy. She never quite understood the idea of having a sister. The only examples were the girls in the village, but they only talked about which boy to marry and which method of proofing bread dough was best. She'd always wondered what it was like to have a sibling but the idea of being in charge of anyone's safety but her own did not sound appealing in the slightest. However, seeing the little glimpses between the Verity sisters warmed a little piece of Fauna's heart.

"One time," Scarlet began a scandalous story as she unpacked some cheese. "Bea got mad at me for something stupid and she threw my poems in the fireplace!"

"I would cry so hard!" Fauna gasped and looked incredulously at the eldest sister, who only shrugged. "I barely trusted Gelon to have my journal!"

"Well, she *thought* they were my poems," Scarlet snickered. "They were some important documents that the Matron had sent Mother... and I was trying to peek at them but Bea threw them in the fireplace!"

"I got in so much trouble," Bea whined as she sat down. "It took me ages to be able to go to the library again. I genuinely thought I was going to be taken to Hurmehovi."

"I don't know why that reminded me." Fauna temporarily changed the subject. "I was able to read the book in your mother's office. The really big one?"

"Oh!" Scarlet paled. "Did you read any of the things that I wrote? Oh, that would be so embarrassing. I could barely spell, let alone keep a rhythm."

Fauna shook her head. "I skimmed it but I didn't retain anything. I mostly was looking for the reason everyone in this castle seems so sad all the time."

"And why we never go to the gardens," Bea said quietly. "I haven't been out here in years, I had almost forgotten how much care goes into it. I should take more time to appreciate this place."

"Rhiannon showed me the window up there." Fauna pointed and squinted at the small but ornate window. "What room is that?"

"Oh." Bea got very quiet. "That was a reading room."

"Is that not a library?" Fauna was a little confused. "I thought they were the same thing."

Scarlet shook her head and popped some bread in her mouth. "A reading room is sort of like a little miniature room with no distractions. We weren't allowed in there—we were quite noisy as children."

"Even as adults, we're rather noisy," Bea laughed softly. "Some-times."

"Do you still want to see the greenhouse?" Scarlet asked though she was still staring up at the window. It was becoming more and more obvious that the prior energy had faded.

"I think we could stay here. The greenhouse isn't going any-where," Fauna agreed.

As the picnic began, Fauna noticed that the girls seemed dis-tracted once again. She ate quietly and watched them give each other silent looks and little calming gestures. Fauna wanted that. She wanted someone to wordlessly make her feel better. But, even though she was more comfortable with it, asking for it was something completely different.

The sisters stared up at the window until the sun traveled too far west. Fauna laid on her stomach and watched the window as well, daydreaming about what kind of love it would take to have someone bring flowers in from so far away. And if that was the same woman that appeared in her dreams, well, it all made sense. It was obvious that the love between the Verity family was very strong, forged by deep emotional bonds. It was nice to see, but Fauna couldn't help but resent the fact that she would never have that for herself.

The sun began to set and the stained glass window slowly became obscured by the twilight. A symphony of evening insects began to play, while the moon started her journey to the top of the sky.

"I… think I'm going to go write a bit," Scarlet said quietly as she stood. "Thank you both for the company. We should do this again soon."

"I think I'll do the same, actually," Bea agreed and stood. "Is it okay if we leave you with the cleanup?"

Fauna nodded gently. "Sure. Let me know when you want to show me the greenhouse."

With that, the girls left, leaving Fauna with a small blanket of crumbs and a lot to think about. Once she had packed up the remnants of their afternoon, she walked back to the angel and sat on the bench once more. As the moon rose higher and higher and the sky got darker, she sat and pondered what Aphrodite would learn on her journey to Hurmehovi and if Fauna truly wanted to know anything at all.

Twenty-Three

Later that week, Fauna once again found herself in the common library, sitting sideways and dangling her feet off the edge of the chair. She knew better than to sit that way, but it invoked a certain childlike glee that she was rarely able to experience. She closed the book in her lap and took a deep breath. It was nice to be able to read without fear in the back of her mind. The pictures in her mind seemed more colorful and clear when she was truly able to *focus*. On a whim, she jumped up and slid the book back into its slot on the shelf. With a little pep in her step, Fauna climbed the first few rungs of the ladder attached to the shelves of books. She hadn't had the opportunity to explore the collection and she always felt like she was being watched when others were around.

The floor-to-ceiling shelves were packed with books of all colors and sizes. It was a nice surprise to see so many different subjects tucked into the shelves. She almost wished she could explore the other libraries, but knew that even the common one would keep her busy for ages.

She climbed two more rungs and skimmed her fingers across the spines of the books on the top shelf. Fauna, utterly overwhelmed in the best sort of way, grabbed whatever caught her eye and slid down the rungs until her socked feet touched the floor.

She arranged the books in a stack on the floor and threw more kindling into the fireplace, adding an aura of warmth and light to the chilly room. She peeked tentatively outside and decided it was nearing midnight by the placement of the moon. After the long day she'd had, she assumed that she would be exhausted, but she still had a flicker of energy in her chest. So, instead of laying awake in her bed doing nothing but trying to sleep, Fauna had come to the library with the goal of calming her mind with a good book.

The crease in the spine on the cover of the first book caught her eye. Someone had read this book far more than once. Though there was no love note in the front of the book like there was in the one she had found in the office, the care taken to the rest of the book indicated just how important it was to someone. All of the books in the library looked as if they were brand new.

For what seemed like hours, Fauna found herself lost in a story. It began with a man recounting his life and turned into something so grandiose and fantastical that Fauna almost couldn't turn the pages fast enough. Oh, the *adventures* her mind was going on.

And then a cough startled her.

"That one's of my favorites," Lady Aphrodite—still in her travel clothes—pointed to the book in Fauna's hand. "I've been searching all around for you. I should have known that you would be found here. You seem comfortable."

"You're back!" Fauna cheered quietly but immediately stopped. "Very early! Too early? You've only been gone just over a week! Is that cause for celebration?"

Lady Aphrodite took a seat in the chair across from her and seemed to melt into it with exhaustion. "I was only at Hurmehovi for two days before I decided to come back and explain what I found. We have much to discuss—there are things I found up there that affect us both."

Fauna blanched. "Both of us?"

Aphrodite groaned in exertion and stood again. "I need a glass of wine and to take off these shoes. Would you care to meet me in my atelier? I know it's late, but you seem awake enough. It could be a while, but I wanted to tell you as soon as I came back."

Fauna nodded, the novel in her hand suddenly not nearly as important as it was. The entire time she spent putting the book back, she wondered just what could have been so interesting that Aphrodite would cut her trip so short.

The emerald green walls of Aphrodite's painting room were much more foreboding when shrouded in midnight's darkness. Fauna wandered into the room slowly and when she noticed she was alone, she dutifully took a seat on the couch. The painting still stood in the middle of the room with a sheet over it again and while she wanted nothing more than to peek at it, she did not. Aphrodite had begun to trust her and that was the most important thing of all.

The door opened again, revealing Aphrodite, still looking rather exhausted but in fresh clothes and house slippers. She held two wine glasses and a dark bottle of red wine, which she carefully sat down on the table closest to her stool.

"Thank you for meeting me here." Aphrodite smiled in a thin, sarcastic line. "I sound like a businessman."

"You're welcome to speak plainly if that helps." Fauna hoped she didn't offend the woman. "We're comfortable here, yes? Don't worry about my feelings in all of this. Regardless of what happened, I am okay."

Aphrodite nodded in agreement and popped the cork out of her wine. "I'll let this breathe while we speak. You might want a glass later as well."

They sat there for quite a while, Fauna staring at Aphrodite, who was staring at the moon through the small slits in the window high above them. The normally regent and stoic woman was clearly uncomfortable—her fingers played with the edges of her robe and she tapped the edge of her slipper against one of the wooden legs of her stool. Each breath she took seemed to be difficult, based on her loud inhales and tight-lipped exhales. Fauna was ready to burst—she *had* to know what was bothering Aphrodite so badly.

"How well did you know your father?" Aphrodite spoke, though she did not turn from the moon. "Were you two close? I know we've talked about him briefly, however, much has happened since and the details have left me."

Fauna took a deep breath to calm her nerves. She identified a fraying gold thread on the arm of the couch and began to pick and pull at it. "In my youth, he tolerated all of my insubordination when it came to the Matron. But, as I aged, he pulled away from me. By the time he died, we hadn't spoken in years. It was almost like he stopped existing altogether. He didn't go outside, he didn't speak, and in his final years he barely even moved. At least, he didn't when I visited him."

"But you were with him until the end, correct?" Aphrodite asked gently. "The entire time."

"Not all of the time. I would pop in once a day and try to engage with him, but he only stared at the walls and ignored me."

"Did he ever mention your mother?"

"When I was younger, he kept her keepsakes safe. And he would stare at a picture of her for a long while. But those days ended before I had hit my teenage years."

Aphrodite sighed before visibly debating her words. "Did you read the book in the office?"

"With Gelon? Yes, I did. Not all of it—it's very large. But, she directed me to the important parts."

"Ah, Gelon, a true friend and very funny woman," Aphrodite smiled, charmingly distracted for a brief moment. "You two will be quick friends. You should see her after a few glasses of wine, she has many stories of being a crew hand on a ship in her youth."

"Gosh, that sounds so interesting!" Fauna replied. "I will make sure to ask her about that. Why do you ask about the book, though?"

Aphrodite tore her gaze from the moon and swiveled on her stool to grab the wine and glasses. As she began to pour, she started her story. "Well, the Matron's island in the sky has indeed fallen into ruin. I had not been there in quite some time. When I arrived, I noticed that there was not a soul left. And when I let myself into her castle, I did not hear a single thing. No bustle, not even breathing. It was extremely odd. The walls were clean and there were no signs of battle, so I investigated further."

"I heard she had armies and lots of weapons up there." Fauna tried to remember the stories of her childhood. "People said she took prisoners and made them her servants."

"Perhaps she did, I was not allowed very far into Hurmehovi—my hunger would grow to be insatiable while I was there. When I was summoned, I would wait in the main area until the Matron came to me. However, if I proceeded toward her laboratories or personal quarters, I would be overcome with a need to destroy—an urge to become feral and quite dangerous. She would never explain why."

"And this time?"

"The hunger was there, but not the urge to destroy anything. I had no aggression, just a burning urge to feed on anything I could get my hands on."

"I wonder what that means?" Fauna pondered aloud.

"I believe that whatever the Matron had in her laboratory, it called to me and unleashed a thirst in I couldn't control."

"How exactly does she have so much control over you? You seem like a very independent woman who doesn't take direction from just anyone."

Aphrodite sighed and took another long sip. "You have to understand, I had known her for years when she turned me. I was dreadfully lonely, spending all my time in my bed and only walking when necessary. She was the one visitor who seemed to want to see me. I held a certain type of love for her—and even a certain degree of respect. I trusted her judgment and even after I was turned... I let her tell me what to do. She gave me life, children, and an estate to run. I did owe her a lot. She felt like a second mother to me, though she was more of a creator than much else."

"Your daughters do not like her at all." Fauna pointed out. "Did that ever weigh on you?"

Aphrodite sighed. "It did, quite a bit. They were right to feel that way. Yes, the Matron gave me children, but she killed their parents and stole their happiness."

"Twice," Fauna added.

"Yes," Aphrodite admitted. "Twice."

The conversation stopped for a moment. Aphrodite poured herself another glass and looked at Fauna for a moment. When Fauna nodded, Aphrodite poured a second one and handed it over. Fauna, who had drank water and milk most of her life, just copied what Aphrodite did.

"Is this blood wine?" Fauna looked at the crimson liquid in her glass.

Aphrodite shook her head. "No, I wouldn't give that to you. I needed something strong after my journey. I couldn't stop worrying over what to tell you and how to say it."

"So far it hasn't been much," Fauna replied. "What else was there?"

"Well, I started to notice that there were dead ravens in the strangest of places. In front of the doors, in the common area, and even in her eating area, When I finally made it to her research areas, I found that her lab was lined with cage-like cells that were locked. Belts and clamps were on the walls, along with some equipment that I didn't recognize. Based on the pile of birds in each cell, I would assume that they were human at some point."

"All of them died?" Fauna gasped. "How?"

"I did not find much, but I did find the equipment for blood drawing and a few bottles of wine. I believe she took the method of feeding that the girls and I did and forced her workers to drink her blood after she turned them. It's how she got me."

"How did the girls get turned then?" Fauna wondered. "I assumed that they wouldn't want to drink her blood knowing what would happen."

"I fed them," Aphrodite's tone indicated that they were in very tender territory. "Once we are bitten, there is only so much time to feed on any blood before the body gives out and dies. She began the process without finishing it, knowing that I would have to let them feed from me. Technically, I am their creator. And that is one of the most foul things that someone has done to me."

Fauna *wanted* to say that it made sense how Aphrodite's wife had died then, but it seemed a bit too obvious to point out. "How did people drink her blood and not know?"

"The wine covers the taste completely."

"And everyone drank her wine at services," Fauna gasped. "But I didn't! I never went. I stayed in the graveyards and then stopped going out at all. Do you think that when she died, everyone with her blood in them died too?"

Aphrodite's eyes reddened with tears as she set down her wine glass. "I apologize for what I am going to say, Fauna, I do. "

The admission shot liquid fear into Fauna's bones, making her shiver and chill with fear. Why would Aphrodite apologize to *her*?

"Why?"

"I don't have anything concrete but a gut feeling," Aphrodite began with a shaky voice. "But considering what she did to you up there," she gestured towards Fauna's prison room, "I believe she stole your father's voice and robbed him of his ability to walk as well. Same as you. Only we cannot be sure *what* he endured, because he could not communicate the way that you did."

Fauna shook her head. "How could you know this?"

"There's more to the story," Aphrodite's voice cracked. "I hate telling you this. I had so much time to think clearly on my journey to Hurmehovi, that so many things clicked into place."

Fauna shook her head. "No, *please*. I want to know."

"Do you remember when the Matron died? She turned into feathers that melted into the floor."

"Yes," Fauna remembered *too* well, as the image was burned into her mind.

Aphrodite took another sip. "You kept saying you were rescued by a large bird. I thought you were just delirious from falling down the stairs. But, the Matron's other form was a raven—one so large that its wingspan was as long as two men."

"So why would she save me? She didn't even know who I was."

Aphrodite set her glass down and clasped her hands in her lap. The tapping of her slipper began to increase and it became very obvious that she was nervous.

"When you were upstairs in the illusion, did you ever see two people at once?"

Oh.

"N-no."

"Did you give any of the fake family members information? It could have been about yourself or your family. You have a journal—were you prompted to write down your feelings?"

Oh.

Fauna began to panic. She downed all of her wine and slammed the glass down a little too hard on the table.

"Yes. All of that. I wrote letters in my journal at first. It was her idea—the fake Aphrodite."

"Did it ever occur to you, that you could not walk or talk... and neither could your father?"

Oh.

Fauna looked at Aphrodite with tears in her eyes and tried to speak. But, when a sob came out instead, Aphrodite slid off the stool and rushed over to the couch to take Fauna in her arms. Fauna cried and cried—harder than she'd even sobbed before. Her breaths stuck and hitched her chest, while her heart pounded so hard that it was all that she could hear. Aphrodite squeezed her tight, pressing Fauna's cheek into her collarbone and gently rubbing up and down her back.

"I'm so sorry," Aphrodite whispered gently into Fauna's ear. "You didn't deserve any of that, and neither did your parents."

"But he... he... never said-"

"Said anything about the Matron?" Aphrodite still whispered with her lips pressed against Fauna's ear. "I can only guess at this point, but I believe that the Matron punished your father for not making you attend her services. I believe that your mother's rebellion made your family a target. The Matron loathed weakness and disloyalty to a fault. That's why I never heard of you or your family—it hurt her pride to have someone not fall at her feet. But if she outright killed someone who was a known naysayer, it would have made your mother a martyr to her cause, and could have inspired others to rise against her."

Fauna did not respond. Instead, vivid memories of her past rolled through her mind like rocks tumbling down a hill. It made *too* much sense. Her father's silence and inability to move, and his constant despondent state. Had he been stuck in an illusion as well?

"Did he even know I existed, in the end?" Fauna mumbled, still in shock.

"I can only guess. You're the only one who knew him," Aphrodite explained. "And I believe that everyone who took her blood has met the same fate."

"The villagers too?" Fauna gasped and pulled away from the embrace to look Aphrodite in the eyes. "All the workers who have family there?"

"We found birds in the castle after we fought," Aphrodite pointed out. "Gelon told me that several staff members are missing too."

"And every one of the maids that are gone turned to birds?" Fauna asked with a teary voice. "All of them?"

"All the ones who drank her blood, I'm assuming," Aphrodite sighed. "I can't say for sure right now, but that's my best guess. The laboratory was clean and so was the castle. I believe when she died, that everyone simply turned into ravens and did the same. Perhaps she was forming her army that way."

"Rhiannon had said that the Matron controlled the birds. Do you think they were humans that were changed?"

"That would make sense," Aphrodite agreed. "It's certainly foul enough to be her doing."

"I do have one question if you're willing," Fauna managed after a shuddering breath. "How did you manage to kill the Matron only now? Especially if you had the power all along. Why *now*?"

"That's a complicated answer," Aphrodite sighed, still rubbing Fauna's back. "She asked my daughters when they would be taking husbands to ensure her lineage would carry on. On the outside, it sounds overbearing, but she was very interested in their... breeding habits. Her words, not mine. She had visited to tell me that she found a nice husband for Bea. And when Bea disagreed, she threatened to kill her like she meant nothing to her. That wretch nearly slit my daughter's throat."

"And that's when I heard the yell." Fauna realized.

"Well, she told dear Bea to prepare to meet the same fate as her mother—not me," Aphrodite spat. "Which was the most despicable thing to say to her."

"Oh goodness," Fauna said. "I can only imagine."

"The woman kills *my* wife and the girl's other mother and dangles it in front of her when she refuses to marry someone picked out for her."

"So you killed her."

Aphrodite nodded and rose from the couch. "Something I should have done a long time ago. It pains me to think that I waited so long, but I always felt as if I owed her something for changing my life. I saw a weakness and I took it. She was trying to maintain your illusion and I could tell she had overestimated how strong she was. So, technically, you helped me kill her."

Fauna scoffed. "She deserved worse."

"I just wonder why she picked that room in our castle. Why not take you to Hurmehovi?" Aphrodite sighed.

"What used to be there? I know it had the pretty painting and the rocking chair, but why that room?"

"It was our bedroom." Aphrodite leaned forward and yanked the sheet off the painting in between them and motioned to it. "My wife died in that rocking chair. I held her while she stopped breathing, and I stayed in it for days afterward."

"And your room now?"

"Was for a third child, should we ever have been blessed with one." Aphrodite's voice broke at that moment. "I think I need to stop for tonight. The rest of the bottle is yours."

"Is that why your wife kept telling me to pretend?" Fauna wondered aloud. "Was she telling me that so I stayed safe?"

"Probably." Aphrodite's voice shook. "That's her, right there."

Fauna stood and wobbled a bit from the *very* strong wine, and peeked around to see the painting. It was the same as before—a beautiful woman with an air of gentility and love around her. She was exactly as the Verity family's book had described.

"This is the first time in almost one hundred years that I've been able to look at this without collapsing or having a mental breakdown," Aphrodite admitted quietly.

"She's very pretty," Fauna admitted. "I heard she sang to the flowers?"

"She made up songs for everything. I swear each day brought a silly little tune. The girls used to try to sing like her. They would walk through the gardens and sing their hearts out. Oh, how far we have come from that time."

"What was her name?" Fauna dared to ask.

"I cannot speak it." Aphrodite began to weep again. "Not ever again."

Fauna nodded. The grief and longing in Aphrodite's voice broke something within her. "Why do we even love, if it ends this way?"

"Because humans were born to love," Aphrodite said sagely. "Grief is one of the most powerful emotions and it touches everyone. We grieve because we love. Love is not a weakness, it is a strength."

"I don't think I'm built for love," Fauna admitted. "I don't think I want to feel anything if it hurts like you're hurting."

"I hurt for many reasons, one being that I miss waking up and seeing my wife bathed in sunlight as she snored softly. The other reason is that the world will never know her kindness again. Those who knew her live here and nowhere else. She is long gone and her legacy will soon die."

"I read the book," Fauna whispered as she walked forward towards Aphrodite. "The castle is silent, there is no music in the walls or songs being sung."

"Who could sing with hearts so heavy?" Aphrodite's face crumpled as her demeanor fell.

"You. You can sing," Fauna encouraged her as she dared to open her arms for an embrace. Twice she had ever initiated one, and both were for Aphrodite. When Aphrodite's arms closed around her, she began to sob again. Never had someone put their arms around her voluntarily. She was not injured and the room was *real*. The comfort around her was *real*. The love she felt in her chest for the Verity women was *real*.

"It's not too late to sing again," Fauna whispered as she pressed her lips to Aphrodite's cheek. "You and the girls."

"Only if you will join us," Aphrodite squeezed her tightly and grabbed a handful of the back of her dress. "Will you sing with us, sweet Fauna? Please?"

It took a moment for Fauna to gather herself, but she nodded—softly at first, but more confidently after a moment.

"Yes, Aphrodite Verity, I will sing with you."

Twenty-Four

The next midday, Fauna woke with a splitting headache and a thirst so visceral that it hurt. The evening prior had been emotionally taxing to the point where she'd collapsed in bed and fallen asleep with her clothes still on. All she wanted to do was lay where she was, but she also wanted to drink a barrel of water.

A soft knock at her door made her jump. After a second, a stricken-looking Rhiannon poked her head in. "You okay?"

"I have no idea," Fauna sighed as she rearranged herself properly on her bed. "Yesterday was okay until Lady Aphrodite came home late and we had a chat. I drank too much wine and cried a lot."

"She's back already? That was fast." Rhiannon slid in and shut the door. "Do you need to talk about it? I was worried when you missed breakfast and lunch."

Fauna raised her hands in confusion before trying to form some sort of answer. Eventually, she gave up. "I genuinely don't know what last night even was. Other than it was really heavy. Everything I thought about my life could potentially be a lie."

"Did the Matron know your mother?" Rhiannon looked up with worried eyes. "I heard some whispers in the castle, but I told them to shut up and mind their own business. I don't like how quickly they seem to hear about things."

"She died right after birthing me," Fauna recounted. "My father would tell me all about the reflection of the sun on the mountains, and the smell of the wind in such detail, that I began to imagine them too. Well, he did in the beginning. Just like everything else, he stopped doing that too."

"But your father never told you exactly what killed her?"

Fauna shook her head. "He just said that she died. We didn't speak at all after I was old enough to be on my own. But, I'm starting to think that the Matron knew me far before I landed at this castle. Did you know that she dropped me on the stairs here?"

Rhiannon's eyebrows raised cautiously. "I did not know that. Who said that?"

"Aphrodite," Fauna admitted. "She thinks the Matron grabbed me in raven form and took me to the castle. And that she was secretly changing her appearance into everyone who visited me in the room upstairs—that's how she knew so much about each person and how they were similar enough to the ones down here, but not *quite* right."

Rhiannon sat down on the edge of the bed and put a comforting hand on Fauna's blanket-covered feet.

"Will you ever know?"

Fauna sighed and shook her head. "I doubt it. And the more I learn about this situation, the more I think I was better off not knowing at all."

"What makes you say that?"

Fauna took a moment to think about the question. It was hard to find the correct words, given that she hadn't had a lot of time to think about it. Her dreams had been chaotic and intense, but not memorable, which made her ever more unsettled.

"I was under the impression that I was hidden in the shadows and comfortable in my solitude. My anger was my safety net—I hated everyone and everything," Fauna tried her best to explain. "And now that I have gone through all of this, my qualms with the village seem so small and unimportant. I hated them, but why? Why was I so angry at them?"

Rhiannon took her hands and squeezed them gently. "Were you envious?"

Fauna groaned and pushed a pillow over her face. The darkness over her eyes helped ease her headache a bit, but the thirst was still there.

"Do you have any family in the village?"

"Nope," Rhiannon explained. "My mother died and I was an only child."

"Well, this may not be accurate, but last night Lady Aphrodite told me that she thinks everyone who went to Matron's gatherings has died. Do you think that could apply to people here?"

Rhiannon's eyes widened as her mouth opened slightly. "We do have some missing staff, and no one has wanted to go down to the village because we've been too busy here. Oh goodness, this is a lot to think about. I suppose we could have Gelon go check, especially if it concerns the rest of the staff. Some of the ones missing have been here their whole lives, and they wouldn't just leave."

Fauna huffed out a short laugh. "That's why I drank so much wine and now I feel like my body is too heavy for me to move. I need to get up and drink some water, but I also want to go back to sleep."

"Well, the girls asked if you would join them in the greenhouse. They invited me as well, but I think they wanted to spend time with you," Rhiannon explained. "I think they like you quite a lot."

"I'll go. I'm curious to see what the greenhouse looks like." Fauna's mood perked a bit. "They talked a lot about it, and everything in the garden is so beautiful. I might take a little bit of time to get ready, but I'll go find them in a bit."

"I haven't been to the greenhouse in ages," Rhiannon admitted. "I don't like venturing too far into the grounds. Well, that was when the Matron used to send birds to spy on everything, but I haven't seen one of those since she died, so I assume that danger has been dealt with. Maybe I'll take myself on a lunch date there tomorrow."

Fauna contemplated just what to tell her friend. "I think all of her birds died when she did. Lady Aphrodite said that when she visited the Matron's island in the sky, she found piles of dead ravens. She thinks that the people on her island were turned into ravens when she died."

"So they turned into birds and died?" Rhiannon shook her head, clearly confused. "Or maybe they were already birds? I always wondered if she brought her army with her when she visited. Were they ever people, or were they just birds?"

Fauna shrugged. "It all sounds so weird to me. Nothing has made sense in a long time."

Rhiannon nodded slowly. "I always wondered why you took all of this so well. I mean, if I had made friends with a group of people and found out they weren't real... I don't think I would handle it as well as you did."

"It hurt," Fauna admitted, "but I had nothing to base it on. I was preoccupied with why the castle held such dark secrets. Besides, my adventure started with the villain *dying*. The night I saw Aphrodite absolutely broken in that rocking chair, I think that I pushed all of my things aside to make sure that she was okay."

"Well," Rhiannon began as she opened the door. "So long as you let yourself feel things, I suppose there isn't a time limit to it all. I should be going—since we're low on staff, I have my own rotation now. Go find the sisters in the greenhouse and let yourself feel things, okay?"

"I will," Fauna assured her. "Also, has Lady Aphrodite talked about the missing maids?"

"Not to me, but I'm not usually in the know around here," Rhiannon explained. "Lots of times the women want an extra day at home, so they stay back and face the wrath of the other maids. I don't mind, honestly. It's nice to see them come back rejuvenated and happy. But, this is something that hasn't happened before. So, I really can't say."

Fauna nodded in understanding as her friend rose off the bed. "Thank you, Rhiannon, for being my first friend two times in a row, and constantly teaching me things. You make me think and I appreciate that so much."

"You've taught us all something in the short time you've been around," Rhiannon said shyly. "Thanks for being my friend too."

The greenhouse was smaller than Fauna had anticipated. It was small enough for the sisters and her to walk around and stay within eyesight, but big enough to house a few rows of different types of plants. In the middle was a circular glass table with chairs around it. At the perfect angle, the glass reflected the plants in such a way that it looked like a mirror image. Each corner of the greenhouse was filled with color-coordinated plants of all shapes and sizes. Purple and yellow were in one corner, and orange and blue were opposite. Green and red were in the third corner, while white and black were across from that. Vines snaked up and down the support beams, making the whole ensemble look like a painter's palette of plants.

Surrounding the table was a series of herbs at knee level. Fauna knew very little about herbs or plants but did recognize a few familiar sprouts. She bent slightly and leaned over to sniff the plant in front of her. "Basil? You guys have so much growing here!"

"Anything but garlic," Bea said with a laugh. "Joking, joking. We have garlic too. Everything in the castle is grown here, but I can't tell them apart. It helps cut costs down and lets us eat without having to deal with the village. Traders don't like the Verity women very much and we can't make contact with people outside the village. Well, I suppose we can now, but that's up to Mother."

"All the years Bea lived on this planet and she still can't tell the difference between herbs," Scarlet teased as she wrapped her arms around her sister's middle. "She would rather be so serious and business-like. She only wears dark clothing, and the only books she reads are *scary* ones about death and math."

"Math?" Fauna grimaced. "Why?"

Bea gently removed her sister and held out her hands to explain. "Numbers don't lie and cheat. You can't be tricked by them, and they're always going to be the same each time."

"See? Boring?" Scarlet muttered as she walked towards some pretty flowers. "She also does puzzles for fun. But, like the kind with a million pieces that all look the same. I think I would rather stare at a wall."

"You would rather write a romance between two walls in the castle," Bea teased back. "So obsessed with fairytales and romance, yet you're scared to talk to anyone who isn't part of the staff."

"I'm shy!" Scarlet frowned and turned around so quickly that her curls bounced against her face. "You try talking to people when they think you're a monster!"

"We *are* monsters," Bea reminded her. "Just not the scary kind."

"All monsters are scary," Scarlet got quiet as she knelt to feel the petals of a flower.

Fauna stepped between them and held her hands out to stop any sibling quarrel that was set to happen. "I don't think you're scary—not at all. Not even when your mother threatened my life. You know what I'm most afraid of now?"

Both sisters look at her with intent curiousness.

"Being alone," Fauna admitted. "It's what I craved for so long, but I've realized that I was missing something in my life trying to maintain my solitude. I thought that I would stay safe if I was alone. People couldn't fail to meet my expectations if I never *met* them. I was so content living my life through books, but there isn't a single book around that deals with what I've been through."

"Write it," Bea offered. "I've seen you writing in your journals. You could write the book!"

Fauna shook her head. "All I have are journals and little bits of prose, nothing important."

"I would read it, even though I was there for some of it," Scarlet offered. "I know how to make a book, I've done it before with poetry. I could help!"

Fauna blushed. It was strange to think that she suddenly had people who wanted to help her do things, instead of chastizing her for simply existing. Only a few weeks ago, she was trapped in a cage without any means of leaving, and now she had a slough of people on her side.

"Maybe," Fauna admitted. "I'll think about it."

"Do it!" Scarlet jokingly sang to her. "I haven't known you for long, but I know that you can do it!"

"Oh!" Bea interrupted them. "Forgive me for interrupting, but I've been meaning to ask Fauna something for a few days now and I keep forgetting."

Fauna nodded. "Go ahead."

"Let's get comfy, this could take a bit." Bea pointed over Fauna's head to a bench under some vines. "I think we can fit there."

"You two have fun," Scarlet said before turning away from them. "I've enjoyed this, but now I want to know why Mother called all the workers for a meeting so I'm going to sneak in!"

"Sneaking into your own home?" Fauna shook her head with a chuckle. "Of course you would."

With that, the pair sat down on the bench. Bea looked as if she was still weighing her words, so Fauna decided to start whatever conversation they were going to have.

"Do you know why your mother called a meeting?"

Bea nodded. "Yes, Mother tells me most things. She also didn't want Scarlet to be there, at first—she's sensitive to things like that. She was *extremely* close to our other mother and when she died, Scarlet took it especially hard. I suppose I did too, but I'm a little more analytical than she is. It's why she writes such good poetry."

"You two are very different from the versions I knew upstairs." Fauna pondered her words. "I think that speaks to how little the Matron knew about you both. She mimicked what she thought you were like, but missed the mark somehow."

Bea looked happy about that. "That's what I was going to ask you about. What were they like—the upstairs people? I don't know what to call them."

"I think that works," Fauna agreed. "Your mother thinks it was the Matron each time, just disguised as someone. I want to agree, considering I never saw any of them together. It makes my skin crawl to know that I let her sleep in bed with me! She made me come out of my shell, just for it to be all fake. The worst part was thinking about how close she got to me, it's unsettling. I feel violated!"

"Did you…?" Bea sighed. "You know what I mean."

"No!" Fauna shouted quickly. "Nothing like that! Oh, that would have been sinister."

"I wouldn't put it past her," Bea admitted. "But I am glad that she didn't do anything that cruel."

"I did have to crawl to the bathroom once when no one could help me. Well, it was Scarlet and she was too weak... but it was the Matron, who never had a problem with it before." Fauna looked away. She'd forgotten about that and the shame of it being a ruse filled her with anger.

"I feel violated too," Bea said. "She used my form—all of our forms—to do things. What else could she do as me? My likeness is mine and only mine. But, she did things as me and I don't like that feeling." She paused, biting her lip ponderously. "Was Mother one of those who visited you?" Bea's eyes were wide as she leaned forward, clearly enraptured. "Like, did the Matron use her form too?"

Fauna nodded. "She did. It was weird though. Almost like she said the exact things that I wanted to hear. Sometimes she would sit in the rocking chair-"

Bea gasped. "The rocking chair? She *didn't*. Oh, that's *vile*. The gall of that woman!"

"She did," Fauna sighed. "And I had no idea of the significance. But the chair was real—when your mother and I went back to the room, it was still there. We ended up sitting in it, just being emotionally damaged. That was right after the incident as well. I think that's what made her trust me—she realized that I was also a victim."

"Was there a painting on the ceiling? Mother painted that right after the funeral, she said it represented 'eternal longing and the evolution of life as seen through grief' but I haven't seen it finished.

She locked the room up right afterward and we never heard about it again."

"There was." Fauna tried to remember it, but the memory was fuzzy. "I remember being obsessed with it. I think once I had a dream about it too."

Bea nodded slowly. "She never let us see her paintings. She keeps her feelings very close, sometimes too close, if we're being honest. I think the Matron dying has her scrambling. She's without a mother now, even if the Matron was a terrible person. We're all hurting, but she bears the brunt of it."

"Also, your mother *killed* someone," Fauna realized. "Is that the first person she had killed since..."

Bea frowned. "I suppose so. She hates it. She says it makes her feel like a monster."

"I feel so terrible for her," Fauna admitted. "I don't know you all very well. I almost feel as if I barged in on a serious family conversation that I wasn't meant to hear."

"Well, we heard her shuffling around her atelier this morning after you two talked, so perhaps she is healing," Bea offered. "I had nearly forgotten about that room. You've seen it? I heard she showed it to you. Did you see the paintings?"

"I did not, they were covered up. She showed me one the second time, but she didn't explain it or anything."

"Maybe we should go back to the castle. It's getting dark," Fauna insisted. "I hope that the staff is okay after the news they're given."

"The only ones left are the ones like us... the immortal ones. They were turned by Mother, so they wouldn't have the Matron's blood in them. The ones that did die...I hope they didn't die in pain. Do you think anyone in the village survived?" Bea wondered. "All those people that hurt you are probably dead."

"Oh!" Fauna gasped as she stood and began to walk quickly back to the castle. "All of them? Even the Merchant? Oh, I hope he survived! I would be heartbroken. There were children in the village, they didn't deserve that!"

"Well, Mother said she would head into the village later in the afternoon to look in on things," Bea replied as they passed through the gardens and into the vast expanse of grass. "You might be able to go with her if you would like?"

Fauna did not answer verbally, instead, she nodded and began to think it over. Was she ready to head back to the village that tried to kill her? What brutal irony that she survived if they did not.

When they got to the castle, Bea pushed on the door to enter the kitchen but turned around for a moment. "I'm going to head in. Are you coming too?"

Fauna shook her head and chose to sit on the grass with her back to the castle. The cool cement chilled her back while the sun warmed her pale legs. She hitched her dress up just a little to take in as much light as she could. As the moon rose higher and higher into the sky, Fauna wondered why she felt so torn up about the village. They had tried to kill her! But, some of them she had never met—they could have been good people. They didn't deserve to die. Not all of them. Hopefully, there were some survivors.

Twenty-Five

The crisp air flowing through her room at the open window smelled like rain. Fauna, stuck in a cycle of melancholy, wanted to see no one and do nothing all day. She'd already locked her bedroom door and only accepted food once Rhiannon threatened to break down the door. Everyone in the castle was giving her a wide berth, considering what had happened. Fauna wanted to confide in her friend, but speaking about the things that had happened brought up images in Fauna's mind that she wanted desperately to forget. Instead of calling for a Verity sister or Aphrodite herself, Fauna grabbed the journal from where Gelon had returned it to her desk and began a new entry.

I am Fauna.

I am not okay. It's been nearly a week since we took the long road to the village to see what remained. And… there was nothing. The silence was the worst part. I can't stop thinking about it.

I thought I would celebrate the loss of those who mocked and tormented me growing up. I thought that I would revel and wrap myself in the warm cloth of their demise. I thought that the men who tried to kill me would cease to exist and know that I have won.

But somehow, due to the time I have spent in this castle, I have learned to care for lives other than my own. I have developed an ability to grieve. And I do not like it. Not one bit.

It was daunting to see the stalls barren, with half-filled cups of water sitting precariously on the edges of benches and clothes scattered about the place taking flight with the wind and landing elsewhere. Half-rotten corpses of birds had been eaten by the abandoned animals out of desperation. I hated those people with everything that I had in me. But did they deserve to die?

Part of me wants to say that they did deserve death after what they put me through. But, as we walked home with somber hearts, I realized that only a few had tarnished my view of the village, not all of them. I cast sweeping judgments upon them based on my own pain, and now I cannot ever show them how much I have grown. That me, the aggressively angry girl who did not speak, can laugh and play like the child I didn't have the chance to be.

I realized too late that my father meant well. However, that is all speculation anyway. I won't ever have the answers and that's a whole other pit of frustration for me to drown in later.

I want to soothe myself by saying that they were all adults, capable of making their own decisions. But... they weren't. All the ravens looked the same but I remember children playing in the streets and causing mischief. I am lucky that I escaped such a fate. I wish others could have escaped as well.

Aphrodite held my hand on the way back and just listened to me cry. She said that she understood my feelings and that opening your heart to those who hurt you is crucial to retaining your humanity. I know it sounds stupid to take lessons on humanity from someone who is barely human, but she knows more about life than anyone I've ever known. We've been talking each night in her atelier, while she slowly uncovers the paintings. I see the grief in her eyes as she revisits the sorrow she poured onto those canvases.

She touches them gently and cries silently. I see the tears, but they are not for me. So, I speak of other things. She's asked me about my life and what books interest me. I told her that I was writing a diary of sorts, and had been ever since I was brought to the castle. It's a mystery to us both why everything was a lie, except the journal.

Aphrodite is planning another journey to Hurmehovi—this time I am invited. To be honest, after my reaction to the piles of birds in the village, I doubt I want to see anything else related to any of it. I feel crushing guilt because, while it is important, I almost don't want to know what happened to my parents. I can't fix it and there just aren't answers up there. Or, so says Aphrodite. And I do trust her, I have no reason not to. But I wonder if there is closure up there. Could there be answers? Can I make it that far? Is it worth it?

Almost all of the paintings are uncovered now. I told Aphrodite that she should hang them in the castle. From an outsider's perspective, they're beautiful and celebrations of love. She disagreed vehemently but did say that she would try to teach me to paint if I found myself curious about it. I have never tried before, but I suppose I have the time to learn now.

The people in the castle are mourning en masse, some of their friends are gone and so are their families. The staff has a month off to do as they please, so it's nice to see the girls and Aphrodite step in and do as much work as they can. Is it strange for me to say that it humanizes them to me? Probably.

I am Fauna… and at this point, that's all I want to think about. Despite the village and Matron's efforts, I am alive.

And I will not squander my second chance.

"Hello? Are you okay?"

Fauna jumped and shook the shock out of her system. She looked around quickly and realized that she'd zoned out while eating next to Rhiannon. Even many days later, the trip to the village had her out of sorts. At least Rhiannon was able to convince her to leave her room.

"Sorry. I'm doing okay, but not much better than that," Fauna answered as honestly as she could. "I can't get the image of the empty village out of my head. I've never seen it so quiet and lifeless. It was unnerving. And to think that if we hadn't gone to check on the people there, we would not have known for a *very* long time, if ever! I can't stop thinking of the food that was still half-eaten in the stalls, or the clothes just laying on the ground where people used to be. It felt like a ghost town! Even now, the images keep flashing through my mind while I'm trying to think!"

"I understand," Rhiannon assured her. "Like, no matter what you do, it's just waiting for you to relax, and *boom* it startles you again. And being comfortable seems like something that will never happen again. I felt that way when I found my mother after she'd died."

"Oh no," Fauna breathed out an apology. "I'm so sorry, I wasn't thinking of that. That was poor wording on my part."

"No!" Rhiannon urged. "Not poor wording at all. I just understand how it feels to not be able to get something out of your mind. It's the worst, especially when it permeates your dreams."

Fauna took a deep breath and nodded. "Yeah, just like that. How are the staff doing?"

Rhiannon sighed. "A few of them haven't taken it well. Most of the workers here stayed here because they didn't have families to go back to. I think the majority of them are just torn between being relieved that the Matron is gone and being afraid for the future of the area."

"No one is in danger, right? Like, there aren't any other threats out there?"

Rhiannon sighed. "I hope we're safe. You know as much about the Matron as I do. Don't forget that we were sent away during most of her visits to the castle. Also, I'm younger than almost everyone here, so I haven't seen her as much as they have."

"Were the ones who died mortals?" Fauna wondered. "Because if killing the Matron took out an entire village, wouldn't Aphrodite be dead as well?"

"You're asking the wrong person, Fauna," Rhiannon laughed a little. "You're better off asking the Lady herself."

"I'm mostly hung up on the fact that I'll never know what happened to those people," Fauna admitted as she pushed her plate away. "I only know what Lady Aphrodite can tell me, and even that is all just a guess. Speculation can get carried away quickly, but it's all we have."

"She knew the Matron better than any of us, though." Rhiannon pointed out. "It might be worth asking her now that it's been several days. I know you've been having evening tea with her. Have you gotten any more information about what happened? Is she doing well?"

Fauna shook her head. "She mostly tells me little stories about her life before her wife died. Little sweet things—nothing overly personal. I think she's mostly just talking and it doesn't matter *who* she is talking to per se, just that there is someone to listen that hasn't been here for ages."

"I think it might matter," Rhiannon added. "She doesn't have those discussions with many people, including her daughters. Scarlet has told me plenty of times that her mother just doesn't want to speak of such things. I don't know if it's because *she* is hurting, or if she's protecting her daughters, but I'm just very happy you came along."

Fauna nodded slowly and despondently laid her head in her arms. "It seems as if they all want to talk about it, just not with each other."

"That's got to be tough on you," Rhiannon insisted. "You're handling triple the grief and your own on top of it. I still don't think you've processed all the things you told me earlier."

Fauna sighed and turned her head to face away from her friend. "I like to write things out… talking isn't my favorite. Words can be tough and misunderstandings happen so easily. I like taking my time. I can scribble out a paragraph, but I can't take spoken words back. Also, talking to others just isn't something I'm good at—it's going to take more than a few months for me to understand how all of that works. I'm working on it though, and you're helping quite a bit."

Rhiannon made a small noise of understanding. "I get it. I've said things on a whim and regretted them deeply. You never know when you're speaking your last words to someone. The last thing my mother told me was that I should live my life alone, rather than spend it with someone who didn't care for me. I think about that often and I wonder if it's made me a little resentful."

Fauna perked up and lifted her head again. "Care for you? Isn't that like… the bare minimum for a marriage?"

Rhiannon rolled her eyes. "Yes, but my grandmother used to tell stories of how angry Lady Aphrodite was while her husband was alive and I think it scared my mother. My father loved my mother quite a bit, but she always worried that I wouldn't find love."

Fauna smiled at her friend. "You've never talked about your father."

"I haven't?" When Fauna nodded, Rhiannon continued. "Well, he was one of the gardeners here! He courted my mother for quite some time, but didn't marry her—it was *quite* the scandal for a while.

But, they loved each other for a long time. I miss him quite a bit, but he wouldn't want me to be sad over him."

"He sounds wonderful, especially if he loved flowers!"

Rhiannon smiled shyly. "He did! If you asked him about any type of plant, you would be stuck listening to him for *hours*. His father and grandfather were groundskeepers, so he inherited his love of gardening. I, unfortunately, ruin every plant that I touch, so I stick to things like sewing and embroidery."

"And reading!" Fauna reminded her. "Did he like reading?"

Rhiannon nodded enthusiastically. "He did! We had a book of fairy tales that were a little *spooky* that I would beg him to read to me before bed. And no matter how much my father had worked that day or how sick he was, he always did."

"My father used to tell me stories when I was very young," Fauna whispered. "He couldn't read, but he had a wonderful imagination. I wish that I hadn't been so angry at him for so long. I was just so hurt that he stopped talking to me and I never really stopped to think about why that could have happened. I was just so *angry* at everyone and everything."

"Anger comes from love," Rhiannon said kindly. "My grandmother used to tell me that. She said that anger at people comes from the fact that we know they're capable of more. We want them to be better than they currently are. Whether that anger is justified or not... well that's not our call. But, anger comes from love."

"Your grandmother was very wise, considering all the things you've told me about her." Fauna grabbed Rhiannon's dishes and combined them with her own. "I wish I could have met her."

"Well," Rhiannon laughed. "You know who her best friend was? The one that taught her all her wisdom?"

Fauna's eyes widened. "Aphrodite's late wife? The Lady of the Castle? You said they were friends! I forgot all about that."

"You're right," Rhiannon agreed while grabbing their dishes. "I have some of her old journals. Would you like me to find them? I used to read them before bed, but it's been ages since I've pulled them out."

Fauna smiled, so very thankful that Rhiannon was in her life. "Sounds great!"

When Fauna went to sit down and write her typical journal entry, she caught a glimpse of herself in the small mirror on her desk and stared back at herself curiously. As someone who rarely looked at herself, it was strange to think that other people saw what she saw in the mirror. She'd spent so much time alone in her life, that being perceived by other people was slightly unnerving. Did they look at her and study her features? Did they judge her based on trivial things? Did it even matter?

Even now she wondered if her injuries were even real. Had she been set ablaze at all? Or was that an illusion too? When she thought back, she could smell the smoke and feel the searing pain across her legs. The memory brought back the full-body panic of imminent death, and the strange feeling of defiant peace whilst others were intent on her last moments being wrapped in fear. But did it actually happen? The transition to her staying upstairs had been seamless, which was terrifying. If the Matron had been able to conjure up such a visceral reality, what else had she changed? Was Fauna even real? Were her parents real? If she thought about it too long, she would give herself a headache and panic until she eventually fell asleep.

Never in her life had Fauna stopped to contemplate if she was considered attractive. There was no one to impress in her life, and vanity took time that could be spent reading, so it didn't have much use in her day-to-day life. But now, with other people around, she couldn't help but wonder. There were plenty of things that Fauna despised before her accident that she now coveted above all else. She *loved* the Verity family and the people of the castle, and she found that, as time went on, there were more and more things she was discovering about herself. Of course, she still loved books quite a lot, but they weren't her only source of enjoyment now.

She didn't think about the initial accident much anymore. For some reason, finding out she'd been lied to was more traumatic than being burnt alive. However, the immolation had still left its mark—mentally and physically.

Now, however, after some time in the Verity castle, Fauna no longer hid in the shadows but *danced* in the grass on her way to the gardens and had a small handful of friends that she could call upon. Even though loneliness still found her, there were people to visit and places to go within the castle. And while she still had many moments where she needed to be alone, Fauna had that choice… and that was the missing piece all along.

A choice.

Twenty-Six

After the bitter bite of Autumn's last dance, Fauna spent more and more time in the common library soaking up the last of the sunlight midday and pouring over every book that caught her eye. Things weren't normal, considering the epitome of abnormal *surrounded* her, but it was stable and that was enough. When she wasn't lying sideways in her favorite chair, Fauna was at her writing table, scrawling her thoughts into her journal. She'd tentatively asked Gelon if she could take the book of Castle Verity's history and turn it into a more mobile anthology.

Everyone had agreed. The only rule was that Fauna would stay in Lady Aphrodite's office and work on it where Gelon could see the book at all times, for peace of mind.

Rhiannon, who still came to greet her daily, even though Fauna needed no assistance, had taken on a more advanced position with the maids and was desperate to unload her feelings about it to someone. This meant that she and Fauna oftentimes took their meals in seclusion and privacy so as to not air all the maids' secrets to the public.

Lady Aphrodite was still evasive and only seemed to be easily located when taking meals with her daughters. After their emotional trip into the village, Fauna had absolutely no idea how to speak with her again. It wasn't the awkwardness that made it hard, it was knowing that Aphrodite was hurting but did not let people in very easily.

Oftentimes Fauna spent her afternoons outside, if the weather permitted. Being contained for so long gave her the visceral urge to sniff every flower and relish in every single sunbeam presented to her. Occasionally, she convinced one or both of the daughters to join her, though they were frequently tied up in their own projects.

On one blissfully underwhelming overcast day with glistening marmalade-colored leaves and woolen gray skies, Fauna, clad in only her nightdress and comfortable socks, had decided to sprawl out on her bed diagonally and read her new favorite book. The scents of an apple-laden candle wafted around the room, making the space deliciously cozy.

A gentle knock on her door put a pause in her reading. Bea, looking dreadfully ashen, even for a vampire, poked her head in and took in the ambiance for a moment before turning to address her.

"Mother wants you."

Fauna slid her bookmark in between the pages of her book and set it gently on her bed. She gazed curiously at Bea, who looked at Fauna with a concerning melancholy.

"Do you know what for?"

Bea bit her lip and looked away guiltily. "Yes, but you should hear it from her."

"The atelier?" Fauna figured it would be in their normal meeting place.

"No." Bea shook her head slowly. "The room you were held in."

As Fauna ascended the stairs, she thought about how she had grown in her time in Castle Verity. She'd walked up to that room only a few times and the last time was when she'd sat with Aphrodite in the rocking chair and pretended their lives were different. She genuinely assumed that the room had been destroyed, considering no one had mentioned it for a while. It wasn't as if she felt a need to go looking for it. Knowing her luck, she would trip and fall into the room and be stuck on the floor unable to yell until she died.

"Fauna?" Aphrodite's unnervingly emotionless voice called from inside the room. The midday sun spilled through the door and into the hallway, bathing the foyer in an appropriately eerie light.

Aphrodite, wearing all black, stood in the middle of the room and held her arms out.

"Yes?" Fauna took a large breath and walked to, but not through, the doorway. "You needed me?"

Aphrodite still held out her arms. "I need help. This room has to go and I cannot do it alone. It means so much to me, but I have put it off long enough. I know you will be helpless for a bit, but I just can't gather the strength to do it by myself."

Fauna's face crumpled as she tried her best not to cry. Going back to that state of dependency would wreak havoc on her mind. But, looking at Aphrodite's watery eyes and shaking outstretched hands, Fauna knew she could do it. She was a simple woman with a brief but intense history at the castle, and the woman across from her had lived lifetimes of sadness and heartbreak.

"Okay," Fauna whispered as the tears fell. She tiptoed on her socked feet and gasped when her toes crossed the threshold of the door.

A numbness traveled from the soles of her feet and up into her calves and thighs. A tingle shot from her hips, up her spine, and into the back of her head. She felt the rumble of her cries snuffed out like a candle and her center of balance disappeared completely. Aphrodite caught her under her arms and pulled her close into an embrace.

Aphrodite swiveled Fauna away from her and had her sit gently on the rocking chair that had been moved next to the bed. As they moved as one entity, Fauna took solace in the comforting scent and feeling of someone so close to her, and she felt her body begin to relax. The feeling in her legs *would* return, and she *would* be able to speak once more. It wasn't permanent—she was moral support.

"Sit here," Aphrodite guided her and placed a calming kiss on her forehead. "Thank you for doing this. I can't imagine how it feels. But, having you here is helping so much."

Fauna smiled weakly and tried not to look anywhere but her feet, lest something in the room trigger a memory.

"Here goes." Aphrodite steadied her shoulders and walked towards the chest of drawers across the room.

With a sickening crack that startled the fear right out of Fauna, Aphrodite pulled a single drawer out and yanked so hard that the wood splintered as the drawer broke free. She threw it down and stomped on it with her shoe until the floor was littered with oversized woodchips.

"She took *EVERYTHING* from me!" Aphrodite began to cry. "My heart, my soul, my children's safety! She took their mortality and robbed me of any humanity that I had! I am a monster, and now I have to live in this castle, surrounded by memories, while she gets to finally rest!"

Fauna, forced to be silent, simply watched with tears slowly trailing down her cheeks. It was unsettling to see someone so put together lose themself completely.

"This is for *her!*" Aphrodite screamed with palpable rage and ripped a painting off of the wall. "The one person in this existence to *choose* me. No one else got to *choose*! My children were ripped from their families and forced to love me! My *disgusting* husband was forced to marry me!"

Aphrodite's heel poked through the canvas as she stomped it into pieces as well. Almost immediately, the decor and furniture faded into nothing until all that was left was the bed. Had it been real the whole time? Was it the very bed that Aphrodite and her late wife had slept on for years?

"She was *pure* and full of *love*!" Aphrodite wailed with such heartbreak that it broke something inside Fauna. "She died in my arms. It took weeks—*weeks!*—for her to finally fade away. Do you know what it's like to watch someone die slowly, knowing that you will have to live the rest of your life without them? Do you know what it's like to wrap your arms around someone and rock them to sleep, knowing they won't wake up? Do you know what it's like to tell two children that their parent is gone and that she chose that ending for herself? How do you call the most selfless human being selfish? You can't! I can't!"

Fauna, sobbing, shook her head, even though she knew that it was a rhetorical question. Suddenly, all her pain and suffering in the room faded away as she tried her best to speed up the process and help.

With each shattered drawer and ripped piece of fabric, Fauna felt a glimmer of her autonomy return. It started with a tingle in her fingertips and a jolt of feeling in her spine. She regained enough movement to hoist her legs to the side so she could grab things from her perch. The pillows on the bed fell victim first as she pulled them apart as hard as she could. Her weak arms shook with the effort, but the satisfying rip and explosion of feathers made her push on. Next, she began to break the things on her bedside table, starting with the damned glass of water that always mocked her.

She threw it against the wall with a yell and realized that she could hear a tiny whisp of a voice when she yelled. Without thinking twice, she threw herself out of the chair and stumbled, but did not fall over. The hardwood burned against the skin of her kneecaps, but Fauna kept pulling at everything in her path. The blanket, the sheets, and even the pillows were ripped into tiny pieces and feathers filled the room like confetti.

After a moment, the two looked at each other and then at the chair. It was the only piece of furniture that remained untouched.

"No," Aphrodite whispered the sparkle of tears on her cheeks. "Not that. I can't. That has to stay. I will put it in my atelier."

"If the curse on this room persists even after the Matron has died, what is its source?" Fauna croaked, her voice still a flaky rasp. But, it was better than nothing.

"The Matron likely hid it within something near and dear to me—something that I could not destroy."

Fauna pointed to the ceiling. "Like a painting? Or the chair?"

Aphrodite looked at her with wide, red-rimmed eyes. A look of understanding slid into place and seemingly gave Aphrodite the final push that she needed. "Like a painting. I hope on *everything* that it is the painting."

"I'm sorry," Fauna offered quietly. Her voice was still barely a whisper, but the mere sound of it bolstered her confidence.

Aphrodite heaved in a very uncharacteristic move of exertion and shook her head slowly. "It needed to be done and I have put it off for far too long. This painting was done during the height of my grief… and now its removal will help close the book on this. I need to let it go, I need to let *her* go. I have a family and an estate to run. I cannot keep hiding away, hoping that I will see her again."

"Do you think the Matron kept her from your dreams?" Fauna's voice creaked. She half-crawled across the floor to grab onto the rocking chair and pull herself into it once again. Being in the chair itself wasn't as frightening as she originally thought it would be, but it still didn't feel quite right.

"At this point, I wouldn't put anything past her," Aphrodite explained as she stepped out of her heels. She set the shoes gently on the remains of the bed and took a deep breath as she scoured the room. Her gaze landed on a splinter of a broken drawer. She grabbed the makeshift stake and climbed onto the bed with surprising grace.

"I can't pretend anymore," Aphrodite whispered harshly as she began to cry again. "No more pretending."

Fauna sat in the rocking chair, gripping the wooden arms so tightly that her palms began to sweat against them. She watched as Aphrodite raised the stake to the ceiling and dragged it across the painting. The lights in the room began to dim as the trinkets on the furniture began to shake and fall.

A sliver of the ceiling tore away, revealing a clay-colored surface underneath it. Aphrodite threw the stake to the bed and grabbed the flap. With a sharp tug, the painting ripped in half like tissue paper, nearly crumbling in her hands. Pieces of canvas fell and littered the bed around her feet as some stragglers floated in the air to each corner of the room.

A feral mourning wail pierced the room as Aphrodite began to scratch and pull at the leftover painting. Her perfect nails scraped and tore the freshly bared ceiling, leaving polish-stained marks on it. After nearly a minute of destroying the painting, the marks turned a dark red as the ceiling rubbed Aphrodite's skin until it broke.

"Aphrodite!" Fauna cried out, startling herself with her volume. She tried her best to stand and was relieved when she was able to balance, albeit just barely. Feeling bled back into her legs and the rumble in her throat began to turn into a fully-fledged yell. "Stop! You're hurting yourself!"

Still, the woman clawed and smeared her way around the ceiling. Her normally warm eyes were startingly unfocused and her face held no emotion. There was a cold determination in her eyes so fierce that Fauna *shivered*.

"Aphrodite!" Fauna tried again, with no success. A tingle in her throat warned her that screaming at such a volume would be painful later on. Seeing her friend's bloody scrawls across the ceiling made her stomach turn.

Hoping for the best, Fauna climbed onto the bed that was her prison for so very long and threw her arms around Aphrodite. After a few heartbeats, the woman stopped and looked at Fauna with such a sorrowful mourning, that it knocked the wind out of her. When Fauna let go, Aphrodite turned her back and fell to the bed below. Fauna, still reeling from it all, lowered herself slowly to the bed and pressed her face against Aphrodite's back before throwing her arms around Aphrodite in a very tight embrace.

Fauna felt Aphrodite's shuddering breaths and listened to the staccato of her breathing. Overwhelmed and unsure of how to further comfort someone in their scenario, Fauna simply held on tighter and continued to press her face against Aphrodite's back. The zipper of her dress pressed uncomfortably into the apple of Fauna's cheek, but she did not dare move. They stayed that way until the arm that was wrapped underneath Aphrodite went numb, and Aphrodite's cries faded to whimpers and the occasional shudder.

A knock at the door started Fauna, but she did not roll over, lest she disturb her freshly calmed friend.

"It's just us," Bea whispered from the doorway. "The lights flickered and then all the candles in the castle lit themselves. Then we heard mother crying. Are you okay?"

"I am," Fauna assured them, though she could not see them. She felt that familiar terror of wondering if they were real, or if destroying the room did nothing.

"We should get her to bed," Scarlet also whispered from behind them. "Want us to carry her?"

Fauna nodded but realized they likely couldn't see her movements. "Please."

"Rhiannon's here too if you need help getting to bed," Bea assured her as she appeared around the bed with her sister. "Can you walk?"

"I think so," Fauna assured them. "My body *hurts* though. That took a lot out of us."

"Oh, you're covered in blood and dust," Rhiannon said softly as Fauna opened her arms to let Aphrodite go. "Want some help with getting to the bath?"

"She can use mine," Scarlet told them both. "No need to be put on display for the rest of the castle and no one will disturb you both."

Fauna nodded and let her be rolled over by Rhiannon. She stood slowly and groaned as gravity took its toll. Exhausted and barely able to think, Fauna focused all her energy on putting one foot in front of the other.

Rhiannon sat against the bath to keep Fauna company, making sure that she didn't have to move much to grab anything. Towels were placed in her hands just as quickly as they were taken. Rhiannon, bless her heart, had offered to help wash Fauna's back, but the familiarity of her former room still hung menacingly over her mind. Unwilling to even *begin* to process the events of the last few hours, Fauna chose instead to make a halfhearted attempt at scrubbing plaster and canvas off of every inch of her skin that had been exposed. Having bits of the painting that had held such a vile curse floating in her bathwater was unsettling, to say the least.

When it came time to wash her hair, Fauna went to raise her arms and realized just how heavy they felt after such a long day. As if she could read Fauna's mind, Rhiannon grabbed a cup from the bath and winked knowingly at her. Without even speaking, Fauna smiled back and let her head loll against the back of the bathtub. Rhiannon washed her hair gently and a sudden wave of emotion that she was *not* expecting surged through Fauna's blood. Being handled so gently brought out a certain vulnerability that remained even after her months of growth. Rhiannon's gentle fingers untangled her hair and affectionately tucked her gray streak back in such a gentle way, that a sob began to build in her throat.

"Why are you crying?" Rhiannon asked softly, though it came out more as one conjoined word. She softly brushed a tear away from Fauna's cheek and tapped it affectionately.

"No one's ever washed my hair before," Fauna admitted with a rough voice. Though she hadn't suffered any injuries from destroying the room, her screaming had done a number on her throat. "I used to think that anyone touching me was disgusting. I think I missed that part of growing up."

"Oh, that's very sad," Rhiannon replied, gently pushing Fauna's head up to rinse her hair. "I love hugs and kisses, snuggles too! My mother liked to hug me because I'm soft—I think that's a wonderful gift to have."

Fauna closed her eyes and smiled. "I guess I'm pretty soft too. I think back to how I used to be, and I barely recognize that girl. She was so *angry* and lonely. But... I had no idea. Like, I had so much hate within me and I still do... but it's directed *at* people and not just at the world."

"What changed?" Rhiannon tapped her forehead gently to have her lean her head back.

"I'm not sure," Fauna admitted. "Maybe it was being dependent on people. Maybe I'm just too traumatized to process it correctly. Maybe it's one of those things I'll understand in twenty years when I'm filled with wisdom."

"Well," Rhiannon added. "My grandmother used to say that sometimes our minds have the answer before we know the question. Perhaps you always wanted those things and you just didn't know how to ask. You never ask for anything, ever. But... you *should* ask for things if you want them. I say that, but it's hard for me too. Maybe we can both work on it together."

Fauna shrugged. "I think of how often I read books—some days I read from sunrise to sunset! And I wonder where my life went. Perhaps it's my age or how much I've experienced in a short time, but my life feels like a big blur that finally cleared up when I got to the castle."

"Maybe it is," Rhiannon suggested. "You have true freedom for the first time in your life and there isn't some big bad thing hovering over you. That must be nice. You're allowed to be happy about that."

"And the best part?" Fauna said. "I'm not alone."

Twenty-Seven

I *am Fauna*

I'm sure of that now.

I slept for fourteen hours after Lady Aphrodite and I destroyed the room. Rhiannon told me that it took the girls almost the entire night to get their mother to stop crying. She said that Lady Aphrodite's cries were almost as bad as the day the Lady of the Castle died. I remember the pain in her voice and the sorrow in her wails whilst we tore up the room. I think that sound might haunt me forever. I can only imagine hearing it right after her wife had died. I don't think that I could have handled that.

The sun is about to rise and I'll admit that I slept a bit too much. I love watching the changing of the days from my room, but I cannot focus on anything else except Aphrodite. I've always looked at her as a very intimidating woman, completely put together. She paints, she maintains an estate, she deals with a sanguine affliction, and she still manages to be a mother. But right now, all I can see is someone brokenhearted and extremely vulnerable. Is this what it is like to see your parents cry? I'll never know and from what little experience I do have on that front… it's unsettling, to say the least.

I have no idea where to go from here. I know that I have so many questions that I want to ask Aphrodite about her time in Hurmehovi and while I want to learn more about my father's silence, I'm not sure it's the best course of action.

"Fauna?"

Fauna's pencil tip broke as she looked up to see Scarlet with puffy eyes and skin even paler than normal. Her usual bouncy red curls were flattened and matted and her clothes looked uncharacteristically rumpled. It was clear that she had not seen a wink of sleep or a crumb of sustenance in a while and Fauna assumed her sister would look the same way.

"My mother would like to see you. She wants to show you something," Scarlet said softly. "She will meet you in the main hall when you are ready."

With that, the youngest Verity daughter sniffled and backed out of the room. She then reappeared once more, as if she had forgotten something.

"I'm sorry for startling you, I keep forgetting to knock."

"It's okay," Fauna assured her. Scarlet nodded and left once more.

Fauna felt a physical pain in her chest—she *hated* how much everyone was hurting. It wasn't fair that this family of women who just wanted peace kept having to rehash the same grief over and over. She desperately hoped that they were on the path to healing.

After a quick change into something more appropriate and a stop by the communal bathing area to freshen up, Fauna made her way into the center of the castle. Gone were the bustling maids repairing the holes in the walls and now the castle seemed tauntingly peaceful. The adrenaline of the fight had long gone and now, weeks later, everyone was scrambling to cope with the aftermath.

From a visitor's perspective, the castle may have looked to be in perfect condition. The holes had been repaired and mortared to look as if nothing happened and the broken windows had been replaced as soon as the replacement panes had arrived. Every trick in the staff's repertoire was utilized to clean the blood from the beautiful wooden floor.

The Matron had inherited Fauna's fiery ending instead. A bitter-sweet ending to a sour individual. Served her right, truly.

Aphrodite sat primly on a padded bench near the front door. From the outside, she looked perfectly splendid in a fresh burgundy dress, tailored impeccably, paired with black heels. Every hair was in place and when she turned to Fauna, her face looked the same as it always did: splendid. Deceitfully so.

However, the slouch in her shoulders, the heaviness of her breath, and the faint marks of quickly healing wounds were what gave her away. Lady Aphrodite could put on a brilliant facade, but she could never quite hide her grief. There was a deep sadness in her eyes and an air of ambivalence around her.

"Good morning," Aphrodite murmured, as if even addressing her was taking all the energy she had.

Fauna sat beside Aphrodite and did not speak. It was nice to casually exist with her, even if Fauna was only *barely* used to sharing space with people.

Aphrodite moved a hand out of her lap and slid it into one of Fauna's. She squeezed reassuringly and took three deep breaths before her thumb began to casually drift up and down the back of Fauna's hand. It was new but not unwelcome.

Fauna eventually shyly replied, "Good morning."

Aphrodite smiled at Fauna's pink-tinted cheeks. "Now that we've gone through that ordeal together, I have something to show you. It's the last secret in this castle, and then you've seen it all."

Fauna gasped. "I don't need to know it *all*. I have no desire to see the cellar."

"It's not a bloodbath, it's a wine cellar—not very dramatic," Aphrodite assured her. "Very organized and cold, if we're being honest. Lots of spiders too. Besides, that's not where we're heading. We're going *up*."

"Either way." Fauna shook her head. "You don't *owe* me anything. So, only show me what you're comfortable with. We have plenty of time."

"We think we have time, but we do not," Aphrodite said wistfully before giving Fauna's hand another squeeze. "I swore to *her* that the walls would not know silence or shadows, and I have neglected both in error. I have been derelict in my promises, and it is time that I do right by my late wife. It may take a lifetime, but she deserves everything that I have to offer."

Fauna, with little to add but a smile, followed Aphrodite's direction and began to travel down the hall with the locked door. She waited nervously for Aphrodite to pull a keyring out of a pocket in her dress and began to thumb through many keys with trembling fingers until she landed on the correct one.

"Did you know she used to sing? Not only to the bees and the flowers but to the girls as well? Nothing serious, just little phrases she made up on a whim. She'd sing to the birds and the sky, or the foxes and trees. Every living thing had a song. Goodness, her voice was *beautiful*. It was effortless—playful. There was whimsy and wonder in every single note. Little Bea found that she loved composing music for her mother to sing—something about the precision of notes combined with the freedom of creativity genuinely spoke to her. She stopped when her mother died. Her love for it was gone, just like that."

"And Scarlet?"

"Liked coming up with the words. That girl's mind hosts the largest dictionary you can imagine. Even as a child, she would find the biggest words that she could and memorize them. I'm sure she's shown you her writing. Beautiful. That girl has a way with poetry that is simply divine. She didn't give up on her craft, but she did retreat so far into her mind that I wonder if she will get lost."

"And what did you do in all of this?" Fauna gently asked. "Did you sing too?"

Aphrodite began to walk down the dark hallway, lighting up one of the dusty sconces and using it to ignite the rest of them down the hall. At the end, she turned to Fauna and answered.

"I watched them with a pride so profound that it made me ache. I was so astounded by them, that no thoughts were in my mind except the overflowing of love in my heart. In those moments, I had no wants or wishes, no needs or aches. I used to want to hurt and destroy things. But, now as time has passed, I only wish that everyone experiences that type of love in their lifetime, no matter how fleeting. Perhaps, if the world could love with all its might, we would know no manmade conflict. I think that the hardest part about losing someone is knowing that their specific type of love in your heart, will never be felt the same way again."

Fauna inhaled sharply, tears already threatening to fall. It hurt so badly to see Aphrodite in pain.

Aphrodite stopped at a dark cherry wooden door and closed her eyes for a moment. Fauna watched as the Lady stabilized herself and turned the knob.

As soon as the door opened, Fauna was *overwhelmed* in the most wonderful of ways. Bright, multicolored beams of light illuminated the room via a single stained glass window that faced the sun. The design, a plethora of flowers in so many colors, immediately captivated Fauna with its intricacy and array of tones. The most beautiful waterfall of sunshine poured from the window over every surface in the room. Books, coated in the most calming blue light, were haphazardly stacked in knee-high piles against a wall, while a yellow-tinted mantle sported little doodles and trinkets that seemingly came from travels. Purple puddles illuminated the wooden floor, traveling up Fauna's legs until they faded into the deepest emerald color that Fauna had ever seen. She held out her arms and walked around into the different colors, turning herself into a human rainbow.

"This is beautiful!" Fauna spun around in the lights. "It looks like we're inside a jewelry box!"

Aphrodite did not answer; instead, she smiled at Fauna and gestured an arm at her at her to explore the room. Fauna didn't want to move from the center of it all but found herself drifting towards the window itself. As she got closer and the little fragments of colored glass got more in focus, she found herself drawn to the sheer craftsmanship of it all. Rhiannon was right, it *was* magical! Underneath the window was a simple daybed with a small blanket and a stack of *very* dusty books at the foot of it. When Fauna looked out the window, she saw the secret pond that Rhiannon had told her about.

"Do you know when women are the most beautiful?" Aphrodite said, so softly that the words nearly fluttered away. The breeze outside in the trees made the old panes of the window rattle, implying just how long the room had been locked away without repair.

Fauna broke herself away from the view and turned around so Aphrodite could finish.

"Right before they wake, they are the sweetest things ever created. Their eyes are a little puffy and their hair is everywhere. Their bodies are warm from blankets and in those moments between sleep and total clarity—they are the most beautiful things on earth. The vulnerability of seeing a woman drift slowly awake is something that many people take for granted. I will never do so again. So many naps I interrupted on that little bed because she would tire herself out and fall asleep while reading. For plenty of days, this was her safe space after tending to so many people in the village. Even when spent, she loved every minute of it. There was just enough room to slide in right behind her on days when I too was exhausted. And if I found her there in the wee hours of the early morning, she was not much to carry down to our room. I miss the little things like that. I miss her so terribly. I'm not sure that I'll ever heal, or that I even want to."

Fauna's chest felt heavy at the description and the look of unbridled longing on Aphrodite's face. The woman's eyes were closed and a hand rested against her sternum. She breathed in long, slow swings. Even in their combined silence, the leaves kept fluttering and the shadows on the wall kept moving in the most surreal way.

"Books are wonderful treasures, filled with so many things," Aphrodite whispered, her eyes still shut. "But living is so much better."

After nearly four hours exploring the bookshelves and trinkets in the room long locked away, Fauna admitted aloud that she was hungry. She didn't *want* to leave, but her stomach made the noise of a feral animal and Aphrodite forced her out while speaking the empty threat of locking the door until she knew Fauna had eaten. She pressed the small key into Fauna's hand without another word and rubbed her back lovingly as she dropped her off at the table where Rhiannon was sitting.

"You girls have fun now." Aphrodite squeezed Fauna's shoulder as she turned away. "I think I'm going to paint."

As she walked away, Rhiannon looked at Fauna with wide eyes and a sandwich still mid-air and ready to eat. After a second, she dropped the sandwich onto her plate and looked incredulously around the room.

"Did she say she was going to paint?" Rhiannon gasped. "I don't think she's ever said that—at least not while I've been alive. What did you do? Did you kiss her?"

Fauna laughed so loudly that she startled herself. "No! She showed me the room with the stained glass window and we talked. She told me some personal things. I think she's just comfortable talking to me because I'm not part of the family."

Rhiannon gasped excitedly. "Oh, that must have been beautiful! I can only imagine!"

"It was! There are so many books and fabrics and even a little piano! I don't know how to play it, but I want to learn! Aphrodite said that Bea knows how to play and that maybe she could teach me! I just can't explain how amazing the light was coming through that window. It was like I was inside a rainbow! I can't wait to spend all my time up there—she said I could! She also said you can come too. I think she likes you much more than you realize."

"I think she *really* likes *you*," Rhiannon chuckled as she picked up her sandwich again. "I'm your friend so I'm part of the package deal."

"There is a small sewing machine up there, one that works with pedals," Fauna remembered. "You could make us those matching dresses you wanted to make! Now you don't have to share the space with the grumpy tailor!"

"I think she died alongside the matron," Rhiannon admitted, trying to not laugh but failing. "I hate feeling that way about someone, especially the dead, but she was so *mean* for no reason. I won't laugh… much. I just won't be as sad when we find a new tailor. We already have maids with ripped aprons and torn blouses.

I know it's a last priority, but maybe I should mention it to her just in case."

"Why don't you do it?" Fauna suggested. "You said you didn't have a proper place on the staff, but this could be it. And Lady Aphrodite already likes you, so it's probably something she would immediately agree to. I assume she needs a personal tailor too. I never thought to ask where she got her clothes."

"Those dresses are so expensive though," Rhiannon admitted. "Like, worth more than you think. She imports them from other countries. They're made by people with names I can't even pronounce! I would be too scared to even touch them!"

"I think you can do it," Fauna assured her. "I think you can do anything!"

"You're still just riding high from seeing that room," Rhiannon shyly teased her. "But, if it makes you happy, I will offer up my services to her. Well, I will tomorrow. Today, I will make us matching dresses. Come with me to the fabric room, there's so much to choose from! Oh, it will be so fun. We can pretend we're twins. You're ten years older and I'm taller and we don't look anything alike in our features, but who cares?"

"A twin sister?" Fauna laughed in amusement. "With different parents? Not the strangest thing these people have seen lately. Lead the way!"

"Come in."

Fauna pushed open the heavy door and entered the atelier. The room looked different than the last time she had been in it. Where long, dark curtains had obscured the light and dusty sheets covered every surface, the room now displayed floor-to-ceiling windows that let in every dewy drop of sunlight. Little specks of dust floated through the air and the duster lying against the wall explained why. The furniture was uncovered and looked freshly primped; however, the paintings were still hiding under their protective sheets.

"It looks nice in here," Fauna said in wonder as she gently touched every new thing she could see. "The room looks more alive, like it can finally *breathe*."

Aphrodite turned on her stool to face Fauna. "It's because I can breathe. The heavy weight against my chest has lifted and while I don't think it will ever go completely away, it has given me reprieve against my sorrows. That is one thing that I truly believed would never happen. I assumed that I was meant to live and die by my grief—that was my punishment for loving as viscerally as I did. But today, the sun rose *just* right and I could hear the bustle of the castle waking up. I smiled for the first time in a long time. I didn't have to force it and it didn't feel as if I was playing the part. I am content. I'm not exactly happy, but I know that I can be in the future, and that makes all the difference."

Fauna pointed to the freshly cleaned couch. "May I sit? What is different now?"

Aphrodite nodded once. "I feel… hopeful. Your crash landing on the stairs brought about a lot of feelings that I did not discuss with anyone. There was a part of me that wanted to just throw you into the woods for the beasts to feast on. But, when I realized how utterly wretched that would be, I was thrown for a loop. Here was a hurt woman begging for help and I wanted to ignore you. And yes, you were a little *too* familiar with us, but you didn't know anything else. It took me a while to believe you, but once I was convinced, I realized that you came to us at the perfect time."

Fauna flushed. She did not think that she had done so. "I arrived on one of the worst days and I threw a wrench into everything."

"You get to see us happy again," Aphrodite urged with tears in her eyes. "My family is everything to me. And because we are immortal, we lose track of time. I had no idea how long I had been stuck in the vicious cycle of grief. I suddenly was faced with two major events: someone who took everything from me had died, and someone who gave me a sense of hope came into my life."

Fauna opened her mouth to speak but realized that she had no words.

"And you were never afraid of us," Aphrodite pointed out. "Not once."

"Well, I was afraid of you, but not like that," Fauna laughed quietly. "You are a very intimidating figure, especially when you're angry. I was not afraid of being eaten, I was afraid you would yell at me."

"Yell at you?" Aphrodite managed a small laugh at that. "That makes no sense."

Fauna shrugged in her defense. "It doesn't, but it's how I felt."

Aphrodite turned back to the sheet that covered the painting. "Well, I had no idea who you were and we had just been attacked, so I was on edge. But I don't yell, not often. Only when someone threatens my children."

"Do you think that the Matron's grasp on me loosened when you started fighting? That explains why I was able to hear you all downstairs. I don't think I could have done so otherwise."

"I think it's the other way around," Aphrodite agreed. "Keeping you hostage up there might have also stretched her a little too thin and left her vulnerable to me as well. I didn't even think about any repercussions, I just went for it."

"What did you even do?" Fauna leaned into the arm of the couch and tucked her socked feet into a cushion.

"I hardly remember at all. I was in a furious rage," Aphrodite inhaled deeply and played with the corner of one of the sheets over a painting. "Instinct took over, I suppose. The details are fuzzy... and a bit gruesome. My hands went to her throat to keep her quiet, and then I let loose all the anger that had built up over the years. I'm sure you remember the aftermath."

Fauna winced. "I remember. When I fell down the stairs, I ended up at eye level with her as she died. It was *disturbing*."

"I still have trouble walking around there," Aphrodite admitted. "Scarlet said she would make me a large rug to cover up the black stain. No matter what the staff does, they can't seem to get rid of it."

"Does Scarlet even make rugs?"

Aphrodite's eyes lit up as she laughed. "Scarlet learns how to make everything. Never once has she lamented over her immortality. She uses all of her time to learn new things. Some days I wonder if she'll just learn everything there is to learn and feel satisfied. But, she hasn't gotten there yet."

"Maybe when she's done learning, she'll begin to teach," Fauna joked. "She and Bea have already taught me how to interact with people. I feel as if I would still be silent and glowering from the bed had I not had them and Rhiannon to help me along the way."

"I know they miss going to the village. They haven't gotten a chance to venture off the grounds for quite a while," Aphrodite admitted. "They used to have full and colorful lives, and now they spend their time locked in here. I hope that someday the village will see the hustle and bustle of life again."

"Did the Matron have a reach anywhere else, or just the village?"

Aphrodite stopped for a moment. "I don't know. There was so much information in her laboratory that it would take more trips to decipher. I know her area of operation was vast, but not to what extent. I should look into that now that she is gone—there is much to look into and I don't have many people to ask about her."

"I would like to accompany you," Fauna decided. "When you go. We could travel to Hurmehovi. And then you can show me the things I need to do and I will be able to go exploring the outer villages. Maybe I could bring the girls with me? If no one exists, there is no danger, right?"

"That is something I will need a lot of time to think about, but in the meantime, the offer is appreciated," Aphrodite replied. "If you're willing to make the journey to Hurmehovi with me, we can go. It will take nearly a month, and you should be sure that all of your things are settled here, as we will not be able to turn around."

"Why so long?" Fauna didn't know what to make of that. "How can it be so far if she could arrive so quickly?"

"She flew," Aphrodite explained. "And we cannot. I have the benefit of not needing sleep or food as often as you, but even I need to rest. There is a staircase that winds around a mountain and towards the end of the path, the weather gets very nasty. Many humans have tried to walk the stairs as some sort of pilgrimage, but they were never prepared for the weather. And it's harder to leave than it is to get there. One wrong move going down the stairs and you're tumbling to your death."

"How did you get there when she summoned you then?"

"She would fly me—flying takes less than a day. No human has gone alone and made it to the top. But, if you're with me I can help prepare you. The air gets hard to breathe and animals will fight you for the resources up there. They'll leave me alone though. They recognize our similarities."

Fauna shot Aphrodite a very serious look. "You are *not* an animal."

"I appreciate your candor. If you had seen me many years ago,
you would not be so quick to defend me. It took a lot of work to
calm my anger. I still have my moments, but I am forever a work
in progress."

"May I ask one question about your late wife?" Fauna was cautious when speaking. "Nothing too personal."

Aphrodite nodded but turned back to her canvas, daring only to
lift one corner of the cover.

"You said that you found her in the woods?" Fauna started gently.
"And that your husband died in the same woods?"

"Not at the same time, if that's what you're asking," Aphrodite
said. "Though that would have been rather poetic... or too good
to be true, depending on who you ask."

"Did you ever ask her why she was in was in the woods? It just
seems like a strange coincidence. And there was a wolf? And it
didn't attack her?"

Aphrodite inhaled deeply and on her exhale, tore the tarp off of
the last canvas. Whereas Fauna had seen part of it before, seeing
the portrait in the sunlight in all its glory, caused her to stop
mid-question. It was obvious that it was painted with so much love.
A beautiful and familiar woman sat in a heap of a gorgeous white
dress, surrounded by flowers and animals. Her hair—red as the final
autumnal leaves, fanned out perfectly against the stark white of her
dress. She fondly gazed at a chipmunk in her hand that seemed
equally entranced with her."

"She truly was a princess," Fauna whispered. "I wish I could have
known her."

"If you want the truth, I think she sought me out. I don't mean
to sound pompous at all, but she would always cheekily avoid the

question when I asked why she was in the woods. She claimed to be picking berries, but the area of the woods where she was found did not host a single berry bush. Also, it was the wrong season. And after nightfall," Aphrodite said nostalgically. "I do believe she was a bit infatuated and was hoping to be spotted by me. Though, as I said, I have no proof of this. I will always wonder how and why she would do such a thing. But is it worth it to look? Or do I just enjoy the years we spent together and move along? The eternal struggle."

"That's quite coy… and a little dangerous," Fauna laughed a little. "You could have been a murderer!"

"Or in the middle of a hunt!" Aphrodite sighed in relief. "That would have been terrible. Imagine if she had appeared from the woods and I had been the one to kill the wolf? That would have been so tragic. Thankfully, that did not happen."

She gazed at the painting for a while, wistful but unbroken. "The things we do for love," Aphrodite mused as she gently touched the edge of the canvas. "She braved the woods, night after night, trying to catch my eye, and in turn, I got her killed."

Fauna stood and walked to Aphrodite, standing slightly behind her and putting a comforting hand on her shoulder as they both looked intently at the canvas. "You did not kill her, she was a victim of the same menace you were. You also gave her… how many years of happiness?"

"Not enough," Aphrodite whispered as she graced the painted woman's face with the gentlest of touches. "Not nearly enough."

Twenty-Eight

"**M**other, come *on!*" Scarlet playfully yelled across the yard. Jumping up and down in her colorful clothes, the youngest Verity daughter looked exactly like a very excited 16-year-old. She turned to run back across the yard, but not before a final shout. "Everyone is waiting for you!"

"Coming, darling!" Aphrodite laughed a true hearty laugh before she turned to Fauna. "It's been so long since I've seen her so bubbly. I've missed it so very much."

"They've been talking about this for at least a week," Fauna admitted, tugging on her new dress. It was a bit tighter than the shapeless ones she had worn for as long as she could remember. It still touched her knees, but the gathered fabric under her bust made her a little self-conscious. Next to her, Aphrodite looked like she'd stepped right out of a book! It seemed like no matter what she wore, she made it look regal and sophisticated, while Fauna was still adjusting to her new wardrobe.

"Stop pulling at the waistline, you'll stretch it out," Aphrodite gently tapped on Fauna's hand. "You look wonderful and that dress was *made* for you."

"It literally was," Fauna complained lightheartedly. "Rhiannon's been doing so much now that she's in charge of the textiles. She's called me over at least once a day to inspect the cut of something or to ask what colors go together. I think I might just start taking my meals in there to save myself time."

"I think she enjoys your company," Aphrodite informed her. "You two are good friends. Is it so strange that she might just want to be around you? I think that's why the girls invited her along today."

Fauna stopped walking for a moment before looking at Aphrodite. "You think so?"

"I know so."

Fauna tried her best not to smile but failed quite miserably. A blush darted across her cheeks as she looked away to not embarrass herself even further. She had friends. People who *wanted* her around. It seemed to be such a far cry from her aggressively isolated former self who wanted to live and die alone.

"Come." Aphrodite touched Fauna's shoulder gently to usher her forward. "Look at how beautiful this all is. It's been too long since I've enjoyed being outside of my own home. The girls have clearly been quite busy."

"It was Bea's idea at first," Fauna admitted. "She said she missed gathering the family. That began a conversation about the games you all used to play. You didn't tell me that you played chess! It's a concept lost on me, but I've enjoyed watching Scarlet and Bea try to outsmart each other. They get so violent sometimes!"

Aphrodite laughed. "Would you believe me if I admitted that I had forgotten all about that? I used to play a lot of games—most of them with the girls, some with my wife. But grief and maintaining the estate took over all of my free time. I haven't even looked at a board in years. I can't even remember the last time that I had any fun at all."

"Well, I think you have some daughters who would love to play a game with you sometime," Fauna said fondly. "They tell me all kinds of stories about your time together and it's very clear that they miss it."

"I have neglected them and I feel awful," Aphrodite admitted. "But I have been shown the error of my ways and I will change. Which is why I've let you lead me here with little to go on, other than I was 'cordially invited to dinner'."

"I'm just the messenger." Fauna pointed to the gardens. "Think you can make it to the greenhouse? I know the memories must hurt quite a bit, but I'm here to help distract you if you need it."

Aphrodite stopped and closed her eyes. She breathed in and out evenly a few times before a calm smile spread across her face. When she opened her eyes, there were fresh tears that had not quite fallen, glimmering in the late afternoon's light.

"Yes. I can make it."

"Those came from a land very far south—so far south that the ground is practically made of sand." Aprhodite pointed to flowers that looked like little black bells. "I used to send people as far as they could go in search of new flowers and these took a very long time to get back to me."

"I heard she liked the new flowers," Fauna added gently. "Your wife."

"And I liked making her happy," Aphrodite said sweetly as they finally exited the garden. "I would wake early every morning, just to watch her get ready for the day. A spritz of perfume and a few twirls in the mirror and she was ready to face whatever was thrown her way. Sometimes she let me braid her hair and sometimes she let the girls practice. My favorite days were when she let it hang free. Something about the whip and twirl of it as she smiled and danced… those are memories that I will keep close to my heart forever."

"How does one even fall in love after hearing that?" Fauna lamented. "I can barely speak to people I don't know, but you make me want something… want to love."

"Do you?" Aphrodite raised a playful eyebrow.

Fauna flushed in a *very* obvious blush. "Well, someday. Maybe. It just sounds nice. I think. True love just always seems so wonderful!"

Aphrodite sighed. "True love cannot be found. You have to live your life and it will find you."

"In the woods?" Fauna joked.

That got a small laugh from Aphrodite.

"Yes, in the woods."

Together, they crossed through the gardens and came upon the greenhouse, where two very impatient daughters were waiting. They had decorated the building with small lights, giving it a celestial quality, as though they had been drawn into a fairytale. Before the duo reached the girls, Aphrodite stopped and turned to Fauna with open arms.

"Thank you, for helping me through these recent times. I don't think we could have healed from this the same way—or even defeated the Matron at all—without you."

"Thank you for taking me in and understanding that I'm not very good at being around others yet," Fauna replied, accepting the embrace. "I still get nervous when I'm alone, and I sometimes have nightmares that I'm back in that room and I'm going to die with no one to help me."

"Well, we destroyed the room," Aphrodite assured her as she wrapped an arm around her shoulders. "And you will never have to die alone. I can promise you that."

"Yeah," Bea interrupted as she ran up to the pair. "Technically we can't die, so we'll outlive you anyway."

It was said so casually by Bea, but the realization hit Fauna much harder than she anticipated. She knew that most of the castle was made up of immortal vampires, but she had never truly *thought* about what that meant. They would outlive her. She would die and they would move on. It was uncomfortable to think about her death in the scope of how others would react.

"I don't want to die," Fauna pleaded. "I just learned how to live."

"Well none of us want you to die, silly." Scarlet ran up to them as well. "It's just a fact. We're going to live much longer than you. We'll outlive Rhiannon too."

"We could get old together," Rhiannon offered. "I'm sure there are millions of books that we haven't read. We have a whole lifetime to do that."

"And you still have so much time to live," Aphrodite reminded her. "We all do—there is no longer any danger. We are safe and no one will hurt us."

"Bea might hurt us if we don't start eating," Scarlet said with the most serious face. "She spent hours making *one* loaf of bread. Who even cares about bread?"

"True craftsmanship knows no time limits," Aphrodite reminded her daughter. "You know that. How many times have you re-written a draft?"

"Yeah, yeah. Let's not dwell on that." Scarlet rolled her eyes and motioned to the blanket on the lawn. "We spent a lot of time perfecting this ambiance, so we need to eat before everything is cold."

"They really did," Rhiannon nodded in agreement. "I heard plan after plan until they decided on this one."

"I know it's not as comfortable as the dining hall, but we wanted to eat together. As a family. Rhiannon and Fauna too. They've been through so much." Scarlet grabbed Rhiannon and pulled her close before laying her head against Rhiannon's shoulder. "She's my friend."

"Family isn't only where you came from," Aphrodite spoke with abundant wisdom. "Family is about *choosing* people and staying close to them, even when it's tough. There is no greater feeling than being surrounded by those whom you have hand-picked to lean on. This family is small and it has been through terrible ordeals. We still have wounds from those we have lost, but soon we will fill them, bit by bit."

"They have nowhere to go," Bea muttered, though the vulnerable warble in her tone gave away exactly how she was feeling.

"We could go anywhere," Fauna said gently. "We have bodies that can transport us and a whole world to explore. But, I *want* to be here. I *want* to spend time with you all. I *want* to belong."

Rhiannon agreed. "Same."

"We're kind of weird." Scarlet motioned to the group and looked directly at Fauna. "You're sure you want to stay?"

"Of course I do. Besides, I think your mother is quite fond of me now."

Aphrodite dapped gently at her eyes. "You're correct, sweet girl. Let us break bread as a family—a family born from the most vile evil known, but bathed in love regardless. We will enjoy all the time that we have together."

"Cheers to life, death, and whatever comes in between." Scarlet raised her glass and looked around. "Stop being so morose, this is a happy night! We're safe, we have good food, and we have room to dance. There isn't much else to ask for."

"You're right," Fauna agreed and raised her glass. Soon the others did the same and little *clinks* could be heard all around. Smiles, as well as gentle touches, were affectionately given freely in the group as everyone calmed from the tender moment.

"I should visit the staff's quarters in the next coming days," Aphrodite told the group out of the blue. "I need to gather them now that the dramatics have passed. Gelon could also get their accounts of what has since happened. Are they well, Rhiannon?"

"They are," Rhiannon replied as she looked around the table. "They're all getting belligerently drunk and playing cards in the maid's hall tonight. That's how we cope down there."

Aphrodite raised an eyebrow. "Interesting, but who am I to pass judgment on anyone's methods of coping?"

"I'm enjoying reading the lore." Fauna raised her hand a bit. "I am learning so much from copying the book down. I'm almost at the part where you arrived to meet Victor."

Aphrodite seemed to think about that for a moment. She took two sips of wine before she answered.

"I was so confused by it all. I truly thought that marrying him was the best-case scenario for me. I wanted to make the Matron so proud and in turn, she exploited me."

"She exploited me too," Fauna admitted. "I don't even know how to heal from that either."

"Time," Aphrodite assured her. "Time makes things more bearable. It helps us learn."

"You're so smart," Fauna admitted with a blush.

"Someone should be," Bea snickered. "Scarlet couldn't even open the bag of flour without making a mess."

"Hey! I tried so hard!" Scarlet shot back.

"So, that's who cooked all of this?" Aphrodite motioned to the blanket, which held all sorts of foods and baked snacks. "This must have taken ages."

Rhiannon agreed. "They did a very good job. Perhaps they should be added to the maid rotation."

"No!" Bea looked aghast. "I almost burnt the kitchen down."

"She put water in hot oil to cool it down," Scarlet told the table. "It was funny."

"Was not!"

"Well, Scarlet, you also dropped a bag of flour on the ground and covered yourself from head to toe," Rhiannon outed her. "You both need more lessons, but I'm a pretty good teacher. You can bake, but your cooking needs work. Bea is too obsessed with measurements and precision, you need to learn to relax when adding things."

"Will Fauna learn to cook? She can't just write all day. What else is there to do here?" Scarlet pointed out.

"Could I help with the garden?" Fauna asked, surprising the whole group. "I think I would like that. Would that be okay?"

"I think I would like that as well." Aphrodite smiled at her warmly. "I trust you."

"I think our food is getting cold," Rhiannon said. "We're too chatty."

Scarlet threw herself back on the picnic blanket dramatically. "We just have a lot to talk about! Silence is *boring*."

"Yes, it is." Fauna couldn't help but smile. "Yes, it is."

As the late afternoon turned into evening, and evening turned into twilight, Fauna found herself swept up into the whimsy of her first official family dinner. They had moved from the lawn into the greenhouse for tea once the evening chill had set in. The lights in the greenhouse twinkled beautifully, reminding Fauna of the dream she'd had ages ago about dancing with Aphrodite's late wife. A half-empty wine glass sat on the table by Fauna's hand. Every so often, she would tap her fingers gently against the thin stem of the glass just to watch the liquid splash about.

She looked over to Aphrodite, who was watching her daughters and Rhiannon talk about something entertaining that had happened a few years prior at the castle. For the first time that Fauna could remember, Aphrodite looked *content*. Normally she wore a serious expression that commanded respect, but now donned a hazy smile. Though her legs were still crossed, it was not done as primly as she would have in front of staff. Her fingers gently curled around the arm of her chair. One of the lights cast a warm glow over her, engulfing her in a glimmering beam.

"Did you and your wife like to dance?"

Aphrodite's slow smile turned into a fully formed grin. "We certainly did. We would dance anywhere. Up and down the hallways, into the dining room, and sometimes on the rooftop. She would grab my hand and *tug* and soon I would find myself dancing through the castle. Oh... how I miss those days."

"She sounded perfect."

Aphrodite nodded. "I remember the strangest things about her, you know? It's been years. The way her hair would swing when I spun her, the color of her favorite lipstick, the tune she would sing when she cooked breakfast. All of the random things that made her so... unique? I feel like the luckiest woman alive to have experienced them."

"How did she react to you having a husband in the past?" Fauna turned and sat sideways but cross-legged in her chair. "Did it matter?"

"Not at all. We barely spoke of him," Aphrodite admitted. "I carried on his estate and that's all the Matron wanted. I did make him a lot of money, though. I never cared that it was in his name, I just wanted to live my life comfortably with my family."

"Did you dance at your wedding?" Fauna asked quietly, hoping she wasn't pushing too far.

"We danced for hours, just us, under the moon." Aphrodite's eyes filled with tears. "The girls took turns with us at first, but they went to bed and we danced until the sun began to peek over the clouds. She'd changed from her dress into something much more casual."

"Was it light green and a little blue?" Fauna ventured a guess.

"How did you know that?" Aphrodite looked at her carefully. "There should be no record of that night anywhere."

"She visited me in a dream. I know I told you that already," Fauna offered. "She always told me to just pretend and that it would all be over soon. But once, she took my hands and we danced a little. She also visited me right before you yelled at the Matron. I think she helped me wake up and hear you."

"We were lying to the Matron when we said she didn't scare us. If we pretended that she didn't matter, she wouldn't. That's why she told the girls to pretend the blood was juice when they were young. It was what she said when they bumped their heads or got into a fight. Pretend it doesn't hurt, and it won't."

Fauna sighed. "Well, it was good advice."

"I suppose that means that it worked?" Aphrodite closed her eyes and let her head fall back against the chair, her blonde waves shimmying as she relaxed.

Fauna thought it over. "It did. But, I think just having her near me made me calmer. Even if I didn't know who she was at the time. I wish she could come back. I would love to talk to her."

"I miss the scent of her hair after she went galivanting around the garden," Aphrodite hummed in delight. "Nice and warm from the sun and smelling like flowers. It was days like that when I would just kiss her senseless in the middle of the castle and run away giggling because I knew she was blushing—she was *always* blushing."

"I'm so happy you got to experience her in your life," Fauna said honestly. "I don't think I'll ever find a love like that. My life is nearly half over and I can barely make eye contact with people most days."

"You've spent your entire life hiding and resisting humanity," Aphrodite sat up and looked at Fauna directly. "That won't just go away in a few months. You'll be working at it for a long time. But, I can assure you that you are always welcome here, and I will help you as much as I can."

"She held my cheeks and kissed my forehead," Fauna admitted with a pink tint to her face. "Was she normally like that?"

Aphrodite laughed at that. "Of course. That's just who she was. So excited to be in love, that everyone around her experienced it too."

With that, Aphrodite lifted her glass to her lips and downed the rest of its contents before turning to Fauna once more. "Would you like to dance?"

The question caught Fauna so off guard that she genuinely believed that she had misheard Aphrodite. However, when Aphrodite repeated the question once again, it was obvious that wasn't the case.

Immediately, Fauna shook her head. "I don't know how."

Aphrodite stood and slipped out of her heels before holding her hand out for Fauna to take. "Just follow my lead and try not to step on my feet."

Fauna, ready to decline once more, made the mistake of looking at Aphrodite, who was wearing the most adorably petulant look. There was no way Fauna would be able to decline her now, so she sighed and kicked off her shoes as well.

It was awkward at first—Fauna had no experience with dancing at all, so when Aphrodite pulled Fauna into a very casually loose embrace and began to sway, Fauna had to close her eyes lest she get overwhelmed. It was strange… she felt safe with Aphrodite, unquestionably so. However, being so close to her brought up some of the nervousness Fauna harbored from being in her room upstairs. It was never quite apparent whether or not the Matron's version of Aphrodite had been meant to seduce Fauna, but even if not, the idea of someone being in her personal space made Fauna a bit squeamish.

"Penny for your thoughts?"

"I'm not used to being this close to someone," Fauna admitted as she let herself be guided around the chairs. "It's uncomfortable—but not *bad*."

"Just a little new?" Aphrodite added while turning them around the table. "You've never gone into too much detail about how close you were with the illusions. Did any of them…?"

"No!" Fauna said very quickly and very quietly. "Nothing that wretched. I don't remember much, but nothing was inappropriate. I mean, no one crossed any boundaries, if that's what you're asking."

"Good," Aphrodite sounded relieved. "I wasn't entirely sure what type of manipulation the Matron used on you and while both are heartbreaking, if you had been taken advantage of… that adds a new dimension of pain."

"I'm fine now," Fauna assured her, as they began to sway back and forth under the lights. "She can't hurt us and all of her followers are dead. So, the only thing I have to fear is losing all of you."

"Which will not happen," Aphrodite said. "Nothing will happen to us or you. We've been through enough. For now, we rest and heal before our journey to Hurmehovi."

Fauna laid her head against Aphrodite's chest and whispered, "And what happens if we find out that there is far more than we realize? Or that we're in grave danger."

"We'll do what we do best." Aphrodite wrapped her arms around Fauna and hugged her closely. "We'll just pretend."

About the Author

Kathy Criswell is a writer, video game enthusiast, and artist. She lives in the United States with her wife Bee and their three cats. As a self-proclaimed professional fan, she takes a lot of inspiration from those she admires creatively. As an amateur adult, she hates spreadsheets and mean people.

Music is one of her major sources of inspiration and quite frequently she can be found singing quietly to herself to keep herself on track. Kathy also enjoys jetsetting around the world to see various concerts and to meet up with her international friends.

www.ingramcontent.com/pod-product-compliance
Lightning Source LLC
Chambersburg PA
CBHW050009120726
47903CB00006B/1701